By William Gardner Smith

ANGER AT INNOCENCE
LAST OF THE CONQUERORS

ANGER

AT INNOCENCE

WILLIAM GARDNER SMITH

THE CHATHAM BOOKSELLER
CHATHAM, NEW JERSEY

All characters portrayed (except known historical
characters) are fictional, and any resemblance to
persons living or dead is coincidental.

The lines from the song "Laura" are used by the
permission of the Robbins Music Corporation. The
lyrics are by Johnny Mercer and the music by
David Raksin.

Library of Congress Catalog Card No. 73-86226
ISBN 0-911860-36-8

Reissued, 1973, by The Chatham Bookseller by
arrangement with Farrar, Straus and Giroux, Inc.

To DR. GERALD HAMM, of the University of Pennsylvania and Benjamin Franklin High School, without whose years of patience and friendship this novel would never have been written.

BOOK I

CHAPTER ONE

AUGUST LAY AGAINST his skin.

A woman floated waveringly, like a heat shimmer, above his eyes in the small dim room and he searched anxiously but in vain for eyes in the soft face he could not see clearly. She seemed near; yet, when he reached for her, she was far away, unattainable, beckoning with her hands, her lips moving without sound. Wearily, he struggled toward her through the dense fluidity of space; but the distance between them remained constant, his strength fled, and finally he paused, exhausted, frustrated, as her lips continued to move and her small faint hands still called.

Then he was awake.

Theodore stretched, wiped the perspiration from his face, and sat exhausted in the wooden chair. The gray night watchman's office surrounded him. To the level of his eyes, just over the rough wooden table, hung the dreary lamp, giving his pale white skin the same hue as the gray office. Beyond the lamp and the table was the door to the main storeroom. On his right were the dull green filing cabinets; to his left was the big window, at street level, and near the window stood the other chair. The one shaded light illuminated the splintery table and his face and the floor nearby; the rest of the tiny room, like outer space, lay in darkness.

He sat motionless, feeling August, staring absently at the

small twenty-five-cent reprint which lay on the table—*Modern American Poetry*. He looked at his Ingersoll watch: two-ten in the morning. A murmur ran through his stomach; he was hungry.

He rose and walked to the window. A thin, concealing rain fell on Philadelphia. He could not see to the other side of the street. It was hard even to see the sign which hung outside the building: "Dranger Pharmaceutical Laboratories." He put out the light and went through the storeroom to the street. Carefully, he made sure the door was locked. Bent forward in the fine rain, he walked to the corner and into a diner shaped like a locomotive.

A man sat at the counter, eating a sandwich and drinking coffee; a boy and girl sat in one of the booths near the wall; behind the counter, pouring the contents of a bag into the net of a coffee urn stood a broad man, the waiter. Theodore sat down on the round stool. The waiter turned around and beamed.

"Hi, Ted? How you been?" The waiter was fat cheeked and squinty eyed.

"Fine, how about you?" The other man at the counter looked at Theodore; Theodore smiled and nodded. The man looked at him blankly, then turned again to his sandwich. You don't know whether to be courteous or not, Theodore thought. You never know what to do.

"What'll it be, Ted?" the waiter asked.

"Hamburger and coffee, Jerry," Theodore said, after all these months still feeling odd when he called the waiter by his first name.

With a flourish and grin, Jerry swung the sandwich and coffee onto the counter in front of Theodore. He smiled, happy, pleased with himself. Theodore smiled.

"Bad rain out tonight, huh, Ted?"

4

"Yes."

"Nice night for pickpockets, huh? Bump into you and *wham*, no wallet." He grinned broadly, imitating the pickpocket. Theodore nodded. He poured catsup on top of the steaming hamburger and added salt and pepper. He bit into the hot sandwich; the hamburger burned his tongue and he had to push it rapidly from side to side in his mouth. Jerry watched him, grinning. "Hot, huh, Ted?" Jerry grinned. Theodore added sugar to the coffee and sipped it.

"I serve my food piping hot, Ted," Jerry said. "That's the way to do business, huh?"

The girl in the booth laughed loudly, and her boy friend chuckled. Theodore thought: I'm thirty-nine. I used to take girls out to diners after dates and sit in booths and make them laugh like that. Then he thought: If we had any children, they'd be old enough to go out on dates and sit in diners like this. He thought of his wife: eighteen years.

"Anything new at the plant, Ted?" Jerry asked.

"No. Same as usual."

"Pretty boring job, huh? Sit there hour after hour."

"It's all right," Theodore said.

"Now *there's* a business for you, huh? Boy, I'll bet *those* people make money."

"Sure," Theodore said. "They do all right."

"Damn tootin'. That's the only way to make money. Have your own business, huh? That's the way to wrack in the dough. Look at you and me. Do all the work, don't make more'n a penny or two. I make thirty-four lousy bucks a week. Bet you don't make much either."

"Not much," Theodore said.

"Hell no. Only way to wrack in dough is to own something. Fellow owns this place don't never come near it. Sam takes it all day and I take it all night. But who makes the dough?"

5

Theodore slid off the stool and walked over to the juke box. He slipped a nickel into the slot and pushed a button. The record rose to the arm and began to spin.

> *Laura, is a face in the misty night,*
> *Footsteps, that you hear down the hall . . .*

He sat down and bit into the remainder of the sandwich. The woman floated gently in the suburbs of his mind.

"You like that record one hell of a lot, don't you, Ted?" Jerry asked, grinning.

"Yes."

"Play it all the time," Jerry said, grinning. Theodore sipped his coffee. "You don't look like the typ'd like that kinda record. Know that, Ted? You look like the school-teacher type, wouldn't like that kinda record."

"Is that right?" Theodore asked.

"Sure," Jerry said. "You look like a school teacher, quiet."

Theodore thought: slide me into the folder and shove me in the file marked "school teacher." He finished the sandwich. He heard the song.

Jerry said, "Hey, Ted, you oughta been here earlier. Man, you woulda seen a show. Had a coupla punks in here."

Theodore said, "Punks?"

Jerry slapped his own forehead and looked at Theodore in amazement. "Goddamn, Ted, don't you know what punks are?"

"No," Ted said, looking at his coffee, feeling the usual shame begin to flow through him. The usual shame: the shame he felt when others talked to him about baseball or football or prize fighting. That shame.

"Goddamn," Jerry said. "Sissies. Faggots."

"Oh," Theodore said.

"You shoulda been here," Jerry said, grinning. "Boy, were they the McCoy. Come switchin' in here to beat the band.

6

Could smell that perfume and stuff clear across the counter. Had their hair all done up and powder all over their faces and moved their hands all dainty-like." He mimicked the men. Theodore watched him, smiled, and sipped his coffee. "I wouldn't serve 'em," Jerry said.

"I don't blame you," Theodore said. He blushed easily; he hoped he wasn't blushing now.

The boy and girl got up and the boy paid the bill. Jerry handed the boy his change. "Rainin' dogs 'n' cats," Jerry said, grinning. "Yeah," the boy said. They left. Theodore sipped his coffee and wanted to play the record again. He did not want to return to the plant.

"How's the wife, Ted?" Jerry asked.

"Fine," Theodore said.

Jerry leaned over the counter. "Any kids in prospect yet?"

Theodore breathed deeply. "You asked that question just last week."

Jerry shook his head. "Tough, Ted. You oughta have some kids. My kids are great with me. Marriage don't mean nothing if you ain't got any kids."

"I'll put in my order," Theodore said.

He looked at his watch. Jerry said, "Well, you'll be getting off soon. Bet you'll be glad. Wife home layin' in bed, waitin' for you. Just like mine. Great stuff, huh?" He grinned and slapped Theodore's shoulder across the counter. Theodore smiled.

"Well, I'll be going," Theodore said.

Jerry said, "Aw, stick around a while, Ted. Have another cup of coffee. On the house."

"No, I'll be getting back."

"Aw, stick around a while, Ted. I like to have somebody to talk to."

"No, I've got to go," Theodore said. He walked toward the door.

7

"Well, see you tomorrow," Jerry said. "Don't be too rough on your wife tonight."

Without turning around, Theodore could see the grin on Jerry's face.

He went out into the hot, thin rain. He raised the collar of his shirt and walked along the dark street toward the plant. At the door, he took the key ring from his pocket and searched for the correct key. The rain was like thin threads. He heard the click of a woman's heels and then the woman bumped into him. He felt her hand slip deftly into his back pocket. He seized her wrist, startled, and whirled to face her.

"What's this?" he said loudly. "What's this?"

The woman, face averted, struggled to free her wrist. He held tight.

"What's this?" was all he could say in his surprise.

She struggled. "Oh, no you don't," he said. "Oh, no you don't. A pickpocket!" Astonishment and excitement were in him. "Well," he said, "I guess I'll call the police."

She raised her head. Her face was somewhat obscured in the screening, thin rain. He saw the dark mass of hair behind her white face; then dimly in the rain he saw the outline of her features. He was shocked. A girl! She was only a young girl!

"You're only a child!" Theodore exclaimed.

She jerked her wrist but he held it tight. Through the darkness now he saw tiny, fierce glitterings of light from her eyes. She stared at him in silence.

"Only a child," Theodore repeated, staring in amazement. He tried to pull her nearer, for a closer look, but she pulled firmly away.

He did not know what to do. "You need to be turned over to your mother," he said, "not the police." He tried to estimate her age. Just eighteen or nineteen. She stared at him without reply.

"I'm going to let you go," Theodore said, "but you might not

8

always be so lucky." He looked at her. "I want you to promise me something. It probably won't be worth anything, but promise me you won't steal anymore. You'll land in jail."

She stared at him, her wrist held tight in his. He saw the outline of the thick hair and the fierce gleaming light from her eyes.

"Promise me," he said.

She nodded, looking at him.

"Do you promise?"

She nodded again.

"What's the matter, can't you talk?" he asked.

She stared at him in silence. He looked at the thick mass of hair.

"Okay," he said. "For your own good, you'd better keep that promise."

He released her wrist and she was gone like a hare from a trap. Theodore listened to the clicking of her heels and watched her back retreating until she turned the corner. He shook his head and went into the office. He sat in his chair. The fierceness of her eyes remained with him.

2

Sylvia moved methodically through the three rooms of the third-floor-front apartment, cleaning up, glancing, every few moments or so, at the clock. She went through the bedroom, sweeping, smoothing the covers of the bed, dusting, putting objects into place. In the parlor she swept the cushions and the linoleum-covered floor and added water to the vase of flowers on the small table. She neatly stacked the pile of papers on the rolltop desk (she paused, looked at the words on the top sheet of paper, shook her head). She wiped the mirror, evened up the shades, centered every ash tray. Finally she moved into

9

the tiny kitchen (into which both the parlor and bedroom opened), wiped the sink and table with the dish cloth, swept the floor, and made sure the salt and pepper shakers were in their places on the shelf near the stove.

She stirred the contents of a white saucepan and a gray pot; each sat over a very low gas flame. With some annoyance, she looked at the plate of bacon on the table: she could not begin to cook it yet. She looked at the clock, ticking noisily on the shelf: five-twenty, almost time for him to be getting home.

She moved nervously, absently, straightening other things. She was not content that everything was as it should be. A mirror hung slanted against one wall: she looked in it at her plain, forever-calm face with the too-big mouth, tired eyes and lines across the forehead. She wore slippers and a nightgown.

I look all right, she thought. She looked around the room again: why do I bother, he never notices anything anyway. She looked at the bacon and the other things on the stove and the just-swept floor and, in the mirror, at the lines over her eyes: this is being married, she thought. At least, this is being married to him.

She sat down at the table; she glanced at the clock again. She felt tired and bored. Her thin hand stared at her from the table, the veins green, bulging through the skin. Life, she thought, slips like waste down a drain.

"Is that you, Theodore?"

The front door closed. She heard his weary step. (He was always so tired.) He came into the kitchen.

"Hello, darling," he said, kissing her lightly on the cheek. "How're things?"

She put the bacon in the pan and listened to it sizzle. "Are you tired, dear?" she asked.

"Not very," he said.

She let the bacon cook slowly while she put the plates, cups

10

and saucers on the table. Theodore sat down and watched her, smiling now and then. The bacon still hissed when she put it on the plates. Theodore said, "Ummm! Smell that!" She put fried eggs on the plates, poured hot water over the tea bags and sat down. Theodore said, "Ummm, tastes delicious, honey." She watched him relish the eggs, then butter his bread and take the bag out of his teacup.

"I love you a lot tonight," Theodore said. "Food like this does that to me."

She put salt and pepper on her food and sweetened her tea. She looked at him and he smiled.

"Anything much happen at work?"

"No, nothing unusual."

She watched his face. "Did you ask Mr. Miller about the vacation?"

Theodore dropped his fork, snapped his finger, and looked at her with self-disgust. "Umph," he said, "What do you know? I forgot."

"Again," she said.

She watched him eat. "You're such a coward," she said softly, almost through her teeth.

Theodore chewed his food and ate silently. The usual heaviness was in the room, as though all windows were sealed and the air were thick with moisture. He did not look across the table. He ate slowly and heard his chewing amplified, sickeningly thunderous in the room. After a while he cleared his throat.

"I've been hungry all evening," he said. "I kept thinking about coming home and getting a good hot dinner. This night work is murderous."

She seemed to wait a long time before speaking. He avoided looking at her. "You seem hungry," she said finally.

"Oh, I certainly am. This just hits the spot."

Then there was silence in the room again. She sat across the table and would not help him. His mind stirred uncomfortably.

"Jerry asked about you," he said, after awhile.

"The fellow at the diner. That's nice."

"He's still anxious to meet you."

Sylvia had finished eating. She sat back in her chair, smoking a cigarette. Theodore could feel her looking at him as he ate.

"Can that fellow talk," Theodore said. "He rambled on, saying nothing much."

"What did he say?"

"Oh, he talked about everything. He told me about homosexuals, about his wife, about children . . ."

He paused and looked at his food. Sylvia, across the table, watched him. In a way she was amused, in a way angered. So sensitive, she thought. So afraid he'll hurt my feelings. So protective. The brave, shielding husband.

"He's still talking about not making any money," Theodore said.

Sylvia asked, "How did you begin talking about children?"

"Oh . . . he told me how crazy he was about his own."

She looked at him across the table, in amusement and anger. She said, "He probably wondered why you have none."

He flushed. "Of course not. It's none of his business. He didn't say anything about me."

"No?" She smoked the cigarette. Theodore finished eating, pushed his plate aside, and said, "That was delicious." He put the cup of tea in front of him.

Sylvia asked, "How many children does Jerry have now?"

"Four," Theodore said, looking at his tea. She watched him lift the cup, drink slowly, and lower the cup. All without looking at her.

"Of course he's right," she said, looking at him. "A married man really ought to have children."

12

"He didn't say that, Sylvia," Theodore said.

"But you really ought to have children."

"Stop it, Sylvia," Theodore said. He looked at her. "I don't even like children. You know that." He smiled. "You're enough for me," he said softly.

She smiled and he averted his eyes. She thought: well, sometimes he tries. She said, "But it would be nice. Little feet around the house."

He said, "Stop it, Sylvia. There's no need to be this way. We couldn't even afford children."

Sylvia thought: That's true enough. She said, "If you had children, you'd be happier." She waited a moment, watching him, then said, "You'd probably have done much better, Theodore, marrying someone else."

"Sylvia, please stop it. Why do you want to go on this way? Why do you always do this?"

"Do what, darling? I'm only saying what's true." She said, "You'd probably have been much happier married to someone else. Your own flesh running about the house. You'd probably have been much happier." Then she said, "But it's never too late, Theodore. I wouldn't stand in your way."

He sat exhausted, his tea finished. "This is all silly," he said finally.

"No," she said. "It's not silly. I just like to clarify things. That's all. I just like you to know these things."

"It's silly, darling," he said.

"No," she said. "It's not silly. I just like you to know these things, that's all."

The dishes had been washed, morning's light filled the room. They sat quietly in the parlor on the sofa: Theodore read a newspaper, Sylvia a book.

"Howard was past the house today," Sylvia said.

"Really? What did he have to say?"

"We just talked, about this and that. He helped do some of the housework. He asked about you."

Theodore lowered the paper, looked at his wife and smiled. The air seemed less dense now. "I should be suspicious," he laughed. "My former rival asking about me."

Former? She smiled tolerantly. The room lapsed into silence again. Sylvia continued to read. Theodore sat at his end of the sofa, glancing at his paper, then at her.

"An interesting thing happened tonight," he said. "A woman —well, a girl, really, not more than nineteen—tried to steal something from my pocket. She bumped into me and I felt her hand slip into my pocket."

"Yes?"

"I'd just left the diner and was going into the office. I grabbed her wrist. She was just a young girl."

"What did you do?"

"Well, if she'd been older I'd have called the police. But she was just a child, no more than nineteen or so. So I scared her and made her promise not to steal any more and let her go."

Sylvia's eyelids lowered sleepily. She yawned. "That was a silly thing to do. You should have called the police."

"She was just a child."

"All the more reason. Now she'll think she can always get off so easily. You don't really believe she'll keep her promise."

"I don't know. Anyway, I couldn't have her arrested. She was so young. I can't imagine why she'd steal."

Sylvia said, "And you, my dear, probably reached in your pocket and handed her whatever little money you had."

"Don't be silly."

She yawned again. "I'm sleepy. You're such a romantic, Theodore. I don't put anything past you." She stood up. "Are you coming to bed?"

He said, "In a little while."

14

"What are you going to do?"

"Well, I'd like to try a little writing."

Sylvia smiled. Again, tolerance was in the smile. "Well, goodnight," she said.

Then he was alone in the room. His eyes traced the flower design of the wallpaper and he relaxed, breathing deeply, all heaviness gone from the air. He walked to the window and looked at the street. There was the stolid face of the row houses, and the moist flush of silence. A man passed on the pavement. Theodore watched him until he was out of sight. This is the still part of life, he thought. If he could put this atmosphere in a poem!

He sat at the rolltop desk with the sheets of paper before him and the pencil in his hand. He thought of his wife, lying in bed in the next room. He stared at the paper and thought of the small, dim office in which he worked and of the diner and the words of Jerry, the waiter, and of the thirty-nine years of life gone by and the years which had yet to come. He thought of failure. And of fear. Life moved so swiftly!

He stood up and looked at the paper, at the desk, at the pencil in his hand, at the wastepaper basket nearby. He dropped the pencil on the desk and looked out the window once more. Then he left the room.

He heard Sylvia's breathing as he entered the bedroom. She was asleep. He undressed quietly in the darkness, then slipped into bed. For a long time he lay beside her wide awake, listening to her breathing. Light pushed through the drawn curtains and lowered shades. Theodore thought: Eighteen years! The hot air flowed through the window screens, passing like breath across his face. His eyes were closed and he sank near sleep. Life was so long!

The woman swam waveringly, like a heat shimmer, above his eyes in the quiet bedroom. He smiled, but did not try to

15

reach her. She returned his smile and beckoned, but he lay comfortable, content to look at her; he did not try to move.

His lips moved; they said, You're beautiful.

She smiled and beckoned, floating in the air over his eyes. He watched her small hand call. He smiled and shook his head wearily.

I'd like to, his lips said. I'd so like to. But I can't.

Her head moved to one side, inquisitively; her hand continued to beckon.

I can't, his lips said. I want to but I can't. I'm really a coward. Really a woman. Just as Sylvia says.

His wife moved beside him, but he did not hear her. Outside, an automobile rolled through the faintly falling rain. Theodore lay on his back, breathing deeply, asleep.

CHAPTER TWO

THE FINE RAIN fell silently on Philadelphia. It lay on the leaves of trees and made fine, screen-like lines in front of the pale yellow-glowing street lamps. Along the pavement of a narrow, quiet street walked the young girl, Rodina Baleza, moving leisurely.

On the street so late at night, alone, walking without sound, she seemed like an animal. Her strides were long, absolutely without awkwardness. There was a certain wildness about her. Her hair was very long and very thick, coal black, shiny, in waves, loose, hanging almost to her waist. Her forehead was pronounced, her eyes dark and deep-set, and her nose was sharp, clean. She had high cheekbones. She wore a fluffy white blouse with short sleeves, a wide plaid skirt, and low-heeled shoes without stockings.

She walked without haste, seeming to enjoy the rain and the night.

"Promise me you won't steal anymore."

She thought of the words and smiled. She thought of the man's voice, and of his face, what she had seen of it through the thin, screening rain. A soft voice. A mature, troubled face.

She rounded a corner. She still felt a thrill of excitement when she thought of the sudden movement, the sudden capture of her arm, the sudden fear of arrest. The thrill of a chase. The thrill of fear. Like driving at breakneck speed on a wet road at midnight. In all this world, there was nothing else like that feeling.

17

Ah, but it was dark! Boys in the neighborhood had smashed most of the lamps, and of course, with the rain, there was no moon, there were no stars. Even this was a thrill. Alone at night. The only sound your footsteps. The world asleep; you alone awake. The darkness roundabout. And the intimate rain.

Near the alley at the end of the street she paused and stood motionless. A group of cats were congregated near the mouth of the alley. They circled each other. They gave their cat cries. From where she stood, in the darkness, Rodina could see the yellow glow of their eyes. She watched them, fascinated. She moved closer to the wall so as not to frighten them.

Cats. How slick their coats were now, wet with rain; how fearfully their eyes glowed in the darkness; how mysterious they seemed alone at night near the alley of a street! In the olden days, in the days of knights, cats rode with witches. In the days of witches. Days passed now, or so they said. (But they said many things which were not true.) Cats had nine lives. Did they really have nine lives? Cats were the animals of evil. Evil. So she watched them circle each other, crying out, their eyes shining, their coats wet and smooth and glossy.

Then they were gone. Up in the alley. Gone, and Rodina seemed to awake, as though from a spell. She tingled; she scarcely noticed that she was wet. For a long moment she remained where she had been standing. The cats were gone and her eyes drifted up to the tree that stood thick and tall near the alley at the end of the street.

A soft wind carried the rain and the wind went through the tree, making the leaves whisper. Rodina saw the leaves sway lazily and heard the sound of the wind. A lovely sound. Sometimes at night she awoke in her bed and listened to the sound of the wind through the tree outside her window. Or when it rained she listened to the rain falling on the leaves. She loved the sounds. They made her feel at peace. And sometimes the

18

moon was out, shining on the leaves, and the shadows of the leaves moved silently back and forth on the wall of her room. Sometimes she watched the leaves on the wall and was terrified. The leaves were shadows, they were dark, and they moved silently, as though dancing, on her wall in the night. Evil spirits used to dance sometimes in the night.

Rodina walked on. She turned finally into a narrow street and walked to the end of it. There was home. The four-story red brick house with the sagging front and the dirty windows and dirty steps. A tenement. Home. She went inside and walked silently upstairs. At the door she paused. No sound. She turned the key silently in the lock and went inside, closing the door quietly behind her. Again, inside, she paused, listening. She heard the sound of heavy breathing. Asleep. Quietly she walked across the room and sat on the edge of the bed. She undressed and climbed quickly in.

All safe! All safe! She breathed easily and soon was asleep.

2

The morning came clean, bright and pleasant. The sun was high, the streets had been washed by rain and the leaves on the trees shone green and fresh. Even the air was clean, for the dust had been weighted down by the moisture.

Rodina awoke from sleep completely and cleanly. She sat upright in the bed, wide awake, and looked around her, then through the window at the clear blue sky. The room was small. There were twin beds, the other occupied by an older woman with thick hair tied in a net and a face lined and without peace. There was a bureau, a chair, a stool, a table and a closet in the room. The paper on the walls was cracked and soiled; the floor was covered with linoleum worn through in spots.

Rodina looked at a clock: 8:00 A.M. She sprang from bed

19

and went to the window, her hair loose and thick down her back, her nightgown drowning her. She inhaled the crisp air and felt good. The great gelatin of sky was flavored here and there with big whipped-cream gobs of clouds. Below lay the street: already children were playing ball and windows of houses were open wide.

Humming, Rodina washed and dressed. She went into the kitchen and prepared two bowls of corn flakes with milk while the coffee bubbled in the percolator. She carried the breakfast into the bedroom on a tray and sat it on the stool near the beds.

The woman in the other bed slowly opened her eyes.

"Morning, Mom," Rodina said. She wheeled the stool between the beds and helped her mother to a sitting position. Rodina propped pillows behind her mother's back.

"It's a beautiful morning," Rodina said.

Her mother looked at Rodina strangely. Her face was small and round and her nose was like a knob. Her eyes were the same as Rodina's; deep set, intense. She said nothing as Rodina lifted the bowl of corn flakes to her hands, smiling cheerfully.

Mrs. Baleza ate in silence while Rodina talked about the beauty of the morning and how well she felt today. They were interrupted once when Mrs. Davis, the landlady, knocked on the door and then wheezed into the room on huge, pain-wracked legs. Every morning Mrs. Davis stopped by to exchange a few words with them. Then she left, to call on other tenants.

"How do you feel this morning, Mom?" Rodina asked.

"I feel all right."

"Good. I'm glad to hear that."

"What time did you come in last night, Rodina?"

Rodina's eyes moved to the bowl in her hands. She paused for a moment. "Oh, it wasn't so late, Mom."

"When I looked at the clock it was two o'clock."

Rodina was silent. She ate the corn flakes, listening to her heart.

"What was you doing all night?"

"Just walkin' around, Mom," Rodina said.

"Just walkin' around. You know how much I believe that."

Rodina did not answer. She found it hard to concentrate on her food. Finally she finished, and took the dish from her mother and gave her the cup of coffee.

"What would your father think of you? Just ask yourself that. What would he think of you, huh? Him a preacher and you his daughter. Sometimes I thank God he's dead." She sipped the coffee. "Layin' up here in bed, can't watch you all the time. You foolin' around out there in the street, no job, supposed to be takin' care of me. Foolin' around with some of them saloon rats, doin' everything you're big enough to. What would your father think?"

Rodina could not answer for her father, so she sat quietly, drinking the coffee. She was used to this. She was affected every time, but she was used to it. Usually, she sat quietly until it was all over.

"Father up in Heaven," Mrs. Baleza said, "me sick down here. Cripple. Can't do nothin' for m'self. You foolin' around till all hours of the night. Straight to hell, Rodina. That's where you're goin'. Straight to hell."

The woman looked closely at her daughter, leaning forward in the bed. "You remember what I told you about hell, Rodina? You remember what I read you? Don't never forget it. Ain't no joke, Rodina. Remember it, it ain't no joke:

> Blow ye the trumpet in Zion, and sound an alarm in my holy mountain: let all the inhabitants of the land tremble: for the day of the Lord cometh, for it is nigh at hand.

A day of darkness and of gloominess, a day
of clouds and of thick darkness, as the morning
spread upon the mountains . . .

And in those days shall men seek death, and
shall not find it; and shall desire to die, and
death shall flee from them.

. . . the fearful and unbelieving and the
abominable and murderers, and whoremongers
. . . and all liars, shall have their part in the
lake which burneth with fire and brimstone. . . .

Mrs. Baleza sat back. "Well, ain't no need of my talkin', is it?
Ain't nothin' I can do. Ain't nothin' nobody can do about it."

Later, Rodina cleaned the rooms. When she worked in the
bedroom she could feel her mother's eyes upon her. Occasionally, her mother spoke again of Rodina's father, what a
good man he had been, what a righteous life he and Mrs.
Baleza had led.

When all of the work was done, and the room was spick and
span, Rodina washed herself and put on other clothes: another
skirt, another blouse. Her mother said, "Out again?"

"Just for a walk," Rodina said. She could never bear to
spend an entire day at home with her mother.

"Always goin' out," Mrs. Baleza said. "Jittery, no respect
for home . . ."

There was a steady stream of words. Rodina opened the door
and went downstairs.

On the first floor at the front of the tenement there was a
little tearoom which many of the tenants patronized. It could
be entered either from the front of the building, or from the
hall. Now Rodina peeked in through the hall door to see if
anyone was inside. The waiter waved to her and said, "Good
morning." Rodina returned the greeting. As she turned to go

out of the front door, she heard a voice call from the other end of the hall.

"Hey, baby."

Rodina paused without turning around. Just my luck, she thought.

"How's the baby today?" the voice asked, drawing close.

"Just fine," she said without turning around.

"The prima donna," the voice said, "the movie queen. Talkin' without turnin' around. Why don't you turn around and greet old Hucks with a kiss."

Strong arms gripped her shoulders and turned her around. Rodina looked up into the face of a man who looked like a prize fighter. He was broad and blond and his face was square and thick; he might have been about twenty-five. Behind his pale blue eyes something moved obscurely. He was grinning, holding her shoulders.

"You ought to give old Hucks a nicer greeting than that," he said. "You ought to show a little affection toward old Hucks. Like old times, baby."

He grinned. His hands were like iron grips upon her shoulders. He lowered his lips toward hers. Rodina did not move; she watched the lips approach. When they were about to touch hers she opened her mouth and bit into his lower lip. He pulled back with a howl.

He was angry, and then the anger fled and was replaced by amusement. "The fiery prima donna," he laughed. "What's the matter, baby? Don't you love your Hucks anymore?"

Her eyes glared out at him, like cat's eyes. She said nothing. She could not pull away from him.

Still grinning, Hucks said, "Okay, baby, I got to get on the truck now. Ain't got time to persuade you to be nice like you used to be. But you'll come around. I'm pretty sure you'll come around. Like you used to, baby?"

Rodina said, "Hmmmph!"

He released her and went outside to climb into his big soda truck. Rodina stood in the hallway a minute, shrugged, then went into the tearoom. The waiter came over to her.

"Hi, Rodina."

"Hi, Glenn."

"I seen that big slug grab you," Glenn said. "Someday somebody's gonna fix his apples. That's one thing sure."

"You're not just chopping your chops," Rodina agreed.

"What'll you have, Rodina?"

"A cup of coffee and some doughnuts."

"Coming right up," Glenn said.

Rodina sat back in her chair, waiting for the coffee, relieved to be rid of Hucks. She looked around the tearoom: it was always clean. Linoleum covered the floor; there was a counter; there were a lot of little tables with chairs around the room, and each table was covered with oilcloth. Glenn came in with the coffee and doughnuts.

"Anything else, Rodina?"

"No, thanks."

"Care for a little nip? No price to you."

"No, thanks just the same, Glenn. This is enough for me."

She sipped the coffee slowly. A few other tenants came into the room, and they spoke to her. Rodina liked most of the people who lived here. Most of them. They were friendly. It was nice to live in a place where there were a lot of people. She drank the hot coffee as someone played a record on the juke box. Then a familiar figure appeared in the door of the room.

"Juarez," Rodina called.

The man smiled and walked over to her table. "Good morning, Rodina," he said. He spoke softly. Some of the other people in the room glanced at him, but no one spoke. He was a

24

scrawny man, with dark skin, thick features, and shiny straight black hair. Everyone noticed his eyes: they were soft and seemed always to be covered by a film of tears.

"Grab a seat," Rodina said. "Have a cup of coffee with me."

"I'd love to," he said softly. His voice was like felt.

Juarez ordered ham and eggs and coffee. He lived on the second floor, two doors from Rodina, in one room. There was no one to cook for him, so he always ate in the tearoom.

"Getting ready for work?" Rodina asked.

"Yes. Back to the hash house." He smiled, and the smile was pleasant. He had very white teeth.

"How's Juanita, Juarez?"

"Fine." Juarez dropped his eyes a moment, then looked up at her again. "Why do you ask that?"

"Well, I like her."

"Oh," Juarez said.

His order came and Juarez ate slowly. Every so often he looked up at Rodina and smiled.

"How's your mother?" Juarez asked.

"All right." A shadow crossed Rodina's face. Juarez, who was looking at her, saw the shadow.

"Is anything wrong?"

"No." She smiled. "The usual thing, Juarez."

"Oh." He sipped the coffee to remove the thick taste of egg from his mouth. "You're not letting it worry you?"

"No," she said. "I can stand hell if I have to go there."

Juarez looked at her with his liquid-filled eyes. "It's not hell I worry about," he said, "it's jail. You ought to stop it, Rodina."

"Yes," she agreed seriously, "I ought to. But what would I do, Juarez? I can't do any kind of job, and Mom's got to eat."

"You could get a job of some kind, Rodina."

She laughed. "Yeah, I guess I could. Do you think I'm lazy, Juarez?"

"No. I think you're wild, unstable."

"Hmmmm," she said, still smiling.

When, later, Rodina left the tearoom and walked down the street the kids playing ball waved and whistled at her. She waved back. The kids liked to watch her walk; every morning when she emerged from the house they paused in their game and followed her to the corner with their eyes, then turned to wink at one another. Rodina liked the kids.

At the corner saloon the men waved and this, too, was usual.

"How you doin', sugar?"

"Ummm, you sure look good to me, sugar."

"Come on in and get a drink."

Every day the men invited her to drink and sometimes she accepted. But now she laughed and waved to them. She knew all of these men, and knew their wives in the brick row houses of the adjoining streets. She liked the men, too.

She walked aimlessly, slowly in the sunshine, feeling good. Presently she was away from her section of town and in a part of the city which was clean, fresh and attractive. The women she passed wore fine clothes and proud faces. She passed the shop windows slowly, gazing at the beautiful clothes on mannikins, at jewelry, shoes, lingerie. Then there were other things: oriental rugs, with gorgeous splashes of color; mahogany, oak and maple furniture; huge paintings, richly bound books, antiques, glassware, china, stationery, lamps and candlesticks. For hours she turned in and out of these streets: Chestnut, Market, Locust, Spruce, Sansom, Walnut, Arch. She paused at each window, fascinated, oblivious of the stares of passers-by. She could see herself in the expensive clothes, sleek and stylish, glittering like a star.

When the sun had passed overhead and the trenchant heat of afternoon assailed the city, she found herself in the northeast section of the town. She looked at the billboard of a small theater: a double feature today, a Western and a love story. She went inside. The theater was air-conditioned and the coldness made her think of winter. Which do I like better, she thought, winter or summer? In winter you had to buy coal and in summer there was only ice, so she supposed she liked summer better.

3

Dusk, like dry fog, was upon the city. Early evening had come. Now Rodina sat in a square, wondering what to do, where to go. She did not want to go home. Mrs. Davis, the landlady, always made her mother's dinner. She could not bear to be at home until her mother was asleep.

From the bench in the park she watched darkness move gradually across the sky. People came through the park in nice clothes; the young men and women held hands. A faint wind stirred the leaves and Rodina listened to their sighing. She thought of the leaves in her bedroom at night and of her mother's repeated recriminations, and a sudden sense of fear rushed through her, making her tremble. It lasted only a second; but in that second she saw the fires of Hell raging through the pages of *Revelations*. Then the fear was gone and the wind still blew and people walked past, laughing, the young ones holding hands.

She stood up and walked, not conscious of the direction she was taking. And then she found herself among lonely office buildings and warehouses and homes lined row on row. She walked among them, fascinated by the night, and came upon a lighted window that brought a sweep of recollection into her mind. The window was part of a diner, shaped like a locomotive.

Excited, she turned into the adjoining street and walked

along, looking in the windows. She could almost feel the rain of the night before. Which building was it? She walked slowly, trying to remember. Then she saw the lighted plate-glass window. She peered inside. Ah, there he was, asleep it seemed. An open book lay on the table in front of him.

She tapped on the pane. The man awoke immediately and rose to look at her through the window. She laughed inside. He came to the door and looked at her pleasantly.

"Yes?"

"Good evening," she said, "remember me?"

He looked at her, puzzled. She kept a straight face. Finally he said, embarrassed, "I'm sorry, but I don't."

"Oh," she said sadly, "then it didn't mean anything? You weren't really interested in me?"

He looked at her as though she were insane. She said, "And we only met last night."

"Last night?"

"Yes. Here in the rain."

His eyes opened wide. He looked at her as though he did not believe her. Then he said, "You're ——"

She nodded. "The same. 'Promise me you won't steal any-more.' "

The man smiled. He had a pleasant smile, Rodina decided. And soft eyes. And a nice voice.

"Aren't you going to invite me in?" Rodina said.

"I can't," he said, embarrassed again. "But if you like we could go to the diner."

"Good."

He paused in the doorway. "It's odd, you know," he said, laughing. "Your coming back here like this. It's an amazing thing."

"Yes? I just wanted you to know I'm grateful to you for not turning me over to the cops."

28

Theodore turned out the light and they went to the diner. The waiter stared at them and Rodina thought: He must not bring many chicks here. She sat down opposite him in the booth and they ordered hamburgers and coffee. He wasn't bad looking, Rodina thought. About forty years old. Probably married with half-a-dozen children.

"My name's Rodina," she said, "Rodina Baleza."

"Oh——," once again the man seemed embarrassed. "My name's Theodore, Theodore Hall."

"Ted," she said. "Hello."

The hamburgers came. Other people were in the diner. Someone turned on the juke box. The words of *Laura* filled the room.

"There doesn't seem to be much to say," Ted said to her.

He's awfully shy, Rodina thought, smiling. "No. Let's see. You're married, aren't you?"

"Yes."

"With six children."

"No. No children."

There was a pause. Theodore was self-conscious. Rodina watched him, amused. But there was something appealing about this shyness.

"You seem like a nice girl," he said at last. "Why do you pick pockets?"

"Oh," she said, "I'm a horrible person. I also kill helpless mothers."

He smiled distantly and said, "You'll end up in jail, Miss Baleza."

"Rodina."

"Rodina, then."

"Do you really think I'll end up in jail?"

"Yes."

"How awful."

Then, seeing his face, Rodina was sorry she had said that. She did not want to embarrass him. Not too much. Just a little but not too much.

"No," she said, "I'll stay out of jail. I'm going to get a job soon and then I'll stop."

"Is that true? Can I depend on that?"

"Can *you* depend on that?" she said, laughing.

He blushed and laughed. "I mean, do you intend to keep that promise?"

"Oh, yes," she said, "positively." And she realized that her joking was embarrassing him again.

"Are you always so easily embarrassed?" she asked.

"No. It's silly, isn't it. And by a mere girl." He laughed and she liked the sound of the laugh.

"No, it's not so silly."

She did not want to tease him any more. She was rarely at a loss for words with a man, but now she did not know what to say. He was so serious. Different from the men she knew. Suddenly she was sorry she had tried to pick his pocket.

"I'm sorry about last night," she said.

"Oh, forget it."

"But I'm glad you caught me. It saved your money."

"I didn't have much," he said.

She laughed. "Then we have something in common."

"Yes," he said, smiling. "We have a lot of company."

"Well," she said, after a pause, "I guess I'd better let you get back to work. Thanks for the hamburger."

"Oh, you don't have to go yet," he said quickly. "It isn't often that I have the chance to talk to somebody."

In his eyes she thought she saw unhappiness. And there was something in the tone of his voice which betrayed some sort of longing. Rodina did not know for what. For some reason she pitied him. The momentary impression passed. She smiled and rose and said, "No, I'd better go. I'm glad we met."

"So am I," he said, and, looking at him, Rodina knew he meant the words.

At the counter, he paid the bill. Rodina thought the waiter stared at him. They went outside and stopped a moment at the corner.

"It was wonderful that you came back to see me," Theodore said.

"Oh, it wasn't anything. I was in the neighborhood, anyway."

That seemed to take something from him, and Rodina was sorry she had said it. Theodore looked at her and said, "Well, will you come again sometime?"

She shrugged a little. "Sure. It'd be nice to talk."

"Yes," he said.

She left him standing on the corner.

CHAPTER THREE

WHAT LATER PUZZLED them—the police, the reporters, the others concerned—was how love ever grew between this wild young girl and this weary, middle-aged man. They shook their heads over the incongruity of it; that the quiet Theodore, who loved poetry, should have been attracted to a pickpocket; that the girl, who had undoubtedly had many men, should at last have surrendered herself to a man they all thought weak, cowardly, a failure.

Hucks could not have understood it.

"Let's get ourselves a cup of tea," he said to Rodina one day, shortly after her first visit to the night watchman's office.

"I could stand a cup," Rodina said, more pleasantly than usual.

They sat in the tearoom and Glenn, the waiter, came over. Juarez passed and Huck made some crack about "the Mex." They talked about the usual things. Hucks was his usual self.

"Still waitin' for that date, baby," he said.

"Yeah?"

"Now is that the way to be? You don't want to play hard to get with your old flame, do you? Can't you remember the good old days?"

"Sure," Rodina said, "and I remember the good old Hucks. He's changed. Aren't you satisfied? You've got a million girls. How's Sally?"

"Fine. The others, too. But there's none nice as you."

Glenn brought the tea and said, "Anybody care for a little nip?" Nobody did, so Glenn went away. They sipped tea. Hucks winked at Rodina.

"You're goin' to waste, baby," Hucks laughed. "You know what I mean?"

"You've got rotten thoughts."

"Normal thoughts, sugar. Goin' to waste. It's a shame."

"Normal thoughts," Rodina said. "That's what's wrong. I want somebody who doesn't have normal thoughts for a change. Somebody who thinks of other things."

"You'd be bored stiff," Hucks said.

"You think so? I don't. Somebody who thinks about other things. There *are* other things, you know."

Hucks laughed. "Look who's talkin'. How many decent things you think about, baby? You musta changed a lot. You'd be bored stiff. Bored to death."

"You think so?" She was annoyed. "Well, I don't."

Hucks laughed. "You better be satisfied with what you can get."

"Which is you, no doubt."

"Which is me."

Hucks could never have understood. Nor could the others.

2

She visited Theodore the first time out of mischief. She went again out of curiosity. After that she visited him many times, because she found in him someone who seemed different from all the men she had known. Someone who was "good."

There was no mystery. When she tapped on the window of the dull night watchman's office Theodore rose smiling and walked to the door and they went together to the diner. There they sat and ate and talked. Someone always played the juke

34

box. They talked about nothing but Theodore smiled when he was with her and she knew, she could tell, that he did not often have reason to smile. He never mentioned his home life, yet she knew it was not happy. He never mentioned his wife, yet Rodina sensed that Theodore did not, could not really love her.

They sat and talked while Jerry stared and Rodina was amazed that Theodore never tried to make a pass at her. She was amazed only during the first visits; afterward she knew that decency was what to expect from him; he was not like the men she knew. That made her happy. Somehow, because she knew him, she, too, felt decent.

"Rodina," he said to her once, "remember that you promised you wouldn't steal anymore?"

"Yes."

"You've kept that promise?"

"Yes."

He smiled and she knew it pleased him. So it pleased her.

Sometimes, when they did not stay in the diner long, they took a walk around the block or sat on the steps across from the night watchman's office. They talked. Theodore asked her questions about herself: where she had lived before coming to Philadelphia, what her life at home was like. She had lived in this city all of her life and for as long as she could remember her mother had been an invalid. Her father had died when she was very young; he was a preacher, and she did not remember ever having seen him. For ten years she and her mother had lived in the red brick tenement house. She had taken jobs for short periods of time: she had quit each of them because she hated the unhealthy work in factories, or because the boss got fresh, or because she felt herself incompetent and destined to remain in one position, poor-paying, all the rest of her life. She had felt nothing wrong in stealing. She had stolen since she was a little girl, beginning with comic books from the local candy store and working up to candy and, eventually, small amounts of money. She had felt nothing wrong in this because, after all, her mother could not work and had to have money to stay alive, and she herself needed more than the four walls and a bed at night: she needed books to read (joke books), lipstick, stockings to wear. She felt nothing wrong with all this at first, but others had told her it was wrong, and her mother had read her passages from the Bible. A deep sense of the wrong of the things she was doing came to her, and for a time she followed the beaten path, working in a lamp factory and then in a cigar factory and finally in a restaurant. She had borne this as long as possible, she said, and then had left the jobs and gone back to the old habits. But she knew that what she was doing was wrong. She hated herself for doing these things. Then, eventually, she had buried the hatred of herself and again become defiant and reckless.

She had seen nothing wrong in stealing, and she had seen nothing wrong in going out with boys or going to bed with them. That was a natural thing, wasn't it? She had seen nothing wrong in this, or in walking alone late at night on the streets, or in swearing. She had seen nothing wrong in letting herself go, in being herself, in having no inhibitions.

Yes, she admitted to Theodore, she had done evil things. Sometimes her very thoughts frightened her. Her mother had told her that many people were born in sin, were sinful from the first day they set foot upon the earth, and perhaps she was one of these. Certainly she acted like it. No matter how hard she tried to change, eventually she slipped into the old habits.

"No one is born evil," Theodore told her.

He said this to her many times. But sometimes, even with him, she could not help but believe her mother's words. Even with him, occasionally, the sense of evil rose up to haunt her.

Whenever Theodore saw this he talked to her softly and patiently, as though she were a little girl, explaining things to her. She was not evil. No one was born evil. She could be what she wanted to be.

That was the miracle. That he believed in her. He was kind, considerate, decent. He was good. And he believed in her. After talking to him she felt that she was worth something, that she was a lady, the same as any other woman in the world. When she returned home and listened to her mother she sometimes doubted herself again; but Theodore was always there, at the night watchman's office, available whenever she needed to hear kind words or a soothing voice.

After a while, when he had come really to trust her, Theodore told Rodina of his desire to write poetry. She did not laugh. She seemed even to understand. And then, when she came one morning as he finished work, he walked her home and told her something else. At first they walked in silence. Dawn's opaque light was in the sky. Street cars passed and workers stood on corners, waiting for transportation.

Theodore said, "Rodina, before I met you I used to fall almost to sleep and see a woman in my mind. She seemed to be calling me. I always wanted to follow her. Away from the old life. You remind me of her. Since I met you, I don't dream of her anymore."

Rodina was touched by this. And as though to reveal some secret of her own, she paused when they at last reached the red brick tenement in which she lived and said:

"This is home. When we first came here I loved this place. I used to pretend it was a castle and tell myself that someday my king would come to live here with me."

Something passed between their eyes. Theodore left her and walked home.

Two months passed. October's wintry wind and changing leaves filled the city. The people changed clothes and changed activities. Now the boys who came into the streets with knickers patched at the knees and socks wrinkled and worn sneakers tied with broken strings—now these boys began to practice football and basketball and brought out last year's skates. The women took out their short cloth coats as the winds whipped them and molded them for the men who stood on corners. There were walks in the park occasionally, for those who could spare the time: long walks, the boys and girls holding hands, walking together, looking at the leaves, feeling the wind, filled with romance because they had read some place that it was romantic for young men and women to walk hand in hand through parks in the fall as the wind hurried by and leaves on the trees turned brown.

Theodore felt sometimes that there had never been another month. Even when not present physically, Rodina was often in his mind. As he sat alone in the office at night. As his wife complained, or cajoled, or whined at home.

Sometimes he went with his wife to visit neighbors. They played pinochle and drank beer and ate pretzels and talked. The women talked about dresses and furniture and motion picture stars; the men talked about their jobs, or, if the women were not around, about the girl friends they had on the side. Theodore did not listen to them. His mind drifted in and out of the rooms, in and out, like an impatient child. He thought of Rodina. He felt an airy lightness. Like a wisp of cotton he floated mentally skyward, coming to rest on clouds. There was Rodina. Beckoning.

Sometimes, inexplicably, he felt a sudden burst of tenderness for his wife. He suggested picnics together. She laughed;

that was for children. Undaunted, he suggested visits to night clubs, or the circus, or any place else that came to mind.

"What's wrong with you, Theodore?"

"Nothing. I just think you don't have enough fun, Sylvia. I want to take you out."

"Like a boy with a guilty conscience," she said without looking at him. "If you were another man I'd think you had a backstreet woman."

Guilt and anger, like waves of electricity, ran through him. Guilt because she had struck the edge of truth. Anger because she dismissed its possibility.

But Sylvia seldom concerned herself with thoughts such as these.

"Howard was by today," she would tell him some night when he returned, tired, from work.

"Yes. What did he have to say?"

"Oh, we talked and talked. He's made such a success of himself, Theodore. Imagine, he owns those restaurants. You should try to be more like him."

Theodore would not answer and Sylvia would say, "And to think he wanted to marry me," shaking her head.

Yes—Theodore wanted to say—Yes, and why didn't you accept him?

But he remained silent.

4

And then came that Sunday afternoon when Theodore visited Rodina's mother. For in some change in Rodina's conduct at home, or in some difference in her daughter's eyes, Mrs. Baleza had sensed the existence of a special man. She had questioned her daughter; she had learned about Theodore; she was anxious to meet him.

Before they went upstairs, they stopped in the tearoom. Glenn brought them coffee and as they drank it, Rodina said:

"Ted, I didn't tell her you were married. And I didn't tell her your age, but maybe she can tell anyway. All I told her was we went out walking sometimes and that you were nice and didn't make any passes."

They went upstairs and into the sparsely furnished room. Mrs. Baleza fixed Theodore with her gaze and beckoned him to the chair. Rodina sat on the stool, apprehensive.

"I wondered what you were like," Mrs. Baleza said. "I wasn't too sure of Rodina's choices. She's picked up so many tramps."

Theodore smiled and said nothing. But he did not miss the mother's purpose in informing him that there had been "so many" before.

"My only daughter," Mrs. Baleza said. "Well, you look all right. Do you know my daughter very well?"

"I think I know her pretty well," Theodore said. "I've only known her two months, though."

"How old are you?" Mrs. Baleza asked.

Theodore hesitated. He was conscious of Rodina's eyes on him. He said, "Thirty-nine." Somehow the lie would not come.

But Mrs. Baleza did not flinch. She said, "Well, then you're old enough to have some sense. Guess you know what you're doin'." She paused a moment, her eyes never leaving Theodore's. "I don't suppose you're very serious about Rodina."

Again Theodore paused. Then he said, "I'm very serious about her, Mrs. Baleza. I love her."

"And what is this supposed to lead up to?"

"I don't know," Theodore said. He looked at Rodina and wondered, really, what this would lead to.

Mrs. Baleza rested back against the pillows. Her eyes remained on Theodore. She seemed to smile faintly. She said, "You think you know my daughter, eh?"

40

"Pretty well," Theodore said. He felt awkward. Why was he answering all these questions? What, after all, were his intentions? He had tried to blind himself to the future; but the future had to be faced.

The woman in the bed leaned forward and said, "No, you don't know her. You don't know her at all, Mr. Hall."

She looked at Theodore and he said nothing. He waited for her to go on. The woman fascinated him. The way her eyes shone: Like Rodina's had shone that night in the rain.

"You only *think* you know her," Mrs. Baleza said. "You've never really seen her."

Theodore glanced at Rodina. She was wide-eyed, staring at her mother.

"Mr. Hall," Mrs. Baleza said, "are you a religious man?"

Theodore was fascinated by the woman's eyes. He said softly, "I don't know."

"You don't know. You don't know whether or not you're a religious man."

"I don't suppose I am," Theodore said. "I don't go to church every Sunday, if that's what you mean."

"Mr. Hall," Mrs. Baleza said, still leaning forward, "I don't go to church every Sunday either. But I'm a religious woman. Since you're not religious, Mr. Hall, you'll probably think this is an old woman talkin' crazy. Mr. Hall, my daughter is as evil as any woman who ever set foot on this earth."

Theodore could only stare at Mrs. Baleza. He could imagine how Rodina felt; a rush of pity for her filled him.

"You see Mr. Hall," Mrs. Baleza said, "you people who have brains and have read books are smarter than us poor tenement people. You people are too smart to believe in God, y'see. But we people are superstitious. Me and my husband were the superstitious kind. My husband was a preacher, Mr. Hall.

And we're dumb enough to believe that some people are born evil."

Theodore could say nothing. The woman's eyes were terrifying. She sat leaning forward in the bed, her deep-set eyes fixed shining and hypnotic on his.

"Rodina was born evil," Mrs. Baleza said with passion. "When she was eight years old, *eight years old,* she was caught on a couch with a man twenty-five. She stole and she lied and was too lazy to work. She didn't go to church. She did just what she pleased. She was evil, Mr. Hall. She always will be evil, and her evil will spread to any man who fools with her. Mark my word."

She paused and breathed heavily. Theodore could not look at Rodina. He could imagine how she felt. His eyes were caught in the woman's gaze and he could not tear them away. A petal of horror closed round his heart. After awhile Mrs. Baleza caught her breath. She leaned back against the pillows. "Now," she said, "I'm finished talkin'. I wanted to warn you, that's all. You look like a decent sort. Too bad you got brains. Brains make you feel too big to believe in God. But if you take my advice you'll leave this house and never come back."

Theodore stood up. He did not know what to say. Mrs. Baleza lay back against the pillows, her eyes closed. Theodore looked at Rodina. Her eyes were on the floor. He touched her shoulder and she looked up, startled, then rose and went out into the hall and down the stairs and to the front door with him. There Theodore paused.

"Rodina," he said, trembling, "you've got to get away from this."

Her eyes were on his chest. She said nothing. Her shoulders slumped and she seemed tired.

"Rodina," he said, gripping her shoulders, "I love you."

She rested her head on his chest. She slumped loosely against him.

42

"Rodina," he said, "I'll find an answer. Don't worry, darling. You can't go on like this. I can understand so many things, now. Rodina look up at me. Do you love me?"

"Yes."

"Enough for anything?"

She nodded. She was far away, weary.

"All right," he said, "leave it to me. Everything will be all right."

She gripped him tightly and tears came to her eyes.

CHAPTER FOUR

HE LAY IN BED that night. A head on his chest. He remembered the afternoon and Rodina downstairs near the door. A head on his chest. That was what he needed: a head on his chest. Someone to lean on him. Someone who needed him. As he was. Without money or success or the need for his changing.

Sylvia awoke next morning and saw that Theodore was not in bed beside her. She sat up and remembered the night before—how peculiar Theodore was. She rose, washed and dressed. She felt apprehensive, for some reason. She went out into the kitchen and through the door saw Theodore in the chair near the window with the morning newspaper in front of him. She knew he was not reading.

"Good morning," she said.

"Good morning."

Something was wrong. There was something strange about that quality of voice. She fixed breakfast, wondering, but said nothing. Finally she called him and he came into the kitchen and sat in his customary place. She sat opposite him. He would not meet her eyes.

"Another day," she said. He did not respond. She watched his face. He ate without talking. *Something* was wrong. Strange; she could think of nothing. Still, he had been strange all last evening and now . . .

"Have you been up long?" she asked.

"Yes. Since daybreak."

"Anything wrong? I mean, weren't you feeling well?"

"Oh, I felt all right."

Something definitely was wrong. He had never been like this. Something was seriously wrong. But she could handle it. She knew how to handle him.

"Howard came by while you were out yesterday," Sylvia said. "We talked and talked. To tell the truth I was really bored after awhile. I wished you were home."

She watched his averted eyes. He lifted the coffee to his lips.

"It's a beautiful day," she said. "A lovely day, isn't it? Cool and pleasant. Let's go for a walk in the park."

He looked up at her and she said, "I get so tired of being cooped up. I think a walk through the park might do both of us good."

Theodore said, "Sylvia, I'd like to talk to you. Seriously."

"Darling," Sylvia said, feeling herself pressed for time, "must we talk seriously now? It's a glorious day. Tell me what you have to say later. Please? Promise me you won't talk seriously until after dinner. I have a beautiful dinner planned."

She thought she saw him weaken. He said nothing. Almost instinctively Sylvia knew she needed time.

After the breakfast dishes were done Theodore walked with Sylvia through the park. She knew his thoughts were far away from her. She felt a desperate fear. Most of the trees were bare and the wind blew sternly. They walked most of the afternoon.

"It's nice to walk like this," Sylvia said. "We haven't done it for a long time. We've stayed in too much." She was silent for a moment. "Sometimes I think I've been a rotten wife, Theodore. I haven't done very much for you. Out here in the park I feel like making a resolution. I'll change. I absolutely promise not to be a stodgy wife anymore. A real promise." She turned to him and smiled.

Theodore said, "You've been a good wife, Sylvia," and she felt that a minor victory had been won.

"No," she said, "I've been a fussy bore. But all that will change. You'll see."

When they came home Sylvia prepared a delicious supper. During the meal she talked pleasantly. She was worried, she said, because he had not written in a long time. No matter what she had said at times, the fact that he wrote was a source of pride to her. Theodore listened to her and seemed far away.

Finally, he said, "Sylvia, I hate to say this. I don't quite know how to explain it." Then he said, quickly, "I want a divorce."

She stared at him, stunned. For a moment she said nothing. All the time she was thinking rapidly. She covered her face with her hands and sobbed. Her voice caught as she said, "Oh, darling, I know the reason. Because I had no children."

Theodore was horrified. "Sylvia, that's not true!" He rose, went around the table and put his hand on her shoulder. "Sylvia, don't think that. It's not true. Really, it's not that at all."

"Then what is it?"

He hesitated. He did not want to tell her about Rodina. That would be the most insulting thing of all: to let her feel she had been defeated by another woman.

"I . . . I don't really know," he said. "I just want to be free. I want to be away from marriage."

"No," she said, her voice broken, "no, it's because I couldn't have any children. I know it."

He had never seen her like this. He did not know what to do. He looked at her helplessly. She looked up at him;

her eyes were wide and red and her face was grief-stricken. With her hands she attempted to wipe away the tears and tried to smile. He felt miserable.

"Don't feel so bad, darling," she said, still sobbing, looking at him through the red, tearful eyes. "I can understand. Of course, I can understand. Every man wants children. Anybody knows that."

"Sylvia! Sylvia!" He stood beside her in the small kitchen, the dirty dishes still on the table. "Please, believe it isn't true!" The water dripped into the sink from the faucet. He was stifling in the small room.

She touched his hand, patted it, trying a smile. "Darling, it's all right, it's all right," she said soothingly, like a mother comforting her son. "It's all right. You don't have to explain. It's all right."

Tears came to his eyes. "Sylvia, please don't think that. Please don't. Please don't think that."

"It's all right, Theodore."

He had known it would be hard. He had not known it would be like this.

"Please darling," she said, "don't make yourself miserable."

She watched his face as his eyes moved beyond hers, as he stared at the sink, as the pain showed clearly in his face. She watched him as he drew his hand away from her, stood tired beside her, moved away to stand at the other end of the table. One phase had passed. Like a general, she planned her successive moves.

"When do you want to leave, darling?" she asked him. He heard the break in her voice.

He did not answer. Sylvia said, "I know you'll want to get away as soon as possible. You couldn't sleep beside me tonight. Not after . . . You'd feel terrible, I know. You shouldn't darling. These things happen every day. To wives lots better

48

than me. Husbands grow tired, things don't turn out as expected . . . That happens every day. But you'll want to get away, won't you darling? You'll want to forget—"

She broke off; for a moment she was silent. He did not look at her. Always a coward, she thought. She said, "Shall I help you pack?" He said nothing so she said, "Yes, darling, I'll help you pack."

She stood up and went into the bedroom and took a suitcase from the closet. She opened it on the bed. Theodore stayed in the kitchen. She went to the bureau and opened the top drawer. Through the mirror she could see the door to the kitchen and part of the kitchen itself. In a moment she saw his shadow moving toward the door and then saw him in the door itself. She lowered her eyes and took the handkerchiefs, socks, shaving utensils and underwear from the drawer. She walked to the bed and placed them neatly in the suitcase. Theodore stood motionless in the doorway. She did not look at him. She went back to the bureau, opened another drawer, and picked up several shirts. She put them in the suitcase over paper which covered the shoes and socks and underwear; she paused a moment, looking into the suitcase. She heard a sound from the doorway; she felt he was coming toward her.

She waited, looking into the suitcase. Slowly she lifted the top shirt and stared at it. Theodore was behind her. She lifted the shirt to her lips and kissed it a long moment, sobbing silently. Theodore's hand touched her shoulder; she felt the hand tremble. She kissed the shirt and felt tremors run through his body into his hand. She waited a long while, kissing the shirt, sobbing without sound. Then suddenly she turned and buried her head in his shoulder and cried out, "Theodore, Theodore don't leave me, don't leave me!" She cried out, then waited, thinking: This is it!

For a long time he said nothing, made no motion. She

knew that tears were streaming down his face. She knew he was being wracked inside by pain. She waited, trembling, sobbing. She held him tightly. She held him as though she could never let him go. If he had never thought she loved him, he must think it now; if he had believed her incapable of emotion, he must not believe that now. She waited.

Then slowly but firmly, his hands gripping her arms, he drew away from her. He turned and walked to the window, then stood staring through it to the street. She watched him, her heart hammering loudly. Theodore turned abruptly from the window and walked past her to the bed; he closed the suitcase, snapped it shut, and walked to the door of the bedroom. There he paused to turn and look at her.

"Sylvia," he said, "I'm sorry, terribly sorry. But I couldn't go on with it. I'll write. I'll send you money. You can start divorce proceedings."

Then he was gone from the room and Sylvia heard the front door open and close.

CHAPTER FIVE

South philadelphia in fall is chill, but the day that Theodore stood on the street outside the red brick house the air was pleasant and the sun shone warm. He murmured: "I'm free, I'm free." It was as though he stood weightless in a dream.

He went inside. He thought: So this will be home. He went into the tearoom and took a seat, putting the suitcase down on the floor beside his chair. The waiter, Glenn, came to the table.

"Tea," Theodore said.

"Tea," the waiter repeated. He added, noticing the suitcase, "Going somewhere?"

"Coming," Theodore said. "Not going, coming. Perhaps here. Do you have a spare room?"

"Don't know," the waiter said. "Have to ask Mrs. Davis. She runs this place."

The tea came and Theodore sipped it, looking around the tearoom, and then he saw Rodina in the doorway. She stood staring at him, dressed in a gingham skirt and white blouse, staring as though she could not believe it was he she saw. He looked at her and smiled. Her eyes dropped to the suitcase. She looked at him again. For a long while she stood motionless in the doorway and their eyes passed messages back and forth.

She walked over to the table and sat down next to him.

He continued to smile; neither said anything. Her eyes explored his face: they went to his mouth, his cheeks, his hair, his forehead, then to his eyes again. Then she smiled softly.

Glenn brought another tea. They drank their tea together. They were alone in the tearoom; the blinds were drawn, and the light which entered was soft.

"You'll want a room," Rodina said finally, speaking softly. "I'm sure there's one near mine."

Afterward they found Mrs. Davis who, wheezing and chattering, led them up to the second-floor room formerly occupied by a gangster, now safely tucked away in jail. The room was fairly large; there was a small stove in a corner, a bed, a bureau, a table, a closet and a night stand.

"It'll be five dollars a week," Mrs. Davis said gaspingly, "'n' I'm sure you'll be better'n the last tenant I had in here. A gangster, old Sam Johnson, bless his bones in Alcatraz."

Only when Mrs. Davis had gone did Rodina throw her arms around Theodore and cry, "Ted, Ted, you came to me!"

Through the evening they sat in the room and talked.

"Oh Ted," Rodina said, "you loved me enough to leave her?"

He smiled and squeezed her hand.

Then her face changed and was serious. "I hope you never regret it. Never."

"I don't think I ever will."

"Ted," she said, earnestly, "I'll make you glad you came. I'll never do anything to make you ashamed of me. I'll never steal or swear or drink or be loud. I'll be a lady, Ted, and you'll be proud of me. I'll do anything you say."

He kissed her for the first time since they met.

"Ted, how did it happen? How did you come to leave her?"

"I've always wanted to," Theodore said. "For fifteen years. For longer. I never had the courage, that's all."

"And how did she take it?"

52

"Hard," Theodore said. A frown came to his forehead. "I can't understand it. I never thought she loved me. I thought she might welcome her freedom."

After a moment Rodina said, "And how did you feel, Ted? Did you feel bad about leaving her?"

"I hated to hurt her. I did hurt her, terribly, and I almost changed my mind at the last minute, when we started to talk about it. I still feel pretty rotten. But I couldn't go on with it. I could never be happy with Sylvia."

Still later, rummaging through the drawers of the bureau and the closet, they came across several belongings of old Sam Johnson. The closet was filled with his clothes hangers. In the bureau drawers there was a stale pack of cigarettes, a screw driver, pliers, a jimmy, a hammer, a dirty handkerchief and a revolver, with bullets in five chambers. Rodina was excited about the gun.

"Do you know what this means? Finding a gun, loaded?"

"What?"

"It means good luck! I'll hold the barrel, you hold the handle. There. That's good fortune!"

"Even if Johnson killed somebody with it?"

She frowned. "No, that would be *bad* luck." She looked at him seriously. "I hope he didn't kill anybody."

Theodore smiled. "Well, let's forget it." He put the gun back in the drawer, along with the tools, and closed it.

"But Ted, suppose he *did* kill somebody with that gun. It means terribly bad luck. For certain. Death even."

"I don't believe in superstition." His mind was elsewhere as he kissed her. "You'll make a wonderful wife."

"Wife?" Her eyes shone.

"Yes," he said, "wife."

Late that night he said, "Rodina, will you sleep with me?"

"Of course."

"But Rodina——" He hesitated, and she saw he was embarrassed again. "Rodina, I don't want to touch you. I just want you to sleep beside me."

She looked at him, perplexed. He went on, "Perhaps I sound silly. But I don't want anything *common* to develop between us. I want to make you my wife. But right now I'm still married, and I'll be married until my divorce papers come through. Until then I don't want to touch you. Can you understand what I mean?"

She nodded. He said, "We can wait."

"Sure," she said. "Anything you say, Ted."

"Darling, I have strange ideas. I have a lot of taboos that I can't do anything about emotionally. This is one of them. Just a whim." He smiled. "Try to understand me."

"Sure," she said, smiling. "I like that in you, Ted."

2

South Philadelphia is a checkerboard of bricks and lots and narrow streets. It is filled with the smells of sheep and of the Delaware and Schuylkill rivers and of fish and horse manure. The two-story dingy brick houses stretch in monotonous squares for miles. There are stables and tenements and railroad yards and iron works and garages and red-light districts. South Philadelphia is heat in summer and an appalling, brick-enclosed cold in winter.

It is another world. In South Philadelphia horses still pull the wagons loaded with fruit and vegetables and ice; the vender still shouts. Any day one can see the pushcarts loaded with bananas coming through, the wizened conductors puffing from the strain. There are many streets so narrow cars cannot drive through; streets still bearing the imprints of the coach paths of another day. There is South Street, the avenue of the

54

Negro ghetto; there is Snyder Avenue, main stem of the Italian and Jewish sections; there is the east section with Poles and delicatessens and Jewish bakeries out of Palestine; there is Grays Ferry with the Irish, where strangers once dared not walk. There is filth such as is rarely seen in a northern American city; there are taprooms which must close weekdays at two o'clock in the morning and on Saturday's at midnight, and speakeasies which are open all night long.

In South Philadelphia the police join hands with numbers writers and the people vote Republican to stay outside of jail. Ward leaders and committeemen pit race against race and nationality against nationality to retain themselves in power. When times are hard there are clashes and gang fights between Negroes and Italians or Italians and Jews or Jews and Irish or Irish and Negroes.

It is a crowded district. At night in hot weather the streets are filled and the corners are crowded with boys in shirt sleeves. They swear and lie. Already they hate the police and the law. Already they hate the discipline of school and work. Already they despise their parents.

Because there are no porches and no lawns, because in summer the heat is heavy and unrelieved by gusts of breeze, the people come out at night to sit on steps and watch the boys play ball. In the narrow streets where few cars come the boys chalk bases on the asphalt and toss a rubber ball which they hit with their fists and they call this baseball. And the older folks sit on the hard marble steps and fan themselves and smoke to keep mosquitoes away and talk about the day. This is their relief from the daytime of unceasing work and worry and speculation on the numbers lottery.

The people are always worried. There are bills to be paid. No job is secure, and some of the men drink. For money, they borrow from the finance people who send their men into the

55

area to paint glowing pictures of pleasures and luxuries to be had at only seven or eight per cent per month.

At sixteen or seventeen the sons and daughters usually have had enough of school; besides, money is needed at home. So they leave school to work. Later they are dissatisfied; they want better jobs; they have no training. They are dissatisfied and so some leave the jobs and spend their days at home or on the streets talking on corners and watching the automobiles which come flashing by. After a time, someone older than they comes around to suggest a way of getting a lot of money fast.

The people know their district; they feel ill at ease outside of it. To them, South Philadelphia is the city, the state, the nation, the world.

This is not all of South Philadelphia, but it is what Theodore most vividly remembered. He knew this section well. He had lived in South Philadelphia for five years, from the age of seven until he was twelve.

Theodore's family moved from Malvern, Pennsylvania, to South Philadelphia in 1916. Theodore attended junior high school there. He did not like the school or the boys in the neighborhood or the streets or anything else about it. He did not like his father, who pushed him out of the house to make him play with the boys; he did not like the boys.

Theodore liked certain kinds of poetry and certain kinds of novels and certain of his lady teachers in the school. He knew nothing about baseball or football or deadbox. He did not like the talk he heard from the boys about girls. He preferred to stay at home and read or draw or talk to his mother who was gentle and protective. His father told him he was a sissy.

The boys did not like Theodore. The boys often fought each other, and several times one or the other of them tried to start a fight with Theodore. But Theodore kept quiet and tried to

56

ignore their taunts and jeers. One day, prodded beyond resistance, Theodore offered to fight one of the boys. The boy laughed.

"You want to fight me?"

"That's right," Theodore said. His legs trembled.

All of the boys laughed and the boy in front of him shoved his face and said, "Run along home sissy. Run along little girl."

Theodore charged the big boy and felt his head jerk suddenly backward and found himself lying on the ground and heard the boys all laughing and felt a circle of numbness spread out from the right side of his chin.

"Sissy."

"Whyn't you smack the hell outa him, Rick."

"Kick him one, Rick."

He got up and charged again. Rick struck him another stunning blow. He rose again and was again felled. Then suddenly all anger and indignation and pride left him and he lay still, afraid to move.

"Well, sissy, whyn't you stand up again?"

Everybody laughed. Theodore lay still. He did not want to be brave. Tears poured from his eyes.

"Whyn't you get up, little girl?"

"Kick him one, Rick."

Then his mother appeared on the edge of the circle; she pressed toward him, knelt down to him and buried his head in her bosom while the boys laughed and jeered, "Little girlie go to his mommy's tit." He cried softly, his mother held him tight, and he felt warm and content.

That was the first fight, and there were others. He was always beaten. Eventually he refused to fight; he would bear any insult; he would circle the block to avoid the boys; he would do anything, endure any humility, but he would not fight. Never again.

There were also girls in the district, girls he would not have touched with a fishing rod.

He hated it all. He was happy when he moved away.

3

The days passed, Theodore wrote many letters to his wife, but she answered none of them; this worried him. Otherwise, he was happy; he felt younger. Rodina slept with him and cooked for him and cleaned his room and washed his clothes for him. She was always near. Every morning without exception they went for a walk. They talked. At night he went to work.

When he went to the diner Jerry, the waiter, never failed to ask him about the girl who was with him those nights.

"Who was she, Ted?"

"Who?"

"You know, that sharp gal. The one with the long hair."

"Oh, her. She's just somebody I know."

"A cousin or something?"

"No. No relative at all. Just a friend."

"Yeah?" Jerry watched him. "Sure is good lookin', can say that. She a good friend of yours?"

"The best."

"Yeah?" Jerry looked at him and grinned. "You ain't pullin' nothin' are you, Ted?"

"No. I'm not pulling anything."

Theodore met most of the people who lived at the tenement in the tearoom or in Mrs. Houston's room where everybody went on Friday to play poker with their week's earnings. Sometimes Theodore played until he had lost a little money; most of the time he was content to watch. But at these games he became acquainted with Juarez and Hucks and Glenn and most of the others. He did not make friends easily, and so

58

Theodore knew most of these people only casually, to speak to.

On weekends he and Rodina usually went to a local motion picture theater. Rodina liked Westerns and love stories; Theodore found himself enjoying them, too.

They lived in virtual isolation. Neither went to see personal friends. Neither wanted any others. They talked; they walked; they went to theaters; they worked. A simple existence. They wanted nothing from anyone outside of or within the castle walls.

Because Theodore worked at night, it was easy for Rodina to deceive her mother. She could sleep at home in her room, and, in the daytime, sleep with Theodore when she chose. Often at night, early, she visited him at the laboratory and they went together to the diner.

"Does your mother know I'm here?" Theodore asked one afternoon.

Rodina shook her head. "I never told her."

Theodore did not like deceit. He hated to think that this, between himself and Rodina, was clandestine. "Does she ever ask about me?"

"Yes." She sat on the edge of the bed while he lay, fully clothed, on top of the blankets. Her hair was done; she wore a bright cotton dress. "Sometimes she asks if I still see you, and I tell her yes. She shakes her head. She says you're a fool."

Theodore grinned. He closed his eyes and she leaned down and kissed him on the mouth. He lay his head on her lap.

She said softly, "Where do you think we'll be, five years from now?"

Dreamily, he replied, "Far away. Far away from Philadelphia, in another state, living another kind of life."

"And what do you think we'll be doing?"

"You," he said, "will be fixing supper for me. I'll be at work somewhere, making enough money for us to live decently on.

59

Maybe I won't be away to work, maybe I'll be at home working, writing or something. Maybe I'll be a great poet, or a novelist, or a writer of articles for magazines or newspapers. Might be anything."

"Yes." She clapped her hands. "And we'll have a nice house. A nice cottage in the suburbs somewhere with white curtains and a lawn and clean, shiny windows. And we'll have a shower in the bathroom and maybe a car."

"Sure," Theodore said.

After a moment's silence, Rodina said, "And we'll be married, Ted."

"Yes. We'll be married."

"And do you know what else we might have?"

He grinned again. "Children."

"Yes."

The thought pleased him. Children. He had forgotten it was possible to have children. And then, as though by a chill blast of air, the pleasant feeling was swept away: he thought of his wife. What was she doing now? Was she able to live as decently as before on the money he sent her each week? He sent half of his weekly pay: was that enough? Did she miss him? Was she terribly lonely? Had she forgiven him for the great pain he had brought to her?

"Do you feel too cold, Ted?" Rodina asked him.

"No."

"You trembled then."

"Did I? I didn't realize it."

She rose and lowered the window. "It *is* cold," she said. "The fall is just about over. Winter's on its way."

"Yes," he said.

"Let's talk about our children," she said. "I like to talk about our children."

"All right," he said. "We'll talk about the children."

60

CHAPTER SIX

JUAREZ STOOD NEAR the window of his room. Softly, he said to himself: "Every day, every day." On the street below Rodina and Theodore walked, waving to the kids, holding hands like adolescent lovers. Juarez watched them walk until they were out of sight; then he turned and lay down across the bed. "Every day," he murmured, "every day since he came here."

His room was filled with shadows. Even now, in the early morning, it lay in semidarkness. The shades were low, the curtains were heavy, little light came in. In the room there was a table lined with books held by wooden book ends. (*An American Dilemma, Black Metropolis, Crime and Punishment, The Brothers Karamazov, The Golden Bough, State and Revolution* . . .) A filled ashtray was on the end of the table. There was other furniture, from which the paint had long ago peeled. On the radiator near the bed sat the top from a mayonnaise jar which was used as an ashtray; it, too, was filled with cigarette ashes and butts.

Juarez lay completely relaxed, breathing easily, staring at the ceiling. He closed his eyes and saw himself standing in front of him. Juarez. What was Juarez? He opened his eyes again and thought of Rodina and the man, Theodore, walking down the street, waving to the kids, holding hands like school children. Every day.

When he closed his eyes he saw himself again and he examined himself carefully. Juarez. A small, insignificant man,

61

stooped, skinny, ugly. A face pock-marked and full of acne with eyes which seemed always filled with tears. Skin like sandpaper and dark as a Negro's. He looked closely at himself. His teeth were all right. He smiled. Yes, his teeth were all right. His teeth and his hair. He congratulated himself. His teeth and his hair were all right.

He tightened the muscles of his body and relaxed them again, liking the feel of relaxation after the strain. Who was Juarez? Juarez was a Mexican. Juarez was a Mexican who had lived all of his life in America with a dark skin and shiny black hair and skin like steel wool. A Mexican. A thin wisp of bitterness, like a curl of smoke, passed through him and blew out. Like smoke his bitterness came and went; like smoke it left its taste and odor behind on the breath, on the tongue. He thought of Rodina. She used to come to him for advice and comfort. Rodina. Like a daughter to a father. For advice and comfort. That was enough. What more could one expect. For what was Juarez? A man with pock-marked skin and darkness with stooped shoulders and skinny arms and legs and torso. A Mexican. Above all, he was a Mexican.

There was a tap at his door. Juarez knew who stood outside. "Yes," he said.

"Jest wanted t' make sure you was up, Juarez, that's all," Mrs. Davis called through the door. "Figured you might be late for work."

"Thanks," Juarez said.

"Oh, it's all right, Juarez. Jest wanted t' make sure. Thought you might be late. Beautiful mornin' outside."

"Yes," Juarez said.

Juarez heard her move laboriously away. He lay still a while longer, smoking a cigarette. Then he rose and lowered his window. He went out into the hall and downstairs to the tea room.

"Mornin' Juarez," Glenn said. "Mighty nice out there this mornin'."

"Yes."

"What'll you have?"

"The same as usual. Bacon and eggs and coffee."

Glenn left. Juarez lit a cigarette and glanced at the clock on the wall. He would have to hurry. When he looked toward the door he saw Hucks coming in.

"Well, how's the Mex this morning?" Hucks said lustily. "You look mighty bright and wide awake."

"Yes?"

Hucks looked at him and grinned. "You seen Rodina and her latest love out for a breather this morning?"

"No, I didn't see them," Juarez said. "I must have been asleep."

Hucks kept grinning. He wore a lumberjacket and corduroy pants. "Bet you boil like hell up there, him beatin' the hell outa you, eh?"

Hucks laughed loudly, pounding Juarez on his back. Juarez said nothing. He had determined, by mental vow, not to hate Hucks. It was a hard vow to abide by. Juarez hated bullies; he hated big men who made too much of their bigness. He hated people who called him "Mex." These were emotional hatreds; his intellect went against them. Still they affected him. But he tried hard not to hate Hucks. Even when he saw him annoying Rodina. He had one consolation: he knew Rodina detested Hucks fully as much as he did.

"What's the matter, cat got your tongue?" Hucks said.

Juarez did not answer. Hucks kept on grinning. He pounded Juarez on the back again.

"Well, I got to be going," he said. He turned and walked toward the door, calling over his shoulder, "Bring one of them

Mex chicks around here for me to meet sometime. I hear they're great in bed."

Glenn brought in the breakfast. Juarez wanted to eat it quickly but he could not eat fast, he had always eaten slowly. When he finished he rushed outside and caught the streetcar. By the time he arrived at the restaurant where he worked, he was a few minutes late. The manager was standing where he always stood in the morning: near the door. He looked at Juarez as he came in.

"Better get up a bit earlier if you want to keep your job, boy," he said. The manager was tall and broad and red haired.

Juarez paused and looked at the manager. Juarez was twenty-eight years old. He did not like to be called "boy." For a long moment he stared into the manager's eyes and the manager reddened.

"Well, get changed and get to work," he said.

Juarez stood still and looked at the manager. Then he moved off to the dressing room and changed into the white uniform and white hat he had to wear. Looking in the mirror near the lockers he saw the starched uniform contrasted with his dark skin; the uniform was too big, and made him appear even smaller than he was. He hated the uniform. He looked at his dark face and thought: "This is what I'm supposed to wear. This is the kind of work I'm supposed to do." He turned and walked upstairs.

The waitresses were already behind the counter; they were loading the steam table with food. Juarez spoke to those who spoke to him. From the kitchen Juarez brought trays of breaded eggplant, pork chops, and other meats to the grill. He checked the eggs and bacon and potatoes. From the oven he pulled the frying pans and containers for poached eggs and placed them over a slow gas flame. When he had finished the preliminaries he leaned back against the grill and waited for the first customers to arrive.

64

The waitresses, too, were waiting. Shortly, the door would be opened to customers and there would be a rush for breakfasts. Now the waitresses relaxed. Juarez looked at their faces; some were pleasant, others were cheap, the scum. His eyes fell on one of the girls and the wisp of bitterness drifted through him again.

Her name was Jean. She had not been working at the restaurant long; she had come there less than two months ago. She lived in another section of town. Juarez had liked her face. She had worked hard the first day, and afterwards when it was dark, she would have had to go home alone. Juarez had wanted to help her. He had offered to escort her home.

"What d'you mean?" the girl asked, looking at him wide-eyed.

Juarez said, "You live so far away. I thought you might not want to go home alone."

Her eyes, on his face, went down the front of his uniform to his feet, then up to his face again. Her eyes were wide. She said, "Don't worry about me, I ain't fallin' for that old line. Never mind. Just get yourself one of your own kind, boy."

Your own kind, boy.

The morning and afternoon were routine. There were two rushes: one for breakfast, one for dinner. Crowds milled about, the lines were long, everyone had to work hard. When they were over everyone tried to recuperate for the final rush hour, at supper time.

During the supper rush a short man with a blue serge suit became impatient. He had ordered a sirloin steak which had to be cooked slowly over a low flame. He fidgeted.

"I have an appointment," he yelled to Juarez.

Juarez would not hurry the steak. Cooking was an art. He would have preferred another, but, if he had to cook, he would do it well. He added butter to the steak and checked to see if it could be turned over.

"Hurry up, boy," the short man said, "I haven't got all day."

Juarez turned around and looked at the man. The man saw the hatred in his eyes. Juarez turned back to the stove and lowered the gas flame still more. He filled other orders. The customer fidgeted. His face became red and his eyes puffed with anger.

"I'll get the manager," he said. "How's that?" He stamped away.

In a moment the man in the blue serge suit was in front of the counter again, and the manager came behind the counter to Juarez. He looked at the steak.

"Well, what's wrong, Juarez?"

He towered high above Juarez; his shoulders were square and made Juarez look like an imitation of a man. Juarez refused to look up at the manager; he did not want to look up at him.

"What do you mean?" he asked.

"Why are you taking so long with this customer's steak?"

"It has to cook slowly," Jaurez said.

"He says you're deliberately cooking the steak slowly."

Juarez did not answer. He continued filling the other orders. The waitresses and customers looked at him. Jean giggled.

"Hurry up with the steak," the manager commanded.

He stood towering over Juarez as the stooped Mexican took the steak from the pan and put it on a plate. A waitress added vegetables. The customer looked at the steak and said, "It's not even done right. You ought to get yourself another short order boy."

The manager glared at Juarez. He walked off.

At the end of the working day Juarez went downstairs and changed back into his street clothes. He went upstairs. As he was passing the manager's desk the broad-shouldered man called to him.

"What's wrong with you, Juarez?" he asked.

"Nothing."

"Listen, you better watch your step. I don't want my customers insulted."

Juarez looked at him and said nothing. The manager tried to stare him down but did not succeed.

"You're sullen about nothing at all," the manager said. "I've been watching you. And late this morning. Watch your step, that's all I've got to tell you. Just watch your step. You're not indispensable, you know. You people carry a chip on your shoulder. Watch yourself. We can get your kind a dime a dozen."

Juarez walked past the empty tables to the door and went out into the cold evening. *Your kind.* He walked down the street.

2

Juanita was waiting for Juarez on the corner of two big streets. She had a round face with small, well-matched features. She was not tall, but she was taller than Juarez, and so she wore shoes with comparatively low heels. She did not know that Juarez noticed this, and that he knew the reason why.

When she saw him coming up the street Juanita wanted to rush to kiss him. But she knew he would not like that; he was terribly embarrassed by such things, and refused even to hold her hand in the movie. So she waited for him to reach her and then, smiling, said simply, "Hello, Juarez."

"Hello, Juanita."

"How do you feel today? Everything okay?"

"Sure," he said.

They walked on down the street. She knew something troubled him, but would not question him. He was so often troubled, mixed up, moody. He was happiest at such times when undisturbed.

"What shall we do?" Juarez asked.

"Oh, I don't know. We could take in a show."

"Did you eat?"

"Yes."

"How long ago?"

"Around six. At supper time."

"Let's get a sandwich first."

"Okay. Let's stop at Rosa's."

"No," he said, almost sharply. Then he said, "No, let's go someplace else. No Mexican place. Someplace else."

"Okay," she said, glancing at his eyes.

They stopped at a little dinette on Market Street, not far from the Fox Theater. Juarez watched the salesgirls, rushed and sullen, in their white uniforms. At the counter with the movie crowd, Juarez and Juanita had a sandwich and ice cream soda each.

Outside, the usual Market Street crowd hurried by. There were many sailors, for Philadelphia was a navy town. The sailors strolled by, big-shouldered, in groups of five or six, and Juarez, watching them, felt the usual mixture of hatred and fear. Once he had been beaten by a gang of sailors.

"Not a bad picture," Juarez said.

They stood outside the Studio Theater. Juanita looked at the placards.

"You feel like going in?" she asked.

"Might as well."

They settled comfortably in their seats. The picture was foreign-made, the kind Juarez preferred. Juanita slipped her hand into Juarez's; she knew he did not like it, but just this once she would do what she wanted to do. She felt warm and affectionate. She squeezed his hand and looked at him; he smiled, looking at the screen.

Afterwards, Juarez seemed more cheerful.

"Let's drop by to see Annie," Juanita suggested. "We haven't been there in a long time."

"Okay."

Annie was Juarez's cousin; she had three rooms in an apartment house on Race Street. Juarez rang the bell, heard the buzz of the lock, and walked with Juanita up the stairs. When Annie saw them she said, "Well, I'll be goddamned!" She was a fat, cheerful, unkempt woman with hair that had not been combed all day. They went inside and sat down. Annie brought wine.

"Frank is out, that goddamn bum," Annie said. "All the time out. Where you kids comin' from?"

"The movies," Juanita said.

"Yeah? Don't you kids go no place else?"

"Where else in this town?"

"Yeah. Where else in this town?" Annie laughed, her fat face wrinkled like a rotten tomato. "Boy, you got somethin' there."

She dropped heavily into a chair and looked at her visitors. Juarez, in the chair across the room, watched her light a cigarette. He had never liked to see women smoke. His eyes left hers and traveled around the room. It was extremely untidy. A picture of Frank hung on the wall.

"You kids ain't been by in a coon's age," Annie said. "Nice to see ya again. 'Member the old days? Brother! You kids lived up here. Y'oughta drop by more often, we could have some more fun. 'Cept that Frank ain't never home, the goddamn bum. Y'oughta drop by more often."

"We will," Juanita said. "We always talk about you and Frank. We missed seeing you. That's why we came tonight."

"Yeah." Annie sipped her wine. "Nice ta see you two kids. When the hell you gonna get married?"

Juanita laughed, feeling embarrassed for Juarez. She said, "Oh, we have plenty of time. Takes money to get married."

Annie said, "The hell with that. Wait for money, you never get married. Do it now, what I always say. You won't be no good for nothin', you wait too long. But I guess you don't need marriage for that, eh?" She winked and laughed loudly.

Juanita smiled and did not glance at Juarez who sat quiet, sipping his wine, slouched in the chair, staring at the wall.

"One thing," Annie said, "glad Juarez had 'nough sense ta get hisself a Mex chick. So many a these bums got ta get somebody else, y'know. Mex chick ain't good 'nough for them. Got ta get themself somebody different. Glad Juarez had 'nough sense ta get hisself a Mex chick. Good sense. A lotta sense."

Juanita smiled again. Annie drank the rest of the wine. She was huge in her chair; that quantity of flesh seemed almost obscene. From across the room, Juarez looked at her.

"You kids want anymore wine?"

"No," Juarez said, "we've got to be going."

"Going? So soon? You just got here."

"I have to get up in the morning." Juarez said, standing up. Juanita rose also.

"Hell, y'oughta wait at least till Frank gets home. He'd wanta see ya. He'd never forgive ya leaving before he got in."

"Give him our regards," Juarez said. "We've got to go."

They were at the door.

"See you, Annie," Juarez said.

"Adios, Annie," Juanita said. "We'll see you soon again."

"Y'oughta waited," said Annie, hurt.

They walked down the street to the streetcar stop and rode to Juanita's house. Juanita said nothing. Inside, her nerves seemed to spin, in turmoil. Only in rare moments had she managed to reach Juarez. He was always, *always* so far away, with a wall between them. A wall, a wall, and she could not break through. She knew the sources of his moodiness, but could not

70

mention them for fear of offending him. She was constantly in pain, wary, on edge, balancing delicately on one toe. He was so easily offended, so easily hurt.

At the door, Juarez said, "Good night, Juanita."

"Won't you come in, Juarez?"

They went into the parlor. Juarez said, "I'll just stay a minute."

"Can I fix you something? Something to eat or drink?"

"No, thanks." He looked at her. "Juanita, you're a wonderful person."

"Juarez." She touched his hand, hesitantly, fearing to take too much for granted. Too much for granted, after three years. Three years, she thought, hearing the tick-tock of time inside her head.

"Juarez, I love you," she said. The words came out without her realization. Tensely, she sat next to him, watching his face. Juarez stood up.

"No," he said softly, "why would you love me? Look at me, Juanita. Why would you love me? Why would anyone love me?"

"Juarez!" She stood up in front of him, searching his face anxiously. "Juarez! You must know I'm telling the truth. I love you."

Juarez sighed. He felt tired. What the hell! what the hell! he thought.

"Look, Juanita, let's not talk about it, eh? Look, Juanita, let's call this off. Please, let's call it off."

"Juarez!"

His watery eyes were on her face a moment, then on the floor; with a sudden movement he took a step, and walked over to the door.

"Good night, Juanita."

"Juarez!" She stood beside him again. "Juarez, please, tell me what's wrong. What's troubling you, darling?"

"Nothing's wrong," he said.

"Darling, there is. I can tell. Tell me, I love you."

"Please, Juanita. Nothing's wrong. Let's call it off, eh? Please, let's call it off. That's best all around."

He opened the door and closed it. Juanita stared at the door. Then she sank to her knees, and her eyes filled up with tears.

3

He went up the street where the kids played noisily and into the tenement and paused outside the door of the tearoom, looking inside. There was Rodina. He saw a mare that had never been tamed; he saw Carmen the gypsy and a dark Egyptian queen. Rodina sat drinking a cup of tea. Juarez looked at the long, thick black hair and the dark, deep-set eyes with their heavy brows. After a minute he went inside.

"Juarez, hi," Rodina said.

"Hello, Rodina. May I sit down?"

"Sure. Grab a seat. What d'you know?"

He sat down. Glenn came out, in his white apron. "'Lo Juarez, what's to it?"

"Hello, Glenn."

"Tea, coffee, what, Juarez?"

"Tea, I guess."

"How about a little nip, you two? What say, Rodina? Like a little nip?"

"No, don't guess so," Rodina said.

Juarez looked at her. "Let's have a drink, Rodina. Let's celebrate. Just a little one."

Rodina shrugged and laughed. "Okay. But I'm broke, I'm warning you."

"It's all right," Juarez said.

He was happy, sitting across from her. He looked at her and smiled. She returned the smile; she, too, seemed happy.

"Thanks," Juarez said to Glenn, who had brought his tea and two glasses of whiskey mixed with ginger ale and ice. Juarez paid the bill. He finished his tea and touched his glass, looking at Rodina.

"Toast," he said.

"Toast," Rodina said. "To what, Juarez?"

"To you, Rodina."

"Okay. You toast me, I'll toast you," she said. They touched glasses and drank the liquid down. Juarez felt the pleasant warmth spread out from his stomach. Other people were coming into the tearoom. Across the room sat Hucks with Mrs. Houston, the tenement gossip. Juarez looked at Hucks and said, "I hate him."

"Who?" Rodina said.

"Hucks."

"Oh." She grinned. "Well, I don't feel much like hating anyone now. I feel like kissing everybody."

Even without asking, Juarez knew the reason Rodina felt that way. The knowledge diminished the pleasure of the drink. For a moment, he sat quietly, turning the whiskey glass on the oilcloth. Then he said, "Why do you feel that way, Rodina?"

"Oh, I just do. I'm healthy, and I'm in love. And I feel wonderful."

Perhaps, Juarez thought, I take pleasure in torturing myself. He asked, "With whom, Rodina?"

"Who? Why, Ted, of course. What a question, Juarez!" She laughed. "I feel like we're married already."

"Already?" He looked up at her quickly. "Already? Oh, are you planning to marry eventually?"

"Sure. As soon as he gets his divorce."

"And when—" Juarez moved his eyes away "—when will that be?"

"I don't know. His wife has to do it. I don't know how soon it will be. But I can wait."

"Of course," Juarez said softly.

For a while they were silent again. Rodina's bright eyes moved from table to table in the tearoom, and she waved as new people came into the room. By now the tables were nearly filled; the room was noisy, the juke box played. Juarez heard all this from a great distance; he spun the whiskey glass on the oilcloth, making designs with the wet rings.

"Rodina, what do you know about this fellow?" he asked.

"That I love him."

"No, seriously, Rodina. Are you sure he's right for you? And that he really loves you, isn't just after what he can get?"

"Positive, Juarez. You have to know him better, that's all. He's a wonderful person."

"Is he?" Juarez said. "And you're a wonderful person, yourself, Rodina." The whiskey crept up to his head. "Wonderful person. Wonderful. So sweet. And really so innocent, Rodina, so unpretentious, so unsophisticated. You're honest, Rodina, honest and simple. Wonderful."

"Well, thank you, kind sir!"

"Is he right, Rodina? Are you *sure*?"

"Yes. He's good, Juarez. Really *good*. Decent and wonderful and he makes me good. You know what, Juarez, he never touched me. Never, and I've slept with him, and he's never touched me. I can tell you that, Juarez; you're my friend, and I can tell you. He never touched me. And he's so smart, Juarez. I can come to him and ask anything, anything at all, and he can answer it. And if I have troubles or don't feel good he never yells or gets impatient with me. I can lean my head on his shoulder and he always listens to me and tells me what's right to do. He's wonderful, really wonderful, Juarez. You'll love him. He's wonderful, like you, and you'll like him."

Like me! Juarez thought, like me! And the love runs only one way? Why, Rodina, why? He said, "I'm sure I'll like him if he's all the things you say he is."

"Oh, you will, Juarez, you will. Just like you. He's wonderful."

CHAPTER SEVEN

OUTSIDE THE DARKNESS deepened and the air grew cooler. Old folks sat chatting and smoking and fanning on their hard, marble steps. The steps, row on row, were filled with people, and the street itself was filled with shouting, laughing, playing children. On the corner at the far end of the street men shouted and swore and laughed and drank beer in the saloon. Then around the corner swung a police patrol car which made its way slowly through the street while the people on the steps stared sullenly and the children, interrupted in their play, stared in silent hatred. A cloud crossed the moon and an old sage called across the street, "Looks like rain." Ringing through the air from a distance of perhaps two blocks came a sound like a pistol shot; two spinsters exchanged glances and one of them laughed, "Bet ole Jeff shot that cheatin' wife of his'n." Mighty warm for November, somebody commented; it'd probably be a warm winter. And from the corner, where the tenement stood, came the sounds of a juke box and people talking and laughing. The tearoom was full; business was good; maybe that was a sign of good times for the city.

In the tearoom Rodina sat talking to Juarez and the rest of the people conducted private conversations at other tables. Only at one table did the conversation center around the wizened Mexican and the wild young girl with the long black hair. That was at the table where Hucks sat listening to Mrs. Houston.

Mrs. Houston was enjoying herself. She was laughing loudly and Hucks, who was not laughing, was staring at his hand on the table. It was a big hand; his eyes took in its strength. He saw hair on the back of the hand and on his wrist and veins which stood out boldly. A man's hand; a strong hand. Mrs. Houston was laughing.

"Just think about it," she laughed, "just think about it." Tears rolled down her face. She was a small woman with a sharp nose and sharp tongue. "A great joke."

Hucks clenched his hand into a fist. He relaxed the hand, looked at it briefly, then moved it from the table into a pocket from which the hand extracted a package of cigarettes. He took out one, tapped it, lighted it. He did not look at Mrs. Houston.

"Just think of it!" she howled.

"You think of it, Sadie," he said. Hucks disliked Mrs. Houston.

"Well, can you beat it," she said. "Can you beat it for sheer irony, baby? You, the great, brawny Hucks, beaten to your knees by a pipsqueak who writes poetry?"

"How do you know he writes poetry?"

"I know everything, baby."

That was true enough, Hucks reflected. He looked at her across the table. She was not really a bad-looking woman. Perhaps her trouble was that she was so damned loud. Sound must be more powerful than sight; after awhile, when you knew her, she became what you heard rather than what you saw.

Hucks shrugged. "Hell, it don't matter," he said. "I ain't lovin' her."

"Bull," Mrs. Houston said. "Pure bull. You think I ain't been watchin' you? I been seein' you. You give her the works every time you get a chance, trying to make a play. Hell, I see you.

And she sets you down just as lightly as you please. She sure tells you off. And then she comes back with this scrawny poetry writer who beats the socks off old Hucks. Can you beat it?" She laughed and the tears rolled down her cheeks.

"Everybody's talkin' about it, naturally. Ain't no needa you tryin' to make out nothin's wrong. Everybody knows. Everybody's laughin' their head off."

"Let 'em laugh," Hucks said.

"Sure, sure," Mrs. Houston said. "Sure. Well, I know one person ain't doin' much laughin'. That's you."

"It don't matter worth a damn to me."

"Sure, sure," Mrs. Houston said.

Hucks rose and stretched. Beneath his clothes he felt the muscles of his body tighten and bulge. He flexed his muscles and looked at Sadie Houston, knowing that she knew the strength contained beneath his skin, knew his iron and his stamina. That was consolation, eh? Sadie Houston knew that strength, damn right she knew it. Hucks smiled at her. Let her rage.

"You goin' someplace?" Sadie Houston asked.

"Yep."

"Where to, lover?" Mrs. Houston laughed.

"To bed."

Mrs. Houston's eyes brightened. Her eyes were small and hard. "Alone?" she asked playfully.

"That's right, Sadie," Hucks said, "alone."

Hucks made his way through the crowded room. He caught Rodina's eye; she did not wave, so he kept his arm at his side. To hell with her. He paused lazily in the hall, then moved toward the front door. Overhead in the cooling evening the sky was clear and star-studded. That was strength: the sky and the stars, stretching forever. His eyes came down to the bricks and stones; to the world.

Hucks watched the kids play "kick the can." Someone would kick a can. The kid who was "it" would chase it, and set it on the base. Then he would search for the others, who had run to hide. When he found them, he had to get back to the base before them, and tap the can. If one of them got back to the base before the person who was "it," he would kick the can again and everyone got another chance to hide. Hucks remembered the game.

Hucks remembered a lot of things. How he hated his brothers who went off to school and became doctors and lawyers and didn't want him to visit them. How much he hated his mother and father, dead, bless their bones, who were always pointing to the other kids and saying, "Why can't you be like them?" How he had an affair with a rich woman out on the Main Line and fell in love with her and how she laughed at him when he asked her to elope with him. ("Cute little boy," she called him.) How he hated living in this rat trap with a bunch of dopes and gossips.

And other things.

Hucks moved back from the doorway and started through the hall toward his room. He stopped to look in the tearoom; there was Rodina, talking to the Mex; there was Sadie Houston, talking to a group of people at another table—probably about him. Damn woman!

Hucks looked at the stairs in front of him. At the top of the landing was Rodina's room. He stood still a moment, then walked up the dark stairway. He tapped on the door and heard Mrs. Baleza say, "Come in."

Hucks opened the door. "Hello, sweetheart," he said.

Mrs. Baleza's eyes flickered. Hucks walked over to the chair and sat down. Mrs. Baleza looked at him inquisitively and said nothing.

"Just paying a social call," Hucks said. He felt odd and guilty,

80

like a little boy hastily explaining something in order to hide some mischief.

He opened a newspaper and looked at the headlines. He was conscious of Mrs. Baleza's eyes on him. He dropped the paper and smiled. She looked at him and said nothing. The only light in the room hung over her bed.

"What's the matter, sweetheart?" he asked.

"Just wonderin' how come you're visitin' me."

"You always suspect something wrong," Hucks said, laughing it away. He felt uncomfortable. He wished he had not come.

He leaned back and closed his eyes. He felt like a heel. Sometimes it seemed to him that he was two people; one was a rat, and the second was somebody who hated the first. If he did something halfway decent, the heel in him sneered and told him he was a sucker; if he pulled off a kind of dirty trick, the other guy kept yammering that he would be better off dead. Seemed he could never satisfy both of them.

"How do you feel, sweetheart?"

"Same as usual."

"Nice night, eh? Kids outside playing kick the can. Noise bother you any?"

"No. I can't even hear the noise back here."

"That so? Wouldn't want anything to disturb my favorite mother," he said.

He waited a long moment, his eyes closed so that he would not have to look at Mrs. Baleza's face. Finally, he said, "Where's Rodina?"

"Don't know. She's always out."

"Sure," Hucks said. "Young kid. Got to sow her wild oats. Guess she's out with her boy friend."

He waited and got no response. He felt rotten. After a moment, he said, "Well, guess you'll be losing her pretty soon, huh, sweetheart?"

"Losin' her?"

"Sure," Hucks said. "Guess she'll be gettin' married soon."

"Married? Who'd wanta marry Rodina?"

"Why, that fella she's been living with," Hucks said. "The guy she's been living with up the hall. I *guessed* they'd be getting married soon. Didn't think you'd let her spend her nights with anybody who *wasn't* going to marry her."

"Spend her nights . . ." Mrs. Baleza stared at Hucks and he was startled because he did not see what he had expected—indignation—in her eyes. Instead he saw something which almost frightened him—a gleam, almost savage, brilliant and joyful. Her whole face lit up. She seemed for a moment to forget that he was in the room as she savored an inner satisfaction. Then her eyes focused on him again.

"*What* man?"

"Didn't you know, sweetheart? I wouldn'ta said nothing if I thought you didn't know. I was sure you knew."

"Sure," she said impatiently, smiling, seeming to look beyond the words into his thoughts. "Sure, I know. I know. But *what* man?"

"The guy who writes poetry," Hucks said, feeling rotten, knowing that Mrs. Baleza saw through him. "Theodore, his name is. I thought you knew."

His words echoed in his ears, and they sounded false even to him. He was at once actor and audience; all of this was play-acting, no audience could be convinced. He was merely reciting the lines. He wished he were offstage.

"Oh yes," Mrs. Baleza said, smiling at him, watching his eyes move away from hers. "Of course I knew. Few details I didn't know, though. I knew he lived here, but for how long?"

"About two months. Something like that."

"Yes?"

"Sure. I hope I ain't giving nothing away, Mrs. Baleza. I'd hate that."

82

"No," Mrs. Baleza said, "you're not giving anything away." Their eyes met; his fell.

For a long time, it seemed to Hucks, he remained in the room with the sharp-eyed woman who pried him with questions. Then, finally, he could say, "Well, sweetheart, guess I'll be shoving off. Just wanted to see how you were and exchange a little small talk."

He went outside and down the stairs. In the hall he glanced again into the tearoom where Rodina sat talking to Juarez. Then he went to his room.

Inside, he stripped for bed. His room was neat and clean. He stood in front of the full-length mirror, naked, and flexed his mucles. His eyes traced the lines of his body. Power, strength were evident in every inch of flesh. He stretched and watched the movement of the muscles from his neck to his ankles. He smiled and slipped beneath the sheet on his bed. He slept without clothes, beneath only a sheet, with both windows open wide, even in winter. He stretched and turned in the bed, liking the feel of strength. All things were possible if a man was strong.

He was in the room again with Mrs. Baleza. He felt again the shame. Well, he murmured inside, it was for Rodina's own good. She's only a kid. But a part of him was filled with loathing of himself. He closed his eyes and sought desperately for sleep.

CHAPTER EIGHT

MORE COOLNESS CAME to the abnormal November night and some of the people moved off the steps of the street to escape the falling temperature. Clouds gathered in the sky, passing like ghosts astride the wind across the moon. The old man in the street, looking at the sky, told his neighbor, "Yep, looks like rain. Told you it would rain." And about half an hour later, the rain did begin to fall.

When the first light slanting drops struck the ground, Theodore stood at a bar in another part of the city, listening to the talk of the men. Their conversation was strange to him. Eventually, he thought, he would have to go home. An orange light hung over the bar; the men talked about football games and women. Eventually, he would have to go home.

He sipped his beer and listened to the music from the radio behind the bar. The dour bartender moved back and forth, filling glasses, collecting money, and pausing, every few moments or so, to look at Theodore. The soft-spoken man who had been called a "school teacher," felt like a stranger, like a foreigner, in the saloon.

Four hours previous, he had lost his job.

"Theodore," Mr. Miller, the manager, said to him, "I'd like to have a word with you."

"Yes sir."

"Theodore, I understand you've left your wife. Is that true?"

"Where did you hear that, Mr. Miller?"

"I was told. Is it true, Theodore?"

"Yes, it is."

Mr. Miller placed an elbow on the desk and leaned forward to look sternly into Theodore's eyes. "I hope that by now you've changed your mind and plan to return to your wife."

"No," Theodore said, "I haven't changed my mind."

Mr. Miller looked at Theodore a moment, without moving. Then he sat back in his chair and said, "Theodore, how long have you been married?"

"Eighteen years."

"Eighteen years. For eighteen years, then, your wife has been faithful to you, loyal, hard-working; now, all of a sudden you just up and leave her. Does that strike you as a manly action?"

"Mr. Miller," Theodore said, "I'd prefer to handle my private life in my own way."

Mr. Miller was taken aback. He stared at Theodore, then he grunted and was himself again. "Of course," he said, "I don't mean to tell my employees how to run their private affairs, although I might add I firmly believe in morality and right living. But being a night watchman requires certain traits in a man, high among which are loyalty, steadiness and dependability. It now occurs to me that we may have miscalculated your possession of those qualities."

"Just what do you mean, Mr. Miller?"

"Well, I don't think we can use you any longer, Theodore. I'm sorry, but I'm extremely disappointed in you."

Theodore drank the last of his beer and went outside. The rain fell lightly; it was a fine rain which did not soak him through. He walked aimlessly in the rain, wanting to put off for as long as possible the time when he would have to tell Rodina he was unemployed and see the shadow of fear upon her face.

86

He stood outside the apartment house where he and Sylvia had lived so many years. There was a light in her window; she would, in all probability, be reading now. Could *she* have told Mr. Miller? Had Howard? That was more likely. Yet he blamed neither of them; it was Mr. Miller toward whom he felt a certain resentment. "Pride," he thought. "Miserable Puritan."

Standing in the rain, Theodore stared at the lighted window and felt a sudden stab of guilt. Sylvia was alone upstairs. What did she do with her days and nights? Life had been drab enough for her while they were still married; what was it like now, with only walls to stare at, living in rooms alone, past all hope of obtaining another husband, living from day to day on the tiny pittance she received from him. Standing alone on the dark and silent street, Theodore felt an inner quickening more like remorse than any sensation he had experienced since that day he left his wife. He stared at the window and forgot Sylvia's drabness, her contempt, her complaints like the buzzing of a million angry bees; he thought only of eighteen years gone by, years of fidelity if nothing else, years precious in a life now without future.

Sylvia, he thought, did you really love me? I could be happier than ever in my life if only I knew that you did not. I could be free and sing if I knew your final words of love were lies, your final tears were false. If I knew you despised me. If I knew you were bored by me. If I knew you really did not want me. Only the doubt, only the thought that perhaps you *did* love me, perhaps still do, makes me miserable.

There was an instant's urge: to ring her bell, go upstairs, sit opposite her in the parlor and talk. To talk of love. To look into her eyes. And in her eyes he would see the truth. Tonight he would see love or the absence of love. He would look into her eyes and talk to her and when he left he would know the truth. For good or ill, the truth.

And then, as quickly, the urge was gone. For what if he saw, in her eyes, that she loved him? Would he have the strength, again, to leave her, to desert her, remembering, as he did so vividly, the eighteen long years of loyalty and sacrifice? And if he did find the strength to leave her, would not the thought of this added and unnecessary wounding of his wife make impossible even such moments of happiness as he now found, when he could forget the past, with Rodina?

He turned and walked, in the rain, toward home.

2

"Hear the rain," Rodina said as they lay in bed the next afternoon. "The rain and the wind make the trees sing."

"Yes," he said.

"Remember it was raining the night I met you. I can't forget it. You know, the rain made my hand wet and that's why you felt it go into your pocket. If it hadn't been raining, you wouldn't have caught me."

"Lucky it was raining," Theodore said.

"Yes. The rain is our luck. I'm so happy, Ted. Except sometimes when I think."

"When you think what, Rodina?"

"When I think about your wife."

"Oh."

Rodina said, "Don't you feel unhappy, Ted, sometimes when you think about her?"

"I feel sad sometimes."

"Sometimes I get scared, you know. Most of the time I say, Well, Ted's happy, and I helped make him happy, so that must be good, and then I feel good and like maybe I'm good,

88

too, you know. But then sometimes I think about your wife and how you were married for so many years and left her and then I can't think that I'm good. Then I feel bad for her, and think that instead of being good I'm worse than ever, because I was the cause of you leaving her and so I made you do something bad, too, just like me. Do you know what I mean? You were good before you met me, and then I changed you. That's what I think sometimes and it scares me. I don't want you to be like I am."

"Don't think about it, Rodina. It was good I left my wife. Neither of us was happy. Now all three of us are better off."

"You really believe that, Ted?"

"Yes."

"Then I'm glad. And, Ted, you really think I've changed. You don't think I'm evil anymore?"

"You were never evil, Rodina."

"No, no, but do you think I've changed? Do you like me better the way I am now?"

"Yes. I love you."

She turned to him and kissed him. "I'll always be good for you, Ted. Always."

They lay silently. Both listened to the rain on the leaves and the wind which now blew cold.

Rodina said, "It's the funniest thing, Ted."

"What is?"

"Momma. Most of the evening I was downstairs in the tearoom. Then just before you came home I came upstairs and went into Momma's room to talk. She asked me about you, how you were, where you lived, whether you were married. Remember, she asked you that when you came to see her. Now she asked me again. She asked a lot of questions. She asked if I saw you often. It's the funniest thing."

"She's asked you about me before."

"Yes, but tonight she was asking the same kind of questions she asked before. She already knew the answers."

"Maybe she forgot."

"Maybe." Rodina paused a moment. "And she had the funniest grin on her face all the time, Ted. The funniest thing. That grin really scared me. I never saw anything like it. And her *eyes!*"

"Maybe you should tell her about me," Theodore said.

"Oh, no. She'd have a fit. Not until you've got your divorce and we can get married. Then I can tell her."

She lay again without talking. From the package on the night table, she took a cigarette and lit it; she blew the smoke toward the ceiling of the dark room.

"Sometimes I get so scared," she said, not conscious of saying the words aloud.

"Let me sleep, darling," Theodore said, "I have to get up early, tomorrow morning."

"All right," she said. Then she asked, "But why do you have to get up early?"

"I have to look for a job."

"A job!" She sat upright. "A job! But you have a job."

"No." Eventually, of course, he had known he would have to tell her. "I lost my job today."

"Lost it? But why?"

"A letdown in business. Things aren't what they were. They don't need so many employees any more."

She was leaning on one arm, looking at him through the darkness. "Ted, is that the real reason?"

"Yes."

"Ted, you know you can't fool me. That isn't the real reason. It's something about me. I know it. From the sound of your voice."

"Of course not, darling," he said, "what could you have to

90

do with my losing my job? That's the real reason. Don't worry. I'll find another."

"Oh, Ted," she said, "I always bring trouble. Just like Momma said."

"You had nothing to do with it. Let me sleep now, darling. I'll find another soon."

For some time she lay there, troubled, looking down upon his face that was hidden from her in the darkness.

CHAPTER NINE

RODINA DID NOT SLEEP well. Early in the morning when Theodore awakened he found her fully dressed, frying eggs on the little stove. He smiled and stretched and then came the recollection of the events of the previous night and with it a sudden chill. He lay in the bed, tired again, watching Rodina.

"Well, we're up early this morning," he said cheerfully.

"Theodore." She turned suddenly to look at him. "Oh, you're awake. Good morning. Breakfast is almost ready."

"How do you feel?"

"Better than last night, Ted. I was thinking maybe things aren't so bad as I thought. There are other jobs."

"Of course."

Theodore got up, washed and dressed. When he sat down to eat the two eggs and drink the coffee he said, "Why are you dressed?"

"I was thinking it would be easier if I looked for a job, too. If you had some trouble, maybe I could find something to hold us over."

Theodore frowned, but he was, in many respects, a realist; it would do no harm if Rodina got a job. "I guess you're right," he said.

They got the morning papers and checked the want ads. Then they went downstairs and out and separated.

Theodore applied, first, for two openings as night watchman, but these were filled already. Then he went to a factory to find a job as laborer, then to an advertising agency that wanted a salesman. Too swiftly, the morning and early afternoon were gone and there was little purpose in continuing his search. He ended the day by leaving his name and address at the office of the Pennsylvania State Employment Service on Broad Street.

Rodina's luck had been as bad as his. She applied for jobs in a beauty parlor, department store, restaurant and office. Her greatest handicap was lack of experience, the receptionists told her. It was very difficult, they said, to get a job without experience.

"The day went so fast," Rodina said to Theodore. "I had to stand in line so long before they'd listen to me, and then had to go pretty far to the next place. Before I knew it, the day was gone."

"Yes," Theodore said. "Well, there are other days."

The next day they applied for other jobs without success. On the third day, the personnel manager of a factory told Theodore to leave his name and he would let him know if any openings developed. On the fourth and fifth days they rose before dawn but again they had no success. There was no word from the factory personnel manager.

"We're vagabonds," Theodore laughed, "living on our credit and our fat. Well, I could stand to lose a little weight."

But later he said, "We'll have to talk to Mrs. Davis. Maybe we'll have to let the rent go for a week or so, until we get on our feet."

With what money they had left, they bought canned goods. Mrs. Davis gave them an extension of time to pay their rent. ("Ain't in no hurry; ain't got no fur coats to rush off 'n' buy.") Part of the canned goods went to Rodina's mother, who complained to Rodina that the food was monotonous and too little. Rodina said she had lost her job, but was looking for another.

94

Theodore wrote a brief note to his wife, explaining about the loss of his job and assuring her he would send money as soon as he found another. His wife did not answer the letter.

"The princess and the pauper," he said to Rodina. "That's us."

Theodore joked and laughed but Rodina saw through this, knew that he was worried. Because of her, somehow, he had lost his job; that was her belief. Now she could not bear to see him smile, because she knew he did so only to allay her fears.

Even worse was her knowledge that he worried about his wife, although he did not mention this. Rodina knew of the letters Theodore wrote to his wife. Sometimes, when his mind seemed far away, she knew that he was thinking about his wife. This pained her. It was enough that he had left his wife; that fact alone must, at times, despite what he said, make him feel guilty, even, perhaps, fill him with regret. Now he could not even send money to her. How could she pay her rent, buy food? Did she really believe that Theodore had lost his job, or did she think he was merely trying to escape his responsibilities where she was concerned? These questions must occur to him, Rodina thought. The misery showed in his eyes.

For eleven days through the strange warm November weather the soft rain fell. Every day, through the rain, Rodina and Theodore hunted jobs. Their initial optimism left them. Theodore's attempts at light-heartedness, his endeavors to escape the present by talking about a bright future, fell heavily on Rodina's ears. Eventually they did not try to escape their worry. Each day was a routine: up in the morning, search for jobs, home, the flat meal, a few hours reading and sleep. They did not talk much. And still no letter came from Sylvia.

"You look gloomy," Juarez said to her one of those dreary, rainy days. "Is anything wrong, Rodina?"

"Ted lost his job," Rodina said. "We're looking for work, but we haven't found anything."

"Can I help you out? I can loan you something, about twenty dollars."

"That would be wonderful," Rodina said.

The twenty dollars was soon gone and still there were no jobs. Mrs. Baleza said, "You're not even lookin', Rodina." Rodina scarcely bothered to argue with her mother. She hurried back to Theodore, who, she thought always, must be sick with worry about his wife. Theodore wrote several letters to Sylvia, but still no answer came. He was very quiet in the apartment. Like a song's refrain, the conviction rang in Rodina: "Because of me, because of me."

2

The sun burst through one morning and people in the block believed that at last the rain was over. But by early afternoon the sky was gray again and by four o'clock the soft rain fell. It was raining steadily when Rodina left the store where she had applied for a job as salesgirl to walk once more toward home.

Her spirits matched the rain. For the first time in her life she felt defeated. For herself she could bear anything; it was Theodore she worried about. When she passed the saloon on the corner of the street the men, as usual, waved and called to her. Rodina hesitated, then went back and into the saloon and stood at the bar.

"Well, baby, how you doin'?" one of the men asked her.

"Not so hot. How's yourself?"

"Great. How's about a drink on me, sugar?"

"Sure."

Rodina finished her scotch and soda and left the saloon. She did not feel like going home. She walked around the block and then walked straight ahead, aimlessly, until she reached Chestnut Street. She walked up the street, looking into the windows, seeing clothes and furniture and food. It was wonderful what money could buy.

She walked for about half an hour. In the rain the streets were deserted except for the automobiles which passed now and then. She came up Walnut Street, in the general direction of home, and passed a restaurant. At the cashier's box stood a man paying his bill; Rodina could see the bulge of his wallet.

Rodina's heart beat fast. She stood, fascinated, staring at the money the man took from the wallet and at the bills the waitress handed him in return. It seemed that time stood still. The man put his wallet in his inside pocket and walked out of the restaurant. He walked up Walnut Street, ahead of Rodina, and turned the corner.

Like a gazelle, Rodina ran off in the other direction, circling the block, turning, eventually, up the street the man had turned. He was coming toward her. Breathing heavily, Rodina slowed her pace and approached the man. Her heart was in her throat. The man stopped to look into a window. She, too, stopped, looking into a store front.

For a long time the man looked in the window. Cars drove past. Rodina was scarcely conscious of them; nor did she feel the rain.

Why did the man hesitate so long? Did he suspect? Perhaps he would turn and move off in the direction he had come. Perhaps he had left something in the restaurant. If he turned, she could not again pursue him. Perhaps that would be better, after all. Yes, yes, it would be better. She had promised

Theodore. Theodore. What would he think? He must not know. What would he think? She had promised him.

Like old times, she thought bitterly. Ah, so she really had not changed. Only on the surface. Now, like old times. How justified this would make her mother feel, if she found out. How much this would please Hucks. How much this would pain Theodore. Theodore. She had promised him. She had promised him, but inside she had not changed. It was true what her mother had said, she thought, watching the man, trembling. And the man did not move. *Why* didn't he? It was true what her mother had said. She could not change. It was true, and Theodore had been wrong in thinking she was good.

What was she thinking! They needed the money. This man, probably, did not. They needed the money. The money could make Theodore happy; he could smile again.

"No reason," she said aloud. Her voice startled her. Still the man did not move from the window. *Surely* he suspected! Perhaps he would call a policeman! Rodina looked up and down the street; there were no patrol cars in sight. And then the man moved from the window, coming toward her.

Don't do it! she told herself. *You promised him!* She bumped into the man. On the wet pavement they tripped and fell to the ground. When they rose the man was gripping her hand, which held his wallet, and grinning.

"Well, sister, ain't this somethin'?" he laughed. "You caught yourself a cop this time."

Cop! With a desperate wrench she pulled her arm free and was gone. The cop followed, shouting. *A cop! A cop!* She was filled with terror, running. Surely she would slip on the wet street. She drew away from the policeman but could not lose him. She turned corners rapidly. Once she fell, but was up again, racing, not feeling the blood from the cut on her knee.

Then she turned the corner of the street and ran into the vestibule of the tenement house and closed the door and looked out, breathless, her heart sounding, to her, like a bass drum.

The policeman turned the corner. There were a few children playing in the rain in the middle of the block, and the policeman shouted to them. Had they seen a girl run around the corner? Rodina held her breath. The children shouted, "No." The policeman stood, perplexed, in front of the house. Eventually, he moved off down the street. Rodina breathed easily and prayed silently. Safe! Safe! She was safe! She lifted the wallet and cursed it silently. Well, she was safe.

"Well, baby, up to your old tricks, eh?"

She pushed the wallet down to her side and turned and looked up into the grinning face of Hucks. He stood close to her, grinning. She stared up at him. He laughed softly.

"How much did you get, baby?"

She stared without answering. Her heart beat loudly. Hucks leaned back lazily against the door jamb.

"Well, well," he said. "And what will your poet-lover think?"

Even in the dim light of the hallway Hucks saw clearly the terror which came into Rodina's eyes. He smiled. He had never seen her tremble, but he knew she was trembling now. The prima donna was trembling now. The girl who set him down coldly was full of fear now. Suddenly he felt angry.

"What would he think, baby?" Hucks asked, his voice full of sarcasm. "Him and the cops. What would they think?"

Hucks grinned and looked up at the ceiling and said, "Let's see. How much time do they give pickpockets? Hmmm. Tell me, baby, would your precious lover be waitin' for you when you came out of the jail? Would he be waitin' to take you back in his arms, sugar?" Then he said, "It's my duty as a citizen, you know, to report this. I'm a good citizen. I'm against crime."

"Hucks," Rodina said hoarsely, "take the money . . ."

"Me?" Hucks laughed bitterly. "That's filthy lucre, sugar. I'm decent. I don't take rotten money. I make mine honest." He smiled at her and said, "But I'll tell you what, Rodina. Why don't you be a nice little girl and be nice to old Hucks. Then maybe I'd be nice to you, baby. Be nice. We could go back to my room and . . . well, talk this whole thing over."

She hated him. Her eyes burned with contempt. "Go to hell!" she said.

Hucks kept on grinning but burned inside. "What's the matter, sugar? Am I so repulsive now? Because I don't write poetry and don't talk with big words? Is that it? You wasn't always so particular, were you now? Am I so much worse than that bastard, that puny something you sleep with upstairs?"

He smiled but his voice was bitter as he said, "I could tell the police, baby. Oh, but I could. I could notify the police and you could be identified and there'd be a nice long stretch in jail. And your darling would be so hurt, wouldn't he. Him with his big words. I could tell the police, baby. Don't you think I would?"

She stared at him. He said, "You'd look pretty in prison uniform, baby. I wasn't always such an awful prospect to you, was I? But you're above all that now, eh? Well, I don't think you are. I still think you're a common little bitch. You fool him but you don't fool me; you ain't changed over night. Now come on back and have a talk baby. A little talk. Or so help me God you'll go to jail."

More even than hatred of Hucks, Rodina felt fear. Theodore *must not* find out! This, with Hucks, would take only a moment; it would be over. The rest of her life she wanted to spend with Theodore. Theodore must not find out.

"Just be nice to old Hucks," he said. "Just be yourself. Your old self."

100

Well, she had gone this far. So she had stolen again. What was this one thing more? She lowered her eyes. She walked with him past the tearoom down the hall and into his room.

From the top of the stairs, Juarez, who was descending, saw her go into the room. They did not see him. He paused on the stairs and watched her go inside. For a long time he stared at the hall, as though unable to believe what he had seen. Then, slowly, he came the rest of the way down the stairs. He walked down the hall and out of the tenement. The light from a street lamp, shining yellow in the rain, showed a face twisted with bitterness and pain.

And later that evening, when Theodore came home, he said, "Rodina, Rodina, I've got a job!"

CHAPTER TEN

FROM THE TABLE in the kitchen where she sat eating, Sylvia could look across the room into the parlor and see the roll-top desk between the windows where Theodore had used to work. She ate slowly—ham, string beans, potatoes, salad— looking, all the time, at the desk. She smiled, remembering. There was Theodore, home from work, seated at the desk, determined to write—all night, if necessary. To write: about "nature," about "love," about "beauty." She remembered the way he looked: his brow furrowed, his face set grimly, so like a little boy intent on repairing a shattered play toy. With as much success. With as much success as the little boy.

Dear, dear Theodore. What was he doing now? She looked at her watch: it was nine o'clock. Possibly he was lying awake in the bed of that old tenement in which he lived, thinking about her. Because, of course, he thought about her. His letters, if nothing else, showed that he thought about her. And then, too, Theodore could never change; Theodore would always be Theodore; therefore, he would think about her. And he would worry about her. The gallant Theodore.

Or possibly, possibly he was not thinking about her; possibly he was at work—if he had found another job by now. She would know soon; for Theodore would send her part of his first paycheck. Or possibly he was neither working nor thinking about her; possibly he was with his beloved "other woman."

That was the most interesting of the possibilities. Sylvia tried to see the other woman in her mind. In broad outline, she knew what Rodina looked like; Rodina had been described to her by one of Sylvia's friends; but that was not enough. She knew the girl might be considered attractive, in a vulgar way; that she was sexy, and that she was much, much younger than Theodore. (Wasn't that just like him?) But she knew nothing of the girl's manner, nothing of her character, nothing of her personality. Was she cheap, a flatterer, good for Theodore's vanity? Was she one of those wind-blown creatures, in love with "art," thrilled to "be of help" to Theodore during his pangs of creation? Was she one of those matronly women, the mother type, suffering Theodore to weep on her breasts?

Many nights Sylvia had lain awake in bed, running over in her mind the various categories of women. As she came to each type, she imagined Theodore talking to her, eating at the table with her, telling her about his "work," making love to her. Making love to her. At this point, Sylvia inevitably smiled. That would be a spectacle. Theodore making love to the young girl!

Now she had finished eating. She lit a cigarette.

Well, Christmas was just about here. Only a few more days. Then Theodore would *really* think of her. Christmastime, the old days, together. She fingered the letter on the table beside her, opened it again, reread it. From Theodore. He apologized because he had no money to send to her. Soon he would find another job, he hoped. He did not want her to suffer any unnecessary hardship. Why did she not write? Why did she not let him know what she thought and felt. Sometimes he was so ridden by guilt; sometimes he felt he had been so unbearably unjust to her. He was continually filled with pain. Would she please write to him? Would she please, please let him know if she needed anything, anything at all? And would she— this was the most passionate plea—try to forgive him?

104

As she slipped Theodore's letter back into its envelope, Sylvia's eyes fell again on the rolltop desk and the sheets of paper piled in its corner. She smoked a moment longer, then rose and went into the bedroom. From a box in the closet she took a sheet of rose-colored writing paper and a Christmas card. She opened the card and read: "From Theodore and Sylvia Hall." She fingered the writing paper: this was a present from Theodore on her last birthday.

She sat at the rolltop desk and wrote a letter to Theodore. She wrote easily and swiftly, pausing periodically to think of a word or phrase, then resuming. Finished, she placed the Christmas card and letter inside the envelope. She shook her head slowly and smiled. "Theodore, Theodore," she said aloud. "Trying to play Casanova."

There was a knock at her door. She opened it and said, "Howard!" As he walked in she looked at him reprovingly and said, "You haven't called in ages. Where have you been keeping yourself?"

Howard sat down. He was a big man, and soft; his face was full, and soft; his eyes were large and soft. He was dressed in a neat blue suit, and his black shoes shone as though they were new. He grinned and shifted in his seat when Sylvia spoke; he seemed to be a little shy.

"I was away on business," he said. "Didn't you get my letter?"

"*All* men say they were away on 'business,'" she said, smiling, teasing him. "More than likely you've been away with a woman. Probably a blonde. I know you men!"

"No, really"—he smiled and almost blushed—"I've really been away on business, Sylvia. Detroit. Went to see about buying a new restaurant, fellow wants to close out. You know, Sylvia, I've been thinking about buying a real chain. I mean, something really *big*. Not just these places I have here in town."

She smiled and seemed to stop her teasing. "You'll go to the top, Howard. It's one of the things I've always admired about you."

He was pleased, but he did not know what he should say to a remark such as that. He picked up the newspaper and pretended to read the headlines.

"Tea?" Sylvia asked.

"Yes, thank you, Sylvia. That would be nice."

Sylvia left the room and returned. They sat quietly, drinking the tea. Sylvia looked at Howard's black, glossy shoes, at his well-pressed suit, at his starched collar, fresh-shaven face and brushed hair. Then suddenly, smiling, she said, "Business!" She looked at him as though he were a naughty boy. "I can *imagine* how much business was transacted. I've heard a lot about those Detroit women. I can see you now, being swamped by them. And liking it, just like all men!"

Howard grinned and protested mildly. Sylvia said, "Come on now, confess!" He sat grinning, feeling somehow more manly and attractive. Only Sylvia made him feel like this. Always, after talking to Sylvia, he felt more assertive, resourceful, confident he could achieve things of which he never, otherwise, would have thought himself capable.

"Well," Howard said, "to tell the truth, I *did* run into a girl or so. Nothing happened, you understand; and I didn't even make the first moves. As a matter of fact, they sort of made a play for me." He looked up at Sylvia, smiling. "Nothing happened, you understand. Just a few pleasant words at parties."

Who knew better than she that nothing had happened? Who knew anything about Howard better than she, who had been the sole object of his adoration since their high-school days, who had always been able to make him do anything, feel anything, with a mere lift of a brow, flash of anger, or assumed pain? Indeed, he was nothing without her, for it was she who painted in his mind his mental picture of himself. He was always surprised that others did not see in him the qualities Sylvia told him he possessed. After a time, he had come to believe that Sylvia alone knew and understood him; he worshiped her, and would do anything for her.

They had been sweethearts, or at least he had been in love with her, long before Sylvia ever heard of a weak, soft-spoken poet named Theodore Hall, long before Howard opened his first restaurant. Sylvia was witty, far smarter than he, and very popular; no wonder, then, that she turned her affections to Theodore when he first crossed their paths. They were all very young; Theodore was a sort of celebrity, for he had just had a long poem published in one of the little magazines which were popular during the depression. He was attracted to Sylvia's sparkle, to her poise, and soon they were going together. Before long they were married.

Sylvia never stopped seeing Howard. It would have been difficult for her to do so, for he was always around, asking how she was, wanting to do favors for her. He bore no malice; he could well understand the reasons for what she had done; he simply wanted her to be happy and like him and, perhaps, depend on him a little.

That had been their relationship for eighteen years.

In 1937 Howard bought a restaurant for next to nothing. He worked hard, built up the restaurant, and managed to save a little money. When war broke out, he was able to buy a second restaurant out of profits from the first; now he owned four of them, modernized and equipped with booths and grills. He, himself, no longer had to work; still, he was up early every morning to visit the restaurants or keep an engagement connected with his business.

Over the years he saw a change come over Sylvia. She

seemed so tired. Her former wit turned to cruel satire. He had never questioned her; he did not want to speak out of turn; but one day she told him she was not happy. They talked about it. Howard began to see that Theodore was no fit husband for Sylvia: he had no conception of her needs or desires; he did not really know her. Someone needed to talk to Theodore; but that was not Howard's prerogative. He remained silent so far as Theodore was concerned; he spoke politely when he saw him, and that was all. As for himself, Howard would never marry. There could never be anyone to take Sylvia's place.

"And how's Theodore?" Howard asked.

Sylvia paused. "Fine . . . I suppose."

Howard said, "I guess he's at work now."

Sylvia closed her eyes and looked away. She said, "I . . . I suppose so," and her voice broke.

Howard leaned over and put his hand on her arm. "Sylvia, is something wrong?"

Sylvia continued to look away; she was silent. Howard moved closer, his hand still on her arm.

"Sylvia, what's the matter?"

Sylvia turned her head to look at him. She shrugged and dropped her eyes. "He left me."

Howard's eyes opened wide. "Left you!"

She nodded. He stared at her, unable to believe it. "*He* left *you?*" He was stunned. "But why?"

She shrugged again. She tried a wry smile. "I suppose I wasn't a very good wife to him."

"Sylvia, that's not true. You were much too good for him. There couldn't be a better wife than you." Amazed, he said, "That cad!"

Sylvia smiled and laid her hand on Howard's shoulder. "You're sweet to say that, Howard."

108

For an instant they looked into each other's eyes. "Dear Sylvia," Howard said. He had hesitated to use the word of endearment. "He's a cad, Sylvia. I've never heard of such ingratitude. You put up with him all these years, not thinking of your own misery, and then he has the gall to walk out on you, just like that. A cad!"

Sylvia said, "Oh, I suppose he has good reasons, Howard."

"What reasons could he have, Sylvia?"

She hesitated a long moment. "Well," she said, "I haven't borne him any children, you know. I think that may be the reason."

Howard snorted. "That's no reason at all. If he were half a man, that would have been an even greater reason for standing by you. He could have adopted a child if it meant so much to him."

"He wanted his own flesh and blood."

"Flesh and blood be damned!" Howard said. His jaw flexed and unflexed. Then he said, softly, "Is there anything I can do, Sylvia?"

She said softly, "I don't know what there is to be done."

Howard put his arm around her; he trembled as he did so. Sylvia lay her head in the hollow of his shoulder. For a long while neither said anything. Howard was acutely conscious of her nearness; an air of peace descended over him, like the aftermath of weeping.

"Howard," Sylvia said, "I'm so alone. You'll visit me, won't you? You'll come to see me all the time?"

"Yes," he said hoarsely.

"You'll comfort me, Howard."

"Yes. Yes, I'll take care of you Sylvia. I always wanted to take care of you."

She lay in comfort in his shoulder.

"And Howard . . ."

"Yes, Sylvia?"

"Howard, remember all those times you wanted to talk to Theodore? About me being unhappy with him. Well, I don't want him back, I'd never take him back . . . but . . ."

"But what, Sylvia?"

"Well, I wish you'd go talk to him. I have his address. I think it's horrid the way he left me for the reason he did, after all these years. I wish you'd tell him just how horrible he is."

"I'd like nothing better," Howard said grimly. "I'll break his nose."

"Oh, don't hurt him, Howard. He's weak, you know, and I think you'd be taking advantage of him."

"He's weak, all right."

"Just talk to him," Sylvia said. "Tell him how horrible he is. Not for my own satisfaction. I have nothing, personally, to gain. It's just that your words might help to make him a better man for some other woman he might meet, and perhaps someday marry."

CHAPTER ELEVEN

THEODORE WAS NOW a salesman in a photographic supplies store on Fifteenth Street near Chestnut. The wages were fairly good; at least they were more than he had made as night watchman.

"I imagine you need money," Mr. Donavan, the owner, said the first day Theodore came to work.

Theodore laughed. "That's quite an understatement," he said.

"Well, suppose we give you half of your first week's pay in advance."

"Wonderful," Theodore said. Already he knew he would like the job.

There were three other employees: a salesman, DeWitt Baker, and two salesgirls who were sisters, Rosalie Lewis (whom everyone called "Ro") and Sarah Lewis, the older (whom everyone called "Miss Lewis").

"What did you do before coming here?" DeWitt asked Theodore the first day.

"I was a night watchman."

"Hmmm. Ever work in a factory?"

"No."

"Ever belong to a union?"

"No."

"Hmmm." DeWitt was a big, round man who rarely smiled.

"Well, I used to be a union organizer. A shame you never belonged to a union."

"Yes."

DeWitt leaned over. "Listen," he said, "you never get any place unless you belong to a union. That's the truth. Only way to fight those bastards."

"Who?" Theodore asked innocently.

"Who?" DeWitt stared at him aghast. "Who? The guys who run everything, that's who. The guys with all the dough. The guys who own everything and make all the laws and write all the religious morals, that's who."

"Oh," Theodore said.

"Bastards!" DeWitt murmured. He looked at Theodore. "They got you coming and going. They own everything, so if they fire you then you and your kids starve, see. Then if you go crazy with hunger after they fire you, or maybe just get tired slavin' in their damn sweatshops, they got the cops on their side to lock you up if you go out and steal."

"I see," Theodore said absently.

"They got the writers and everybody else on their side, too. All this moral bunk. Just to keep you from any kind of action. Keep you in chains. Listen, suppose you did something wrong, see. You look like a sensitive guy. Do you know you could drive yourself crazy just worrying about it?"

"Yes," Theodore said. "I know that."

"Sure. And you'd worry because you've been believing in their laws, just like they want you to." He paused, fairly angry now. Then he looked at Theodore again. "You ought to join the Socialist movement, Ted," he said. "I'll bring you some stuff to read tomorrow."

Theodore liked the employees, even DeWitt, who all through the day battered him with propaganda. They were pleasant people. He would enjoy working here.

112

"We're rich," he said to Rodina when he went home that day. Deliriously, he took the money from his pocket and threw the dollar bills on the bed. "Rich, rich," he shouted.

He went downstairs and paid Mrs. Davis part of what he owed her. "I'll have the rest soon," he said. "I've got a job now." He put a little bit of the money in an envelope and mailed it to Sylvia.

"Now we're poor again," he laughed to Rodina. Then he said, "Imagine, darling, a job as salesman. We're moving up in the world." He thought of Christmas. "It's a wonderful time. We'll go for a walk on Chestnut Street, and look through the department stores on Market Street. We've got an awful lot to be thankful for."

"Yes," Rodina said.

"And the tree. You spoke about a tree not long ago. Well, we'll get our tree. A small one. We'll set it over there in that corner."

He thought of the odor of a Christmas tree. He was like a happy little boy.

"Kiss me, Rodina," he said.

She came to him, hesitating slightly, and he kissed her. He held her at arm's length and frowned; her lips were cool and fragrant, but unresponsive.

"You seem distant, Rodina. Is anything wrong?"

"No." She looked at him and smiled.

"Good. If anything ever goes wrong, if anything ever bothers you, you must tell me. Always tell me."

She said, "Can I, Ted? Can I always do that? Can I always lean against you and tell you anything?"

"Yes, darling. Of course you can."

"Anything? And you'd still love me?"

"Anything."

"I wonder," she whispered.

113

"Rodina!" He looked at her closely. "Something *is* wrong."

"No," she said.

"There *is* something."

"No," she said. "Nothing's wrong."

2

She seemed almost to shrink from him when he kissed her in the morning; she would not meet his eyes. He wanted to ask again the question: "Is something wrong, Rodina?" But he held his tongue; if something disturbed her, and she wanted him to know, she would tell him in her own good time.

"I'll fix your breakfast," she said.

"No, don't bother. Get some sleep."

"I'm not sleepy. I'll fix breakfast."

Something troubled her: it was in the room with them, between them. She cooked eggs and bacon and they sat down and ate in silence. Afterward she walked downstairs with him.

"Hurry home," she said, and smiled. But even the smile was shadowed.

"So long, darling," he said.

He kissed her, and was startled by a laugh. "Well, well, the lovers." He turned and saw Hucks leaning against the wall, grinning. He did not notice how Rodina's body stiffened or how her eyes widened; he did not notice the wallet Hucks dangled carelessly in his hand.

"Well. And how's little Rodina this morning?" Hucks asked. He smiled; he saw the terror in her eyes. She stared at the wallet.

Hucks turned to Theodore. "And the lover. How's the lover this morning?"

Theodore did not answer. He looked at Hucks, and saw himself through Hucks' eyes. Lover. A ridiculous picture.

114

"So cozy," Hucks said. "I envy you." He smiled at Rodina and put the wallet in his pocket. "People always forget where they leave things," he said to her. Then he said, "Well, got to get off to work. I'll be seeing you"—he looked at Rodina—"both of you." He went out.

A vague uneasiness had moved through Theodore as Hucks stood there in the hall. Now he was relieved. "So long, Rodina," he started to say, but was arrested by the terror in her eyes.

"Rodina. What's wrong?"

"I hate him," Rodina said savagely.

"Why?"

"I just do."

Theodore patted her arm. "No sense to that, darling." But he did not want to admit to her the sudden fantastic flood of fear which had poured over him as Hucks talked. He hardly knew the man; he had seen him around the tenement and spoken only to be polite. But there was something familiar about Hucks' grin; there was something familiar about the sarcasm, even contempt, in his voice as he spoke to Theodore; there was something familiar about his mocking eyes. Hucks was a big man with a loud laugh and broad, stupid grin. And Theodore had felt the instant fear.

"I've got to run," he said. "I'll see you tonight."

"Ted," she said, "kiss me again."

She held him tight, with savagery. She trembled.

"Good-bye darling," he said.

Reluctantly, she released him. She waved as he went out the door.

Occasionally, throughout the day, Theodore thought of Rodina and felt again concerned because something seemed to be troubling her. Occasionally, too, he thought of Hucks: the man had made a deep and disturbing impression on him. Unconsciously, Theodore hoped he did not run into him too often.

"Here's the stuff," DeWitt said in the afternoon. He handed Theodore a batch of printed material. "Read it. Everybody needs to get educated to the facts."

"All right," Theodore said, amused.

"Lots of tragedy in this world," DeWitt said. "People don't hear enough about it."

In the evening when Theodore came home he saw Howard Grever sitting in the tearoom. Howard saw him when he came in. Puzzled and apprehensive, Theodore went into the room and over to Howard's table. He extended his hand, but Howard refused to acknowledge it.

"Hello Howard," Theodore said. He looked at the man closely. "Is something wrong with Sylvia?"

Howard grunted. "Little you care."

"What's wrong?" Theodore asked, ignoring the remark.

"Sit down," Howard said. Theodore took a seat. "There's nothing wrong with Sylvia," Howard said. "But that's no fault of yours. I just dropped by to take a look at you, and see if you were really human."

Theodore relaxed. Now a slight amusement and a slight annoyance touched him. He looked across the table at Howard, the indignant gallant. He waited for him to go on.

"I dropped past the house to see Sylvia the other night," Howard said, "and was pretty surprised to find out you'd left her. She was sitting alone in the apartment, with nothing to do, with practically no money. She doesn't know many people, so she's very much alone. She told me the story, and I just took it upon myself to stop in here and tell you that I think you're a no-good ingrate."

Theodore looked at him and said nothing. Much as the words, coming from Howard, annoyed him, he was more deeply touched by the picture of a lonely Sylvia. All these

116

weeks he had wondered what she was doing. Now he knew, and was saddened.

"What did she say?" Theodore asked.

"Say? What was there to say? That you'd left her after eighteen years for the most despicable of reasons. That she was in dire poverty, almost friendless, loveless. And alone. Most of all alone." He indicted Theodore with his eyes. "She doesn't whine, mind you," Howard said. "She's not a cowardly woman. She has more courage than you and all the men in the world like you have put together. But I could see these things."

Theodore felt suddenly weary. "Yes," he said, "it did seem like a raw deal." For no reason at all he started to explain, "But I was unhappy with her. I couldn't make her happy. For all those years both of us were unhappy. It was just as well that I left her."

"Without money—"

"I send her money, when I can," Theodore said, tired.

"*You* send her money?" Howard laughed contemptuously. "If you sent all the money you earned each month, it wouldn't be enough to care for her decently for one week." Then he said, "But she lost more than money when you left. She lost companionship. She lost emotional security. Do you send those things to her, too?"

Theodore was silent.

"And your reason for leaving. Because she couldn't bear any children. That is the most despicable thing I—"

"That's not the reason I left," Theodore said quietly.

"She thinks so. If that's not the reason, what is?"

"Both of us were unhappy."

"Nonsense!" Howard said, the color rising to his face. "Arrant nonsense! You're such a coward that you can't face your own guilt."

Coward! The word, from Howard's lips, caused near panic

117

inside of him. Coward. How many times had Sylvia called him that? How many times had he been called coward in his youth? Coward. He hated the word.

"No," he said, still quietly, "it wasn't cowardice that made me leave. It was cowardice that made me stay with her all those years before. It was cowardice, fear of opinion, fear of a million things, that kept me from leaving years ago. By the act of leaving, the cowardice was purged."

He said the words slowly, but did not convince himself. Howard said, "You are a coward. You're acting like a woman. You always did act yellow like a woman."

The severest sting. Still, Theodore controlled his temper. He felt the weariness. He looked up at Howard and smiled and said, "You and your puppy love!" He bit off the words and was satisfied when he saw the red flush of anger explode in Howard's face. But even in this amusement now he felt the sadness for Sylvia.

"Puppy love!" Howard almost shouted. "Puppy love! It's a love more sincere than any you'll ever know. God willing, I'll make her my wife. God willing, I'll make her more happy than you ever could!"

Amen, Theodore thought. Amen, so that the guilt could leave him in peace. Amen, so that he might be rid of thoughts of her which came in the midst of joy, sudden and painful, like the champing of teeth on a sore jaw.

Howard rose in anger to leave. Theodore, too, stood up. Now he was not angry: that had lasted only an instant. He thought about Sylvia. He could only hope that eventually, perhaps with Howard, she would find happiness. Guilt throbbed in him, achingly.

Rodina stood in the door to the tearoom. She smiled as Theodore and Howard walked toward her, and said, "Oh, Ted, I wondered why you were late."

118

She smiled at Howard, thinking him a friend of Theodore's. The big soft man glared at her in surprise, and then turned suddenly to stare in hatred at Theodore. In disgust, he hurried out of the tenement.

Rodina, puzzled, turned to Theodore. "Who was that, darling?"

Theodore said, "A friend of my wife's."

She was suddenly apprehensive. "What . . . did he want?"

"Nothing." Theodore smiled wanly. He looked tenderly into Rodina's eyes. "To talk. To tell me I'm a heel."

She did not need to ask why. He saw her eyes search his, and he smiled.

"Let's go up and eat," he said.

She looked at him anxiously. Then she turned and went upstairs before him.

CHAPTER TWELVE

Now, IN THE EVENING, as the ragged boys and girls played games on the street, Mrs. Baleza slept. Once she awoke and blinked, thinking she heard voices; then the illusion fled and she lay back in her eternal bed, feeling the pain in her eyes and legs. She returned to sleep.

She dreamed of a riotous picnic; all of her old friends were there. They danced and laughed and leaped and sang. Mrs. Baleza, who could not move, sat under a giant tree and watched them. Suddenly it seemed that everyone was naked; but the people continued to dance and sing and play, ignoring their nakedness. Mrs. Baleza shouted, "You're naked, you're naked, put on some clothes." In panic she pressed some leaves around her midriff and shouted continuously for the others to do likewise; but they ignored her. Mrs. Baleza shouted, "put on some clothes," and Adam, eating the apple, did so while everyone laughed until suddenly the dark clouds formed and burst overhead and the storm broke and the wind rose, whipping them while they danced and sang, and streaks of lightning shot across the sky and boulders fell and ashes fell and the sky turned black as ink and everyone continued to dance and sing while Mrs. Baleza shouted, "Put some clothes on, put some clothes on!" Then she woke up.

Her heart raced; she was filled with anxiety. Gradually, she realized she had been dreaming; she lay without moving as perspiration covered her. "Gettin' old," she thought. "Gettin' old to let a little dream bother me." She lay back, relaxing; finally she was calm.

The door knob turned. Mrs. Baleza closed her eyes as Rodina came into the room. Rodina moved softly. Mrs. Baleza yawned and stretched and slowly opened her eyes to look blinkingly at Rodina.

"Hello, mom," Rodina smiled. "Enjoy dinner?"

"Yes," the old woman said sleepily, "tasted good."

Rodina gathered up the dishes and took them into the kitchen. Mrs. Baleza watched her movements, watched her as she walked, watched the way her hips moved, noticed the slimness of her legs.

Rodina returned to the room. She opened the bureau drawers to clean them, and Mrs. Baleza looked at her: full lips and long, black hair and piercing eyes and good skin. Breasts small but firm. "A day of reckonin'," Mrs. Baleza whispered. Then she thought: be a day of reckonin' comin'.

Well, I tried, she thought. Tried hard. Tried hard to make somethin' out of that girl. Lord knows I did. Tried to teach her the right way, how to conduct herself. How to keep from sinnin'. Tried hard, Lord knows. Nothin' come of it. Still the same. Look at her. Well, a day of reckonin' be comin'.

Satan in that girl. God knows I tried to run him out. But she didn't help none, did she? Well, God's will, God's will. Don't question the will of God. Day of reckonin' comin', not just for her, either. For all a them. All this stuff, so important now, won't be then. They'll scream and howl but it'll be too late then. Bertie and Sarah and Lania and the rest. Warned all of them. Be sorry they didn't listen. Day a reckonin' comin'.

Well, I did the best I could. Sinned at first myself. Everybody sins some. All over now. All these years up here in bed, prayin' and livin' right, tryin' to make somethin' decent out a my daughter. No use. Did best I could. That ought to count

122

for somethin'. She don't think I know about that fella a her'n, livin' here. Must think I'm mighty dumb. Always knew she was doin' somethin', couldn't never prove it. Can prove it now. That Hucks; sneakin' up here to tell me. Well, always knew it, just didn't have no proof. Got it now. Day of reckonin' comin', sure as you're born . . . Lies, lies, lies. Always knew she was a liar . . . Bertie and Sarah and Lania and the rest. Still at the old place, still doin' the same things. Still hangin' around the same bar, still sellin' theirselves to every Tom, Dick 'n' Harry comes along an' waves a fin in their face. Warned em. Well, their business. End in hell, sure as you're born.

Some people suffer hell right here on earth. Ain't got to be scared about hell 'cause got it right here . . . Sick or somethin', pent up, caged like a dog . . . Ain't got nothin' to worry about. Time to think an pray, ask forgiveness all that stuff from before. Hell right here on earth. Nothin' to worry about. No man, no money. All right, all right. Ain't complainin'. Hell right here. Day of reckonin' comin', though.

Bertie and Sarah and Lania. Them three especially. See em now, sittin' there at the bar, grabbin' off first customers come in. Beer and five bucks, all it took. Bingo. Havin' a grand and glorious time. Be a day of reckonin' comin', though. Sure as you're born.

2

A pale moon moved overhead. All through the evening Rodina worked in her mother's apartment: she swept, dusted, washed windows and floors and clothes, and rearranged articles in the drawers. All through the evening her mother lay propped up by the pillows, watching her.

"Cold," Mrs. Baleza said. "Cold and clear."

"Yes," Rodina said absently. Her thoughts were elsewhere.

She was thinking about Hucks and the wallet she had left downstairs in his room. She was hating him and thinking of his words: "Be seein' you," and knowing what he meant by them. So it was not all finished. Sometime, somehow, there would have to be a showdown, a defiance of him. Rodina thought of the showdown and shuddered.

"Cold and clear," Mrs. Baleza said. "Not like the summer. Fall and winter are better than summer."

Rodina stacked the sheets and pillow cases in the drawers.

"Summer's hot," Mrs. Baleza said. "Like Hell. Makes me think of Hell. 'Cept Hell is even hotter; a million times hotter. Summer makes me think of Hell. Fall and winter's much better."

Now Rodina dusted. Mrs. Baleza watched the trembling of her daughter's young breasts as she moved the cloth across the top of the bureau in swift, short strokes.

"Been wrong about you, I guess," Mrs. Baleza said. "Been wrong thinkin' you was bad. Want to apologize."

For a moment Rodina did not grasp her mother's words. When finally their meaning drove home, she turned to stare at her in surprise, almost disbelief.

"Watchin' you work," Mrs. Baleza went on, as though talking to herself. "Workin' around here day after day. You been a pretty good daughter, considerin'. Stay out half the night, but you been a pretty good girl, considerin'. Guess I been wrong."

Rodina could only stare at her mother. Her lips parted, but only breath came out.

"Been a little too harsh," Mrs. Baleza said. "Your father a minister and all. Made me kind of strict. Guess I been wrong. Just wanted you to know I been thinkin' about it. Maybe I been wrong." She looked at Rodina. "That make you feel better?"

124

"Yes," Rodina said weakly. She could not understand this.

"You ain't evil. Been comparin' you, that's what. Been comparin' you with some women I know, makes you look like a angel. I been wrong. I been thinkin' about the others, and you ain't evil at all."

Mrs. Baleza's eyes fixed on her motionless daughter. "Sarah and Bertie and Lania and them. Been thinkin' about them this afternoon. You ain't evil at all when I think about them. They're the people going to hell, not you." She paused a moment. "Go to bed with every Tom, Dick and Harry. You seen 'em up here, ain't you?"

"Yes, ma'am," Rodina said.

"Them's the ones. Goin' out with every Tom, Dick and Harry, married men even. Men with wives waitin' at home for 'em. Wives that love 'em; wives who gave 'em all they ever had. Lania and the rest of 'em don't care nothin' about that. Go out with 'em anyway. Break up a Christian home. That don't bother them none. Just think about themselves, that's all. Don't care nothin' about the wives."

Mrs. Baleza fixed her gaze increduously on Rodina's horrified eyes. "Could you believe it, Rodina? People like that, no heart? Remember once Lania *lived* with a married man for months, ain't cared nothin' about the wife, what happened to her. Lived with him. Slept with him, ate with him, took money from him, bold as you please. Ain't cared about how it's a sin to live with a man when you ain't married to him, and how it's so much worse when he got a wife at home. Could you believe there's such kinda women?"

Rodina looked at her mother and said nothing, and her mother went on, "*Them's* the kinda people goin' to hell. Them's the kinda people gonna burn forever, praise God, in the fires of hell. People with no hearts, people cause wives and children to suffer. Them's the worst kind of all." Her voice

125

had risen in intensity; the fire behind her eyes burned more fiercely. "Them's the kinda people really evil, God knows. But be a day of reckonin' comin', Rodina. Praise God, be a day of reckonin'. Burn forever in Hell. Not people like you. People like them. Burn forever in the unholy fires of Hell."

Rodina did not realize how she stared at her mother; she could not see the way the color had drained from her face; she did not know she leaned, for support, on the bureau; she did not feel her entire body trembling. She was conscious only of the bell tolling in her ears.

Mrs. Baleza looked at her with concern. "Rodina, somethin' wrong?" she asked.

"Me?" Rodina jumped as though a gun had gone off beside her. "Oh, no ma'am, I'm all right."

"You're so pale."

"Am I? I don't know why," she said rapidly. "I was just thinking about something."

"And you're trembling, darlin'."

"I don't know why, mom." Rodina thought she smiled; in reality, her face twisted hideously. "I was just thinking."

"And you seem weak, darlin. You're leaning on the bureau."

She stiffened like a soldier called to attention. "Don't know why." She shook her head; she turned to the bureau and rubbed the dust cloth across its top. "Don't know why," she repeated nervously.

"Maybe you ought to see a doctor."

"Oh, I'm okay, mom."

"Well, take care of yourself, Rodina."

"Oh, yes ma'am. Don't worry, mom. I'm all right."

3

She awoke to the sound of a woman's cry, and sat upright in bed. Instantly, she was aware of ants, thousands of them it seemed, swarming over her skin, tumbling toward her face, her eyes. For a moment she stared at them, more horrified than she had ever been, and then she opened her mouth wide and shrieked . . .

Theodore was shaking her and the ants were gone. She stared at the blanket and at her arms and her body, dewed with perspiration. Her thoughts spun.

"Where did they go?" she asked, and her voice trembled.

"What, darling?"

"The ants. The ants. My body was covered with ants. Where did they go?"

Theodore sighed with relief. He kissed her softly on the cheek. "It was a dream, darling," he said. "Only a bad dream. Lie down and relax. Soon you'll be asleep again."

A dream. She lay down, cold and trembling. Soon Theodore was asleep again. Rodina lay wide awake, shuddering now and then, her body damp with the perspiration. Moonlight came into the room. The wind blew through the trees outside the window, and shadows of the leaves swayed and danced and merged on the walls. She watched the shadows dance. She pushed the covers from her and was alternately hot and cold.

Her mind spun. She saw the policeman in the rain. She wanted to cry out again. There was the cop and she felt the first beat-skip of her heart as she saw the money; there she was racing around the corner; there she was walking and he laughed and seized her wrist and she was gone in terror, racing around the corners, into the tenement, thinking, "Theodore mustn't know, I mustn't disappoint him," running into Hucks, the leering Hucks, saying, "Let's go into my room and . . . talk," shrieking, hating him, seeing her mother's eyes.

She closed her eyes tightly and the vision was there against her eye lids; she opened her eyes and the vision was there, on

127

the wall, amid the leaves which would never cease their dancing.

There had been nights like this in her childhood: the nights after her mother's words, lying in bed, the evil leaves dancing like spirits on the wall, she taut inside, straining, like a coiled spring. Nights like this with God in the room, when she had closed her eyes and wanted to shriek; nights seeing God in her mother's unbending eyes, clawing at the eyes, hating them, shrieking inwardly: to hell with it all, to hell with momma and with God!

It was all lost! she almost cried in the darkness, turning to Theodore. It was all lost! this hope of love and a life of goodness. How foolish it had been to hope or dream! How foolish it had been to think she could deserve his love—the love of him, who was good! Ted! Ted! she thought, You don't know about things like this! She could never change; Judas could not change! And an angel could not long love Satan.

"Oh," she cried, and felt the long low wail of despair course through her. The wind raced through the trees. Her terrified eyes watched the leaves dance wildly on the wall.

CHAPTER THIRTEEN

THE NEXT MORNING was very cold. There was a steady wind, not too high, and the sky was overcast. It would be a cold, dull day. This was the beginning of winter; the false warm weather, with its soft incessant rain, seemed gone for good.

Kids were reluctant to leave the warmth of their beds and go to school. The windows in the block were open wide; some had no panes; few had curtains though most had worn, green shades; the steady wind blew through the houses, sweeping them of their summer odors.

The kids were noisy on the street. They shouted and threw cans and swung their books to keep warm. They hated school; the only good thing about it was the recess; during recess they could play squeeze the lemon, and get warm, and feel forbidden parts of the girls' bodies.

Men rose for work. Yes, this was the winter. They cursed their jobs, the need to work. What did they get for their early hours and hard work? They cursed their wives for having children. They went outside and waited on the corners for street-cars. A dull, gray day.

Hucks rose and did his exercises. He opened the windows still wider and lay on his stomach and arched his back and rocked, back and forth, like the bottom of a rocking chair. He did push ups; he did deep-knee bends; he chinned himself on the door frame between his bedroom and bathroom. Finished, breathing hard, filled with the consciousness of his strength, he washed and slipped into his clothes. He put on his lumber jacket and went out into the hall.

Mrs. Davis was turning to go up the stairs. She was wheezing hard. She saw Hucks and grinned, trying to catch her breath. "Hello, Hucks," she said. "How yew doin' this mornin'?"

"Fine, sweetheart," Hucks said. He liked Mrs. Davis; she always spoke to him; she seemed to like him. He said, "You sound like you been running a mile, sweetheart. What's the matter? Gettin' old?"

"Yes, guess so," Mrs. Davis breathed. "Guess so. Legs ain't what they used to be. Hard navigatin' these stairs eight 'n' nine times a day. Ain't what I used to be."

"Oughta be ashamed of yourself," Hucks said. "Somebody'd think you was forty or fifty years old, sweetheart."

"Lawd, Hucks, wish I was that young."

"Well, you are, aren't you sweetheart?"

"Lawd, Hucks, you know I seen the last stroke of sixty years ago. Wish I was that young."

"Don't try to kid me, sweetheart," Hucks said. "I know you're just a chippy."

He walked over to her and said, "Well, let's see if we can't give you a little help in gettin' up these stairs." He lifted her, as she protested that she was much too heavy, and carried her up the stairs. At the landing he placed her gently on her feet.

"Elevator service at your beck and call," he said.

"Lawd, Hucks, thought yew'd break both our necks." She looked at him with warmth. "You're a fine boy, Hucks. A fine boy. Been a fine boy since I first knew you."

He felt a tremendous surge of emotion he did not recognize as gratitude. He could have kissed the ailing landlady. Inter-

130

mixed with the gratitude was embarrassment. Hucks said, "Well, you're a pretty slick chick yourself, sweetheart."

He started down the stairs, still feeling the gratitude. As he neared the bottom Mrs. Davis called, "Hucks, would yew do me a favor? Would yew just take a look at the furnace before you leave, see if it needs any more coal?"

"Sure, sweetheart," he said. "Anything for you." And, at that moment, he meant those words.

He went down into the cellar and looked at the fire; yes it needed a couple of shovels of coal. He put the coal in the furnace and, as he moved the shovel forcefully, saw something drop from the pocket of his lumber jacket. It was the wallet Rodina had left in his room. He put down the shovel and opened the wallet and counted the money inside; thirty dollars, mostly in five-dollar bills. Should he give the money to Rodina, cram it down her throat, shame her with it? Yes, he might do that. Hucks took out the bills and threw the wallet into the flames.

When he passed the tearoom, other people from the tenement were seated at the tables. Some saw Hucks but did not wave or speak. To hell with them, Hucks thought. He would not speak to them either. To hell with them. He did not care whether they spoke or not.

The kids were on their way to school. Hucks walked to the corner, watching the men who cringed in the face of the cold wind. He stood straight and tall, enjoying the wind, defiant of it. What did a little cold mean to him? He watched the kids going by, looking closely at the face of each. Finally he saw a husky youngster carrying a football along with his books.

"Hey, kid, comere," Hucks said.

The kid walked over. Hucks said, "Let's have a look at that football." The kid handed him the football; Hucks inspected it. "Good ball," Hucks said. "You like to play football?"

131

"Sure," the kid said.

"I used to play football. Liked it a hell of a lot. Was good at it, too. Played in the Army. Who you play with?"

"The Bisons. We got a good team."

"Yeah? You like to ride bikes?"

"Sure," the kid said. "Who don't?"

"Some boys don't," Hucks said, "but they ain't real boys, are they?"

"Must not be," the kid said. The kid's hair was cut short and he wore knickers.

"You got a bike?" Hucks said.

"No."

"Why not?"

"Where'm I gonna get one from?"

"Ain't you got no money?"

"No. Not that much."

"Here," Hucks said, "buy yourself a bike." He put the thirty dollars in the hand of the startled kid, and walked off.

"The hell with that bitch, Rodina," he thought."

2

Rodina was awake, thinking. It seemed to her that she was always thinking, these days. There was a rap on the door.

She lay still. The most fantastic fear sprang into her heart: Theodore's wife was at the door! It was a conviction. Theodore's wife was at the door; she had come to take her husband home. The knock came again. Rodina looked at Theodore; he had not stirred. If his wife was at the door, Rodina would send her away; she would say that Theodore did not live here; she would say anything. She got out of the bed and went to the door.

"Who is it?" she asked.

"Me," came Mrs. Davis' voice. "I got a letter for Mr. Hall. Shall I push it under the door?"

"Yes," Rodina said. She was relieved, but only to a small degree; who was the letter from? She picked up the envelope and read the name in the upper left-hand corner: "Mrs. Sylvia Hall."

She stood at the door with the letter in her hand. She looked at Theodore; he was still asleep. She fingered the letter, the flywheel spinning in her mind. She should hide the letter; she should destroy it. She stood motionless, thinking. Then she thought: Suppose Mrs. Davis says something to Ted about the letter. She could not destroy it. She laid it on the dressing table and got back in bed.

What had his wife written? First, yesterday, she had sent a man to talk to Theodore—a man who left Theodore obviously disturbed. They had talked about her, Rodina, for why else would the man have stared at her like that? Now she had written a letter. Why? She had not written all this time. Why did she write now?

She wants him back, Rodina thought. Of course, she wants him back. The man, yesterday, had told Theodore he was a heel because he left his wife. No doubt he wanted Theodore to go back to her. Theodore had not talked to her about the man; he wanted to forget whatever the man had said. He had been disturbed. He was trying to make up his mind.

Look at him now. He lay asleep on his back, his head on one side, his lips parted. What was he dreaming? Of his wife?

She turned her head toward the ceiling. I know he wants to go back to her; I know he misses her. I'm not his kind. She is. She's his kind. He can't fight himself. He likes me and he wants to help me, but I'm not his kind.

She felt a sudden, savage bitterness, a rage against heaven. It seemed so terribly unfair to be condemned at birth. There

133

must be a reason for it; her mother said there was always a reason to God's works. But it seemed terribly unfair. Why let a person be born, if there was no hope for him?

Theodore rarely talked about his wife. Rodina tried to picture her; Theodore had never described her. Probably his wife was quiet and sweet, good, kind and easy-going. Probably these things had bored Theodore; usually they bored a man after awhile. Then he had met her, Rodina, and seen something romantic in her. Then he had met her mother, and afterward felt sorry for her. So he had left his wife. And after awhile he had realized how much he missed his wife, how much he really wanted those very things which had seemed so intolerable because they were unexciting. He had realized that Rodina was a common slut, a street girl, a bitch. Even though he did not yet know about the wallet, he must now have become aware of the cheapness, the evil, which she, Rodina, radiated.

Before this he had been legally married to a woman who had been a virgin before their wedding; now, like a slum lover, he slept with a woman who had slept before with many men. Before this he had been married to a woman who was cultured, composed, a church-goer; now he lived with a woman whose grammar was bad, who did not know how to act in public, who defied and sometimes slandered Almighty God.

She should let him go, she should let him go. But she did not want to lose him.

"Rodina! You're awake. Good morning."

Theodore kissed her. Seizing this moment, like the one before death, she clung to him. Ted, Ted, hold me! She kissed him hard and pressed hard against him. She wanted to split him open, enter his body and be a part of him. For a long

134

while she lay warm and comfortable in his arms. Then, coming back to the world, she said, "You have a letter."

She watched his face. He read the name and she was sure she saw a great change come over his face: his jaw seemed to set, lines creased his forehead, his eyes became serious. He tore open the envelope; he seemed to hesitate before withdrawing the letter. Finally he opened it; a card fell out; he looked at the card and the unmistakable shadow of pain moved across his face. He read the letter slowly; his eyes remained serious, with the pain. Rodina sat watching him.

Finally he was finished. His eyes lingered on the page. Rodina missed nothing in his face; from the corner of her eyes she could see the small, neat handwriting of his wife. Theodore seemed far away from this room; he seemed to be again at home with his wife. (He must have gone there so often, unknown to Rodina, since the day he had come to the tenement.)

"It's from my wife," he said.

A moment before, his voice had been vibrant and gay. He had held her tight, kissed her, and she had felt affection like a warm bath surrounding them. Now the letter; now his voice and his mood were changed. The letter, the wife, was between them. Of course. The wife must always be between them. How had she ever hoped for, ever dreamed of more?

He passed the letter to her. He did not look at her. She said, "Do you really want me to read it, Ted?"

"Of course, darling."

"She looked at the paper and saw the small, neat writing. She inhaled deeply, like a swimmer about to plunge, and read:

Dear Theodore—

I don't know what you must have thought of me all this time, not writing to thank you for your letters and the money you sent. Don't think me ungrateful. The money I

135

needed desperately, as you may well imagine; the letters, of course, I treasure.

I have not written because I have not known what to say; for what is a wife to say when her husband has gone from her? I am reconciled, as much as I shall ever bé, to living alone for the rest of my life. Howard has called on me, and offered me his attentions, but I sent him away; I cannot bear his company. I realize that you did what you did only after careful thought; that you did what you thought best for the happiness of both of us; that there was no malice in your action. If I feel that you were wrong, if I wish that that might never have come to pass, it is only, perhaps, because I am selfish. I still love you; I will always love you. But what is done is done.

Looking back, I have many regrets. That I was not a better wife to you, could not better fulfill your ideal of a wife. That I was often cross or nagging or boring. That I could bear you no children, for without that ability I was not a whole, a complete wife. That I did not display sufficient faith in your capabilities. That I am not beautiful, for you love beautiful things.

I am ashamed to admit that I have not yet begun divorce action. I hope that this does not inconvenience you. I dread starting that final action which will take us apart from one another forever. I shrink from this and from the ugliness that courts have, the lies we both must tell, the wounds we must inflict on one another. I dread these things. Eighteen years is no brief infatuation; it is a priceless portion of our lives, and I, at least, dread to see those years become all I have to live for.

I hesitated to write these things before. I write them now because this is the Christmas Season. The holly, the trees, the lights bring back so many things to me—our first Christmas together, friends around the tree, presents, roast turkey, wine, church, laughter, good feelings.

Memories will haunt my Christmas Day. They are pleasant ones. I will never forget you; I will never stop loving you.

Your
Sylvia

She gave the letter back to Theodore, and tears came to her eyes. So much goodness sprang from the letter. So much sincerity. Rodina could not look at Theodore; he, too, must feel this thing, the quality of his wife, and the cheapness of the woman now beside him.

It was all so hopeless; already she felt lost, as though her love were already gone from her. A matter of time. Only time, time, time. Then it would be over. Why delay?

Theodore was looking around the room; Rodina glanced at him and could see he was trying to appear composed, but unsuccessfully. She knew how the letter had touched him. She wanted to help him.

"Ted," she said, "I'll fix your breakfast."

He did not bother to object. Rodina felt sorry for him. As she cooked, he said, "It was quite a letter."

"Yes."

"I can't understand it. I would never have believed she felt that way."

Rodina said nothing. It was only a matter of time, time, time. A sudden terror shot through her. It was the terror which comes suddenly to the condemned man as the moment of death approaches, the one fleeting moment in which the terror, the starkness, the finality of his extinguishment confronts him. Then it was gone, as it goes from the condemned man; the realization of the impending end remained, but it was hazy and dreamlike.

"So long, Rodina." Like a farewell. They were finished eating and he was about to go to work. He kissed her on the

137

mouth, but it was a distant kiss. He smiled before leaving, but it was a faraway smile. He went out of the door, leaving Rodina and the letter in the room.

3

She lay on her back on the bed, too empty to dress, too tense to sleep. The letter hung above her eyes; she saw every word.

The letters, of course, I treasure. What had he written? That he was sorry he had hurt her. That he wished he could send still more money. These things Rodina knew; but they were not things to treasure. What else had he written? That he missed her? That he wished, sometimes, in the night, that he had not left her? That he was unhappy without her?

I still love you; I will always love you. There had been a wife, yes, she had known that. A wife, distant, insubstantial, something which existed and yet was unreal. There had been a wife, but Rodina had never seen her, never heard her voice, and Theodore had not spoken of her often. Now these words. With them came the sudden full realization that the woman, the wife, was *real*, and that she *loved* Theodore, had *kissed* him, had *gone to bed* with him, had *said sweet things* to him and *heard* sweet things in return. It was, strangely, a shocking realization, one that caused pain.

I have many regrets. Yes, his wife was a good woman; it was a good woman who could admit her faults. Even now she felt no malice; even now she was willing to say that she was to blame. She wanted to make him happy; she believed she had failed; for that failure, she blamed only herself. She was a good woman.

I am ashamed to admit that I have not yet begun divorce action. No, and she would never begin such action. Nor did Theodore want her to. The dread she felt, the remorse, the

138

pain, were felt also by Theodore. There would be no divorce. She, Rodina, would never be the wife of Theodore. And Theodore did not want her as his wife. He would never say this, but it was true. And justly true. Years later, Theodore would think of his narrow escape, and he would shudder.

I hope this does not inconvenience you. Then the wife did not know about Rodina. Theodore had never mentioned her. The wife had no idea that Theodore had intended another marriage. Why? Because, somehow, Theodore had always known he would never marry again. Somehow, even in those first days, he had realized that this thing they talked about would never be. He did not mean to lie; he thought, when he proposed, that he wanted to marry her; but underneath everything he had known the truth.

The holly, the trees, the lights . . . our first Christmas together ... friends around the tree . . . church . . . good feelings . . . Memories will haunt my Christmas Day. So different, those Christmases his wife described, from the one he would observe this year. So different, and so much more holy. Not the wife alone would be visited by memories.

Well, what should she do? For once, for once in her life, she should do what was correct. What would a correct person, what would a good person do?

A good person would say, "Theodore, go back to your wife. She needs you, and you need her."

No, that was not what a good person would say. That was too noble, it smacked too much of self-sacrifice. No, a good person would not try to be a hero. A good person would say, "Theodore, listen, when you came to me I made a promise not to steal anymore, to be a respectable person from then on, a person you'd be proud of. Well, I broke that promise. I snatched a wallet and nearly got caught, and then I went to bed with Hucks. I never changed and I never will change. So

139

you'd be much better off without me. Go back to your wife."

No, no, that had the same fault. That, too, smacked of martyrdom. No, a good person would not allow Theodore to feel such gratitude toward her. A good person would be absolutely honest, without pretense, without drama.

A good person would say, "Theodore, when you came to live here, I thought I loved you and could change to suit you. Now I know I can't. I went out and snatched a wallet from a cop. Then I went to bed with the fellow downstairs, Hucks. If I hadn't snatched a wallet that day, I'd likely have done it another. If I hadn't gone to bed with Hucks, I'd have gone to bed with somebody else. Chances are I'll go to to bed with a lot of other fellows before a year's gone by. As a matter of fact, we're from two different ways of life, and I'm as much a part of mine as you are of yours. I can't change. As a matter of fact, I don't really want to change. I want lots of men and I want to get my money the easy way. I don't love you; I only thought I did. So you'd better pack up and leave. It would save you a lot of misery in the future."

Yes, yes, that was what a good person would say. A good person would say this. A good person would take responsibility for the break-up, state that she was tired of him, kick him out so that he would feel he had no alternative but to leave. That way, Theodore wouldn't feel sorry for her. That way he'd go back to his wife with a clear conscience.

That was what a good person would say. Tonight, when he came home, she would be a good person. She would kick him out. And, when he was gone, the act might even make her feel good—because the act was good—for a time, at least.

Content, she dozed off. When she awoke it was noon. She was amazingly buoyant; now that she had made up her mind to do something good, the horror of his leaving was not acute. She was resigned; and she was doing something good, good, good!

140

She went downstairs into the tearoom. Juarez was alone at a table. Good old Juarez.

"Hi, Juarez," she said.

He looked up at her. He said, "Hello, Rodina."

"Can I grab a seat?"

"Of course."

She sat down, Glenn came in, and she ordered tea. The Mexican was silent, eating his lunch. Rodina remembered the days that seemed long past, the days when she had confided nearly all in Juarez, had asked his advice, had cried, figuratively, on his shoulder. A burst of affection went out from her as she looked at him. Juarez. Good old Juarez.

"I want to talk to somebody," she said. "Juarez, can I talk to you? Like I always used to?"

"Of course," the Mexican said.

CHAPTER FOURTEEN

EVERY TIME HE SAW Rodina smile, every time he saw her eyes opened wide in apparent innocence, every morning that, from his room, he saw her walk hand in hand down the stairs with Theodore, Juarez felt hatred seeping like hot lava through his veins. Ever since *that night*.

(Himself about to descend the stairs . . . the sound at the front door . . . Rodina and Hucks coming in through the hall, taking care not to be heard . . . then into Hucks' room. . . .)

Every time he saw her he wanted to spit or cry. (She was so beautiful: long, thick black hair; white teeth; dark eyes deep-set and intense; mouth full and red and soft in his imagination; and skin so flushed, smoothly downward-flowing, a dainty shield. She was so beautiful: skirts swinging, strides long on legs, long and lovely . . . But beyond, beyond! One did not see beyond!)

Every time he saw her, he wanted to tell her of his hatred. But he could not; and she gave him no chance. She passed; she waved (so nonchalantly, as though all were as it had been); she walked on her way. He did not answer her greetings, but she did not care; his eyes were full of bitterness, but she did not notice. (Should she be disturbed by a Mexican's disapproval?)

She had betrayed a dream.

If a woman were born on a deserted island, reared by birds,

143

neighbor of the sun (Juarez had mused as a romantic young man), she would grow up to be the most perfect woman who ever lived. She would know nothing of hate, have no need for vanity. She would not be buried under the stifling mountain of inhibitions and repressions and frustrations which so disturbed domestic woman. If she loved, she would love freely and faithfully; if she did wrong (according to the laws of God or man), she would do so innocently, without malice or cheating or deceit. In all things, she would be sincere.

She would not wear paint or lovely clothes; she would need no scent from a bottle, nor hair sheen from a can. She would walk naked over the island, or perhaps clad in leaves, or perhaps she would wear the dried skin of a gazelle. Her hair would grow thick, black and healthy and her eyes would be deep-set and her skin would be smooth, the lines of her body gently downward flowing and she would walk proudly without vanity, strides long, legs long and lovely, body swinging free in the sunlight.

A man could worship such a woman (Juarez thought, as a romantic young man) until death.

2

Juarez was a Mexican.

Hucks had said, "Well, how's the Mex today?"

Hucks had said, many times, "Say, introduce me to one of them Mex chicks, will you. I hear they're great in bed."

Hucks had looked at him and grinned, and he had turned his eyes away. Hucks was a loud man without intelligence. Hucks was a strong man who knew he was strong. Hucks was a self-styled ladies' man, who liked to boast of his conquests, to whom love was to be laughed at, something for the sissies,

144

to whom a woman's body was some dishrag to be wrung out and thrown aside for later use.

Hucks, or men like Hucks, might one day rule this country. Juarez had seen them many times. He knew their lust for power. He feared them.

Juarez was a scrawny man with pockmarks and watery eyes. Juarez was a Mexican.

All these years living here in this country in this house or that house with this job or that job he had known he was a Mexican. In New York, when he was young and living with his parents (who spoke such poor English) he had known he was a Mexican. And his brothers and father had Mexican kinds of jobs and wore Mexican kinds of clothes and lived in a Mexican kind of tenement house with dirty wall paper and soiled sheets and loud profanities. And the Irish Catholics and tough Italians of the neighborhood had reminded them with sticks and stones that they were Mexicans. And, later, when the first of maturity brought the first of full comprehension and full hatred, the haughty Nordice of Manhattan had reminded them on streetcars by looks or in the motion pictures by stereotypes or in employment by the type of jobs they gave them that they were Mexicans. They could never forget they were Mexicans. Although Juarez wanted to forget.

In youth when he saw kids with better toys and in young manhood when he saw boys with better clothes and more money in their pockets and smiles more free than his own, Juarez wanted to forget, to change his nationality. Those were the days when he had hated all who reminded him who he was. So he had hated all those who were treated as inferiors: the Jews and Negroes as well as the Mexicans.

Early, when the girls at school treated him differently from the other boys, and he knew the reason why, Juarez felt the beginnings of the hatred of the Negroes. Seeing them dressed

145

loudly on the streets; hearing them talk loudly in the restaurants or saloons.

"Brother that was some chick. Did you see that chassis sway?"

"Didn't miss it. Remember that girl in Chi? Looked like her. We had a ball, didn't we? All those juice-heads around."

He had hated talk like this, not perceiving, in those years, the pain behind the vernacular, the misery behind the brave clothes, the hatred behind the grin he so despised. He hated them, and hated the Jews who were beaten and cowered, the Mexicans whose clothes and voices and manners were as loud as those of the Negroes. With talk of illegal drugs and prostitutes and parties all night long.

And he went to school and became older and began to understand. And then his hatreds changed. He could not love, could not embrace, the people who were as oppressed as he; for secretly he hated them for allowing such oppression. But even more he learned to hate the ones who thought him different, the girls who would not consider going on dates with him, the fellows who did not consider him their equal. Slow hatred burned. But indiscriminately, until the slow-gathering frustrations and resentments gave birth to hatred of all who were considered normal in this country—all those who could walk with their heads up high and their smiles unrestrained by fear or bitterness. Until he breathed hatred.

And then he met Rodina.

Rodina. In all this world there was Rodina. Desert island princess, woman without vanity, to whom a man was a man to be respected as a man. Rodina: honest, untouched, who did what she did, right or wrong (according to the laws of God or man) with freedom, without malice, in innocence. Who was in all things sincere.

Or so, up to *that day*, he had believed.

146

Now he sat opposite her at a table in the tearoom of the tenement house.

"What's the trouble?" Juarez asked. He did not meet her eyes. He was enraged that she should again seek his sympathy, as he was sure she would do. Glenn stepped into the room and out again. For the rest, the room, shaded from the pale sun's glare, was empty.

"Me," she said. "I'm the trouble, Juarez. I'm all mixed up. I just feel like talking."

"About what?"

"About Ted," she said.

He waited. She said, "Ted's unhappy with me, Juarez. I'm sure of it. I'm not his kind. I'm not good enough for him. After he met me and knew me awhile he thought he loved me, but he didn't really. He didn't really know me. Now he gets letters from his wife, and I can see he's unhappy when he reads them. I know he doesn't want to hurt me, but I can see he's not happy."

The same old train, Juarez thought. The same old train, Juarez the blind conductor, guiding her through cool pleasant valleys of soothing winds and sighing, leaning trees.

"There's things he doesn't even know about," she continued. "I promised him I'd change when he came here. I love him, and I know he doesn't like me to steal or get in any kind of trouble, so I promised I'd change. I promised I wouldn't steal anymore. But I did steal. Remember when you loaned us the money and he was out of a job? Then. That's when I stole, from a cop, too, and I almost got caught. He doesn't know me. I'd have stolen again anyway some time or another. I lie and steal and don't even think too much about it. He's different, and he can't be happy with me for long."

"I see," Juarez said.

"Mom says you're born this way, and I guess she was right."

"It seems that way," Juarez said.

"So, tonight, when he comes home, I'll make him leave. I'll make him go back to his wife where he'll be better off. I can tell she's nice. I read her letter. That's the best thing."

"A noble decision," Juarez said.

She looked at him with anguished eyes. "But what do you *do* about a person like me, Juarez? What can be done about it? Being born a certain way, I mean. Nothing you do can change it. You just go on, trying to be something else, but you can't. You were just born to be a certain way, and later on you get punished for it."

"Yes," Juarez said, "you're punished for being born what you are."

"It doesn't seem fair, does it?"

"No," Juarez said, "it isn't fair."

He watched her now across the table. His eyes seemed the same as always behind their watery film. Rodina's eyes were focused on the flowered design in the table cloth. Outside, the heatless sun shone bright in Christmas week.

From the first, when she spoke, Juarez had listened to the usual words silently, filled with hatred. But gradually he seemed to detect some small note of sincerity in her voice, and the sincerity puzzled him. What was this? He could almost believe that she actually meant to send her lover back to his wife. What could one know about another person? Except what one had come to feel—hatred or love, or a portion of each?

"So you're going to send him back to his wife?"

"Yes," she said. "That's the right thing. I decided just before I came downstairs that I could do one good thing in my life. I'll send him back, and then he'll be happy. And his wife will be happy. Maybe he doesn't think so now, but he'll find out."

He could almost believe she meant it. "Don't you love him?" Juarez asked, a note of sarcasm in his voice.

She looked up at him; now he met her eyes and saw the depth of passion there. "Yes," she said. "Yes."

What could one believe? Before—those many times before —she had also seemed sincere. She had seemed sincere when in moments of anger she had shouted her hatred of Hucks. She had seemed sincere in innocence, the heroine raped but unmarred—but how many other men, cheap men, vulgar men, men without compassion or the knowledge of love, had known her intimately?

What could one believe? And yet, in this moment, she seemed so sincere.

"What will you do after he's gone?" Juarez asked.

"I don't know," she said. Her eyes went back to the flowers.

"You'll be unhappy?"

"Yes."

"Day after day after day without him. Can you think of him gone forever? Can you think of never seeing him again?"

She squeezed shut her eyes. "Juarez," she pleaded, "don't make me weak."

"Gone for ever, never to kiss again. Gone, never to sleep beside you again. On whose shoulder then would you lay your head? On whose breast then could you cry?"

"Juarez! Please!"

"To whom would you talk?" He felt the long dormant hatred rise and rise. "Who then would you love? Who then would be left for you? Hucks?"

"No!"

"Hucks!" he almost shouted. "Hucks would be left. Only Hucks. Hucks, the lover Hucks! That would be your substitute."

"No, no," she almost shouted. "Not him! Not him! No one. Not him. I hate him! Oh, I hate him, I hate him!"

"Hate him?" Juarez felt the bitter acid in his throat. "Hate him? Do you hate him, Rodina? Do you really hate him?"

"Yes, I hate him! I hate him, Juarez!"

"You're lying!"

"Juarez!" She stared at him.

"You're lying!" Juarez shouted.

Then the room was quiet. There, outside, was the sun. Here, in the room, were the tables and the chairs and the warmth. Here, in front of him, Juarez was now aware of his tea: tepid now, he was sure. He looked up at her and the anger retreated from his eyes.

"No," he said softly. "No, Rodina, you don't lie. Of course you don't lie. I'm sorry."

There was nothing, now; even in that moment he had failed. Wearily he wondered strangely of the worth of life itself, the endless days following days, the past repeated, with the horizon unapproachable. Motion was necessary and so man moved on: going where, doing what? What was the sense of it all?

He looked at Rodina again, and for a moment felt almost a trickle of tenderness. Quickly that faded. Here am I, he thought, seated across the table from a deceitful bitch, who lies and perhaps does not lie. Why should her bitchery concern me? Was I ever so foolish as to nourish a hope? Am I now so stupid as to try to destroy her?

"Why do you think Theodore loves his wife?" Juarez asked calmly.

"She's just like him. Sometimes, when he looks off and seems far away, I can tell he's thinking about her. When he read her letter this morning, he seemed so sad. He's always sad, I think. And he doesn't really know me. He doesn't know what I really am."

150

Juarez said, "I think he does love you."

She stared at him. "How can you say that, Juarez? He doesn't really know me. He doesn't know what I really am."

"No," Juarez said, reflecting, "perhaps he doesn't."

"And if he did, he'd be miserable. I know how he is. He couldn't still love me."

Juarez looked at her. All that he considered decent in him rebelled against the trend his thoughts now took; but the thick slow hatred, unfelt for a moment, stirred again, crushing the protest.

"There must be a common meeting ground if two people are to know eternal love," he said softly, almost as though speaking to himself. "Satan could not wed an Angel. Good cannot love evil. Lovers—if the love is to last—must be akin, each fulfilling the moral ideal of the other."

The dissimulation came to him easily. His soft and forever moist eyes looked into hers. "And you, Rodina, cannot change. You cannot become good."

He watched her wide eyes; he stared almost hypnotically. "But could *he* become *evil*?", Juarez asked.

Rodina looked at him blankly; for the instant, his meaning was not clear. Juarez lifted the cup of tea and sipped the contents; his eyes had moved away from hers. When he lowered the cup he leaned back comfortably in his chair, feeling a strange thrilling chill, eager, now that he had set his course, for the journey.

"Ted? Become evil?" Rodina said softly, as though only repeating his phrase in her mind. "Ted? Juarez, you're kidding."

"No," he said, "I'm not kidding." He waited again. "There're good and evil in everyone, Rodina. It's hard to change from evil to good. It's hard to change from black to white. But the opposite is easy. Theodore could become the same as you."

151

"But I wouldn't want that," she said. "I wouldn't want him to change."

"Ah, only now you think that. But you cannot know; you haven't seen him as a changed man. Imagine—only then could both of you be free. Only then would he be able to stop worrying about his wife, and only then could you cease worrying about a little theft, or a little lie. If you were alike, nothing could prevent your being happy. It's only his goodness that prevents that. His goodness is the wall between you; if you would be happy, you must break down the wall."

She was puzzled. She could only stare at him, stricken.

Juarez said, "You have only two choices. To send him back to his wife, or let him stay. If you send him back, he'll be unhappy. He was unhappy before; that's why he left her. He doesn't love her, as you think. He simply feels guilty, because he thinks he's done something wrong by leaving her. If he returns, he'll be unhappy, and therefore his wife, too, will find it impossible to be happy. And you? What of you, Rodina? Would you be happy with him gone? The years stretching ahead—years of loneliness, years of the Huckses and the Toms and the Glenns."

He waited, watching her eyes, seeing her shrink from the picture of loneliness. He said, "And the other choice is to let him stay here, with you. This is what he wants to do. But, so long as he is the type of person who is troubled by feelings of guilt because he left his wife, or indignation because you've stolen or lied, you two cannot know happiness. Because you can never change."

She could not respond.

"Change him!" Juarez commanded. "Change him, and both of you can be happy. Are you a woman, Rodina, or a mere girl? Are you a woman who loves like a woman, and acts on that love regardless of the consequences? Or are you a snivel-

152

ing girl, seduced by puppy-love, too weak to take the steps real love demands? Is your love the feeble kind which would permit a weeping wife to destroy forever the chance of Theodore's happiness? He's weak, you must give him strength. Change him. Make him strong. Make him capable of laughing at the verdict of the world, as you can laugh at it. Change him. Make him happy. Only *you* can make him happy."

Panic rose in her. Yes, yes, perhaps he was right—and yet . . . and yet . . . Oh, she could not think! She wasn't as intelligent as Juarez, as Theodore, they were the thinkers. She was stupid and she was evil and she could not think, she could not know! Juarez would know. And yet . . .

"In time," Juarez went on, "you will thank me for telling you this. When the unpleasantness is forgotten. This is the means, but the end is just! Change him and be happy. Change him and make him happy."

"Oh, Juarez," she said, in tears.

"It will take strength. If you weaken, he'll never be happy. Nor will you, nor will his wife be. Think of him. Think of yourself; years without him. *Think of those things.*"

"I don't know!" Rodina said, "I don't know!"

"Break the wall between you. Break it, Rodina, and both of you will know happiness." Juarez stopped; then he said, softly, "For the rest of your lives, Rodina."

BOOK II

CHAPTER FIFTEEN

IT WAS an ordinary Christmas. The day came cloudy, threatening rain or snow, and the air was cold. Kids came into the street with their skates or scooters or wagons or footballs or whatever it was they got. The women walked back and forth across the street, visiting, drinking a little wine or gin, beginning, as the afternoon approached, to feel a bit gay. Rain threatened but did not come, and this distressed some of the fathers who thought that it would rain and their sons would come into the houses and they could play some of the indoor games, or build something with the erector sets.

Crowds collected in the center of the city, where the movie houses were advertising "Special Holiday Shows" which were the same as the shows presented on any other day; except that today they were more expensive because this was Christmas, a holiday. The movie houses were the only place to go, because in Philadelphia on any holiday or Sunday no place else was open.

The city lay under tinsel and angel hair and snow and bulbs and balls and Christmas trees. Church bells rang and pastors preached special Christmas sermons over the radio and choirs were imported from other cities to sing Christmas carols. Some church groups gave performances of Dickens' "A Christmas Carol." Negro preachers went to white churches and white preachers went to Negro churches and every kind of preacher went to the Jewish Synagogues to speak on Brotherhood. Em-

157

ployees spent bonus money given by some of the employers; in some industries and factories and shops there were employer-employee Christmas parties.

Tomorrow would be Monday.

2

On the table in the corner of Theodore's room stood a tiny Christmas tree, decorated the night before, under which lay two presents: a gold necklace from Theodore to Rodina, and a set of bronze bookends from her to him.

They had risen early in the morning and smiled and kissed each other and said, "Merry Christmas."

They ate breakfast, opened their gifts, kissed each other again, and then Rodina went into her mother's room to give her a gift—two gifts, in fact, a rose nightgown and a bed lamp —which she had purchased two days previous. Mrs. Baleza smiled, one of her rare smiles, said thank you and looked at Rodina with those sharp, deep, fiery eyes which John the Baptist must have possessed.

Rodina stayed with her mother until lunch, which they ate together, and then returned to Theodore who lay across his bed on his back with his eyes open, staring at the ceiling. She kissed him, and both of them smiled again. They were together through the afternoon. Toward early evening Rodina left him to return to her mother's room, where she prepared a big supper. Mrs. Baleza watched her, smiled a little, her eyes bright and somewhat glassy. Mrs. Baleza was pale.

"Momma, don't you feel good?" Rodina asked.

Mrs. Baleza said, "He died to save us on this day."

Rodina went out of the room and into the kitchen to see how the food was coming. She stayed in the kitchen as long as she could. She felt that tiny circle of fear, like a spot on the lung, inside of her. When she thought her mother was asleep, she went back into the bedroom to clean things up a bit.

"He was a good man," Mrs. Baleza said. "Your father was a good man, Rodina. Usta preach special kinds of sermons on Christmas. Repentance. Your father preached about repentance. Christ died to save us. Repent all ye sinners. Your father used to preach that. Repent all ye sinners. He was a good man."

"Yes, ma'am," Rodina said.

"Repent all ye sinners, he used to preach." Mrs. Baleza's eyes were glassy.

"Momma," Rodina asked cautiously, "are you—do you feel all right? You look pale."

Mrs. Baleza looked at her. "The mind, not the body. The mind, not the body. The soul, not the body." She stared at Rodina and smiled. "Are *you* all right, Rodina?"

"Yes ma'am," Rodina said.

"The soul, not the body." She was still smiling. "The soul, not the body. Are *you* all right, Rodina?"

"Yes, ma'am. Momma, why don't you try to get some sleep while I'm straightenin' up?"

"I'm not sleepy. I'm all right. Are *you* all right? The soul, not the body."

"I'm fine, Mom. You ought to get some sleep."

When supper was ready, Rodina pulled up the stool and served her mother. She herself ate very little, for afterward she would have to eat also with Theodore. She smiled as she thought of this dual life. Everything had to be repeated between these two rooms. It was quite a strain, sometimes. She thought of Theodore in his room alone and she felt happy, thinking about him, and then she felt sad. Her mother ate slowly.

Afterward, there was dessert. Mrs. Baleza said, "My, ain't we rich, tonight!"

159

Rodina said, smiling, "Yes, ma'am."

"Where'd we get the money?"

"Oh, I worked for it, Momma," Rodina said. "Down on Chestnut Street."

"That so." She smiled. "You doin' a lot of workin', lately. In that restaurant."

"Yes, ma'am," Rodina said, and felt uncomfortable.

When her mother had finished eating, Rodina took the dishes out into the kitchen and piled them in the sink. She could wash them later. She came back through the bedroom and Mrs. Baleza said, "Goin' out again, huh?"

"Yes, ma'am," Rodina said.

"You go out quite a lot, lately."

"I'm generally with some friends," Rodina said.

"That so?" Mrs. Baleza said.

Rodina had cooked most of Theodore's meal earlier in the afternoon, and only a reheating was necessary now. They ate and talked, not saying much. After the meal, as Rodina washed the dishes and Theodore dried them, they kissed again. Then they took out the wine which had become lukewarm and drank it in celebration of the first of many Christmases together.

Now, in this part of the evening, they lay across the bed and felt the solid comfort of full stomachs and physical relaxation.

They did not talk. Outside, through the window, both of them could hear the hiss of the cold wind through the trees. In the room it was warm, and consciousness of the warmth was luxurious.

Rodina had gone through the day as though it were a dream, or a play in which she knew instinctively what lines were called for. She had felt little that day; somehow, her emotions seemed dulled. Perhaps this was the aftermath of the other days just past: days when she felt much like a child waiting for her father to come home and strap her. She had dreaded the

160

strap; but she had almost longed for the blessed hour when the beating would begin and then swiftly be done, with only the aches, resentments and self-pity to be gone through later. The tension was worse, too, when there was uncertainty, when someone had suggested that there was the possibility of reprieve—the pain of hope added to the already unbearable torture of the waiting.

It was pain, of a sort, to have him kiss her—wondering, as she did, whether he was perhaps thinking about his wife on this day of days; wondering whether he really wanted to be kissing her, or whether he would still want to kiss her if he knew all there was to know. She had pride at least; pride of a sort, pride which did not want charity, or what was not given freely. If only she knew what went on in his mind! He was kind, he was gentle—but this was Theodore, who would always be this way. This was no clue to what he really felt. He had withdrawn from her emotionally, she felt, like a snail into its shell. How could she know what actually he thought or felt? How could she be *sure*?

She thought of Juarez. No, she would not do the things he had told her to do. And yet—and yet, she had *not* sent Theodore back to his wife, as she had vowed. She had, then, listened to him. "I will send him back to his wife," she had vowed, and had known a kind of peace. "I will send him back." The one good thing she could still do. And it would bring the inner comfort of goodness; the quiet happiness of rightness. But she had not sent him back. ("I will! I will!") She had talked to Juarez and come away puzzled but with that deadly speck of hope. She would send him home later. (Was it possible that it would not be necessary?) Later. After Christmas. After New Year's. (Was it possible Juarez could be right? He was always right.)

Change him. That's what Juarez had said. Change him. She

161

turned to look at Theodore, lying on his back on the bed, and her heart swelled. Change him. Break the wall. Change him? She closed tight her eyes and stifled a sob merely at the thought.

Something troubled her, Theodore thought briefly, lying on his back on the bed. She had laughed, and she had kissed him, but she seemed distant. She was far away, as she had been far away for so long now; as though she were troubled and trying to hide her troubles. Or as though she did not love but was pretending to love.

Pretending to love? His mind swept swiftly over the thought. Pretending? No, he smiled faintly inside, she was not pretending. If she were pretending, he would know it immediately. He would not have to speculate on it. He would have seen the absence of love in her eyes and in her actions; there would be no mistake; she could hide no emotion. No, love had not gone (the mere playful thought filling him with the usual terror, the usual fears); but something was amiss (love gone, what happened? Rodina gone, what next? Love, Rodina, wife gone, the past gone, the future a nothingness—what happened?). Something troubled her, and when he questioned her she withdrew from him. Was it something he had said or done? He did not think so. Did she perhaps worry about her mother? That was possible; he was sure Rodina loved her mother. Was she concerned, perhaps, about the delay in getting his divorce? He, too, was concerned. Or was the source of her discomfiture something he knew nothing about, something from her past, maybe some former lover now molesting her again (the fear again, the hollowness, creeping hot through him; he the champion, he the white knight, and the laughing lover looking at him, pointing at the child on horse with lance).

He felt with rage the varying inflections of the senseless

162

fear inside of him. Fear at a thought. Fear at a speculation. Fear based on nothing but the idle wandering of his mind. Always, always, it had been like this. Always! (A child, he saw himself the world's greatest boxer, the world's greatest pitcher, the world's greatest soldier, the world's greatest lover, the hero defeating the bully of the block and then, mercifully, allowing the bully to arise from the ground and go sobbing for mercy on his way.) Against his desires, his mind now moved to thoughts of his wife. He heard her words: "You're such a coward, Theodore!" hissed softly in that voice which neither rose nor fell but flowed monotonously like the droning of a hundred sleepy bees. And the words were true. The words were true.

Sylvia. He thought of her letter and felt again the sad suction deep in his throat and stomach that he had felt upon that first reading. The letter: so sad, and yet so brave; so kind, and yet so damning. Was this Sylvia? Was this gentle, sensitive creature the woman he had left? He was confused. Had this sensitivity and love in truth been buried deep inside of her through all those years of misery? Had she in truth loved him as much as her letter indicated? A double curse on his desertion if this were true!

Christmas alone. He could see it now: the hollow room, the lonely tree (if indeed there were a tree), the gift he had sent her, and Sylvia there alone. He could see the room: haunted by the ghosts of eighteen Christmases past, when there had been two of them and, in the early years, laughter. Poor Sylvia. A broken and frustrated woman, without happiness before and with even less happiness now. Poor Sylvia, despite the droning voice and incessant complaints, for these were merely the outward show of the inward misery; these increased, rather than decreased, her command of his sympathy. Pain and guilt suffused him, and he did not push them away but lay stoically

163

in their bath, seeking atonement in the tradition of Job. But there could be no atonement for his act, he thought; and yet, this very knowledge seemed itself, in its horror, to be atonement of a kind: for all of his future days and nights must be haunted by this Christmas, and by the Christmases to come, when his wife sat and would sit in the parlor of the dull gray apartment alone, solitary, detached from the world.

The loud knock at the door jarred them into full consciousness. For a moment, shocked, they sat staring blankly before them. The knock came again, louder, and the door knob turned and Mrs. Houston peered into the room and grinned.

"Hi," she said. "Game a poker down in my room. Can't let Christmas go flyin' by without a little get-together, can we? How's about you two comin' down and joinin' in the fun?"

"Well . . ." Theodore began, astounded by the woman's brazenness in bursting into his room.

"Gang ain't takin' no for an answer from nobody. Ed upstairs decided he wanted to sleep instead of comin' down, and the gang went up to his room and dragged him down—in his shorts. Christmas, you know, and everybody likes to socialize a bit. Don't be stuck up, now. Come on down and join the fun." She looked at Rodina and grinned. "How's the chippy?" she asked. Then she said, "I was kinda sure I'd find you in here."

Theodore could only stare at the woman. He was sleepy and did not feel like being bothered. Still, he did not want to appear aloof or superior.

"The gang'll drag you out if you don't come," Mrs. Houston said. "We got wine, and we're playin' a little cards. You don't have to get in the game if you don't want. Just come on down and join the crowd."

164

Theodore shrugged. He looked at Rodina and smiled with resignation. "All right," he said to Mrs. Houston. "We'll be down."

3

They were milling about in the room downstairs—the very walls seemed in motion. A small group, six, sat around the table in the center of the linoleum-covered floor, playing cards, while the rest, at least eight or nine, shuffled around, peeking at the cards, pouring wine from the gallon jugs Mrs. Houston had bought (she could afford this gesture once a year, on Christmas, someone remarked, since she supported herself on 'cuts' from the poker games which were constantly in progress in her room). Some typical players were at the table: the one who talked incessantly about how close to winning that last hand he had been, the overcautious one, the one who talked loudly when winning but glared everyone else into a guilty silence when he was losing, the one whom the others had to watch for palmed half-dollars and switched cards and fast movements. Hucks and Mrs. Houston were among those playing.

When Rodina and Theodore entered the room, Mrs. Houston greeted them loudly (she was the talkative one; she never played long, since by playing she risked losing her profits from the percentage), and Hucks looked up and grinned.

"So you finally got here," she shouted. "What kept you?"

"We had to wash up a bit," Theodore said.

"Well, well," Hucks said, "the lover and his love. An honor to have you with us."

Theodore felt the inside of him shrivel and was conscious immediately of eyes upon him and heard the sudden reduction in the noise of the room. (Though, in truth, not many people looked at him; and though, in truth, not many people stopped talking.) He was indignant, but did not want his indignation to

165

show: he did not want to make a fool of himself. He looked at Hucks and tried a faint, rather ridiculous smile.

Then suddenly, inexplicably, he was acutely aware of a fact: that Rodina stood beside him, a little behind him. For a moment, after Hucks spoke, he had felt himself alone in the room among hostile strangers. But Rodina was here. Rodina. He was ashamed because he had, in his own mind, been humiliated in front of her. He was filled with anger, staring at the brawny Hucks who moved easily, gracefully, even sitting in a chair playing cards. At that moment he hated Hucks more than ever.

The momentary amused attention had left him, the spectators were concentrating now on the poker game or on their own private conversations, but Theodore stood embarrassed just inside the door, conscious of Rodina and of Hucks; he felt that the thoughts of everyone in the room must now linger on him, had stopped suddenly in transit to hover amusedly over that speck in time when Hucks had raised his head and grinned and called him "lover." He felt this, even though he knew that it was not true; so he dared not move, dared not change his facial expression (could not, in fact, since his muscles, like those of a vain woman posing for a photographer, were frozen hideously), for fear that the disturbance of the very air might again rivet attention on him. He wished that he had not come; but, like a fly in a wire trap, he knew that exit was much more difficult than entry.

Mrs. Houston laughed uproariously at everything, raking in her ten per cent, the half-filled glass of wine in front of her. Hucks, too, must have drunk a great quantity before Theodore came down. These two made more noise than the others combined, it seemed to Theodore, and he hated the quality of their laughter; loud, arrogant, the laughter of people who physically dominate a group. Once Hucks looked up at him

166

and winked and then he looked at Rodina and grinned and winked again.

What was it, Theodore wondered bitterly, that made a man a coward? Was it some physiological factor, like the simple flow of hormones from a gland? Was it sexual, stemming from some early childhood experience? Was it environmental, fear left over from a yesterday filled with fears? Or was it simply introspectiveness which made a man a coward? Was it not nimbleness of brain, the habit of thinking and weighing and self-analyzing, which led one, in the face of a challenge, to weigh all consequences of one's reply (thereby hesitating), while another fellow, the stupid man, the man who did not think, acted on the emotion of the moment, rage or outrage, charging into the fray? For thought, inspection, confused and weakened an emotion; persistent questioning led to inactivity, to impotence; the introspective fear of fear produced fear in its greatest intensity.

"Well, lover," Hucks said, as one of the men at the table rose, "there's an empty slot here at the table. How's about sittin' down and tryin' your luck?"

"No, thanks," Theodore said. Then he said, "These other people"—beckoning with his hand—"were here before me. Maybe one of them wants to play."

"But I want you to play, lover," Hucks grinned. "I'd like to see how you play poker. Don't worry. We know you work hard for your money. We won't take it all. Matter of fact, if you lose much, I'll make it up to you. Now how's that for a bargain?"

Theodore did not wish to play in any game with Hucks. He did not know what to say. He felt the eyes of a few of the people turn on him again.

"Come on, lover. You can associate with men. We don't bite."

Mrs. Houston laughed loudly, bending and rising, and the

167

people in the room looked at Theodore curiously, with amusement. Theodore felt that unfathomable and boundless hatred rising up within him again; he felt, too, that maddening impotence which came because he could not decide what his reaction should be, and so did not react at all. For a long moment, for an infinity, he stood staring at Hucks, noting and hating the fact that he strove mightily to keep his hatred from coming into his eyes; for a show of hatred might lead to other things. All the time, through all this mental churning, he was conscious of Rodina only two feet in back of him—he was wondering what she was thinking. Finally, with an awkward movement, he sat down.

"That's the stuff," Hucks said.

Mrs. Houston dealt, the first card down, the other four up, smiling her malicious smile every time she looked at him. He was some curio, Theodore thought bitterly, a museum piece, invited to this gathering for the amusement of the paying customers. Now he was certain that Mrs. Houston or Hucks had suggested inviting him down only as a lark, much as the wealthy, in the dark days of the Depression, used to pick up the ragged unemployed and take them to parties for the entertainment of the elite. And he could not escape. That was the horror. He could not escape, leave, because to do so would provide these people, really, with their money's worth: after his departure the laughter would be uproarious; he had to remain, knowing he was the butt of their ridicule.

He played the game stupidly, for his mind was not on the cards. Hucks began the betting and Theodore, without even a high card, called him. Hucks won with a pair of jacks. He grinned at Theodore and dealt the cards and again Theodore, without any reason for so doing, called on each play, for he did not want to be considered a penny-pincher. And even as he played carelessly, losing his money, Theodore cursed himself for caring so much what these people thought of him.

"Great game, poker, ain-at right, lover?" Hucks said, smiling his big-man's smile, feeling the effects of the wine. "Great game, hey lover? Way to get rich."

Theodore did not answer, nor did he look at Hucks. It seemed to him that the room was deathly quiet.

"Lover don't talk," Hucks said, poking out his lips, staring in sad astonishment at the others. "He don't talk. Cat's got his tongue. He don't like us people, common people, bums who can't read poetry. Lover only loves. Don't talk."

Mrs. Houston sniggered. Theodore felt the tenseness grow inside of him. This could not go on. He had seen situations similar to this before, and it could not go on. It went up, up, up and up, and then something happened. There was an explosion. He saw a card tremble in his hand and cursed himself. He cursed all of them. He wanted to be out of the room, but that was impossible, and so he sat there, tense, waiting for the rest to happen.

Glenn, the waiter, had been watching the game in silence. Now he glared at Hucks and said, "Whyn't the hell you cut it out, Hucks."

"Cut out what?" Hucks asked innocently. "Cut out what, Glenn? What'm I doin'? Just playing cards, that's all. Ain-at right, Sadie?"

"Sure," Mrs. Houston said.

"You ought to cut it out, Hucks," Glenn said. "Just play the game, that's all. Don't run your mouth all the time."

"Sure," Hucks said. "Run my mouth. *My* mouth, ain-it? Got a right to run it much as I damn please. Wasn't nobody talkin' to you, nohow. Goddamn people stick your noses in other people's business."

"That's right," Glenn said.

"Sure," Hucks said. "Damn right it's right."

He looked at his cards. From time to time he mumbled to himself. Theodore looked at his hand, grateful that for a

169

moment he had been shoved into the background. But there was something pathetic, he thought, about the fact that Glenn felt called upon to come to his defense. As though he were not capable of defending himself.

Well, what was he expected to do in a situation such as this? Quarrel with the man? Where would that get him? What good would that do? Fight him? He had to smile as he pictured this: he, the middle-aged man, engaged in a free-for-all with the young, brawny Hucks. Of course he would be beaten, but that was not the principal objection. There was the simple fact that he would cut a ridiculous figure in the arena—he could see himself, movements awkward, joints practically creaking, while Hucks danced around, toying with him before the kill. He could hear the others laughing. He could hear this laughter ringing in Rodina's ears. That was it: above all, he did not want her pity or her sympathy; he did not want to be ridiculed before her. That would be worse than any mere physical thrashing.

As these thoughts ran through Theodore's mind, Juarez, who had stood all this time silently back against the wall, watched him carefully. Occasionally his eyes moved to Hucks, or to Mrs. Houston, or to Rodina. But, principally, he watched Theodore.

Hucks asked, "Were you ever in the Army, lover?" and Juarez watched Theodore's eyes. Theodore did not look at Hucks. For a moment it seemed that he would not answer. Juarez looked at Hucks and could see he had been offended by Glenn's intervention a moment ago.

"No," Theodore said finally.

"No!" Hucks stared at him, and then at the others, aghast. "You mean you weren't in on the big doings with the Nazis and the Japs?"

Theodore looked at his cards. He placed a bet, but Mrs.

170

Houston, the next in order, paid no attention to it. She was grinning, looking at Hucks and then at him.

"You didn't see them storm troopers in shiny black boots with bayonets through their noses, like all us other all-American boys?" He shook his head, looking at the others. He turned to Theodore again: "Why wasn't you in, lover? Too busy with the girls back home?"

Theodore did not answer. Hucks shook his head.

"Too busy with the girls. Bein' a lover. Keepin' in practice. Protectin' the girls we left behind. Well, they got kind of lonesome and needed a little bit now and then. Good thing we had boys back here."

Theodore looked up at Hucks a moment, hating him, and then he looked down again. Well, he could wait. To hell with all this. To hell with this leering bastard. It had to come, so let it come.

"Army's a great place," Hucks said, "full of men, y'know, and women, too, the WAC's, nice uniforms, and boxing and football and wrestling. Life in the great outdoors. Long marches and stuff. Manly stuff. Just like you'd like, eh, lover?"

Hucks looked at Theodore, who did not answer. Hucks snorted and looked again at his cards. He was thinking: Goddamned sissified bastard, got a peter big as my thumb, thinks he's Holy Moses just because he can read a spot of poetry . . . and that goddamned dumb gullible Rodina, like a goddamned fool . . . Goddamn 'em both!

Now all of it was over—at least for a time. Hucks seemed to have subsided and everyone placed his bet and played the game. Slowly, conversation caught fire and spread again around the room. Rodina, who had said nothing through all this, but had stared in fierce hatred at Hucks, holding her tongue by supreme effort, stood partially relieved in the precise spot she had occupied since they arrived. Theodore played the game.

171

Juarez moved from his spot by the wall and drew up a chair behind Hucks. He looked at his cards. Softly, almost whispering, he said, "I'm glad you've stopped talking, Hucks. You must be pretty high, eh? I think you ought not to have baited Theodore like that."

"What's that?" Hucks said, startled.

"He's a guest of sorts," Juarez explained. "We're veterans. He's only been here a relatively short while. We should treat our guests with respect. It's only common decency."

"What the hell?" Hucks exclaimed. He stared at Juarez. "You goddamn Mex bastard, who the hell asked your opinion?"

"No one," Juarez said. His soft, watery eyes did not change as he looked at Hucks. Nor did the epithet affect him overmuch: it went clanging and clattering down the hard stone steps into the catacombs of his heart, to fester and rankle amid the bitterness there. "No one," he went on in his soft whispering voice, "I just ventured an opinion. I like Mr. Hall."

"Nobody asked you who the hell you like," Hucks said.

"No," Juarez said thoughtfully. He waited a moment. "But you ought not bait him about the Army, or about poker. How would you feel if he baited you about literature and science? Your interests differ, that's all I was trying to say. You can't expect everybody to like the same things that you do. He has brains and sensitivity. You're different."

"You tryin' to be funny?" Hucks asked. "What the hell you talkin' about? You act like I ain't got brains."

Juarez laughed it off. "Of course you have. Maybe I shouldn't have opened my mouth."

"That's right. You shouldn't of."

Juarez shrugged apologetically. "I'm a rotten arbiter," he commented wryly.

"That's right," Hucks said, although he did not know what the word meant. He looked at his cards again. Goddamn that goddamn Mex! "Poetry and literature!" he snorted. He looked at the others and sneered. "Ain't that a goddamn shame! Poetry and literature. Act like I ain't got no brains. Hell, I know a little something about poetry and literature, too, you know. You ever think a that?" He looked at Juarez. "You ever think of that, Mex boy?"

"No," Juarez said, "I never thought of that."

"Well, you oughta." Hucks looked at his cards. Then he mumbled, "I'm just a *man*, that's all. I like football and boxing and baseball. That don't mean I'm dumb. I just like sports, that's all. I could write poetry if I wanted to, but I leave stuff like that to the lover. But I'll bet the lover don't know nothin' about boxin', ain-at right, lover? You, too, Juarez."

"No," Juarez admitted, "I don't know much about boxing."

"Goddamn right, you don't. I just ain't inclined toward writin' poetry, that's all. People use different talents, that's all. I use other talents, that's all. Ain't that right, Sadie?"

She looked at him in mock indignation. "Why the hell ask me?"

Hucks grinned brightly, and looked at Theodore. He was pleased with that one. He said, "I got other talents, lover. Big talents." Sadie Houston laughed loudly, and Hucks' grin broadened. "Yeah," he said, "big talents." He looked at Rodina and winked. "Ain't that right, Rodina? Big talents. Way bigger talents than the lover here."

"Go f—— yourself!" Rodina hissed.

"That ain't no way to talk, baby," Hucks said reprovingly. "That ain't no way for a lady to talk. You ought to watch your language."

She stared at him and he could see the hatred in her eyes. He turned away from it. Now he looked at his cards again and placed his bet. Theodore won. Mrs. Houston dealt and Hucks glanced up to see Juarez looking at him; then Juarez's eyes

173

moved to Rodina, then back again to Hucks. Juarez smiled and beckoned with his head toward Rodina.

"What the hell you grinnin' about, Mex?" Hucks wanted to know.

"I was just thinking."

"About what?"

Juarez shrugged. "It wasn't anything. Just a little thing that crossed my mind. Not important."

"Dammit, what the hell you grinnin' so damn pleased with yourself about?"

"I was just thinking," Juarez said, whispering again, "about the fact that you and Rodina used to go together. Seems fantastic now."

"Yeah?" Hucks looked at Rodina and grinned. "What's so fantastic about that? You used to love me madly, didn't you, baby?"

He was beneath answer. Rodina merely curled her lips and nose in contempt. She snorted.

"Used to love me madly," Hucks chuckled. "Used to swear undyin' love, didn't you, baby? Used to tell me how much you liked my talents, didn't you, baby? Tell the lover here about my talents, sugar. Tell him how big my talents are. A whole lot bigger than his, eh?"

Theodore said, "Why don't you go to hell!"

A stunned silence burst into the room. Mrs. Houston's eyes widened and she grinned with glee and moved her eyes back and forth between them; one could almost see her licking her lips. Rodina was tense, silent. Juarez's calm eyes watched them both.

Hucks, recovering from his first shock, stared at Theodore and then began to laugh. He laughed loudly, deafeningly, while Theodore stared at him angrily. When finally his laughter had subsided he said, "Well, well, will you look at this"—catch-

174

ing his breath—"will you look at this. The worm turns. Whatsa matter, lover? You sick or somethin'?"

Theodore stared and felt called upon to answer and said, "I feel fine."

"That right, lover?" Hucks, at ease, looked at Theodore, resisting the urge to burst into laughter again. "Well, well. Lover don't like all this. Don't like hearin' about what used to be. *Used* to be?" He looked at Rodina and winked. "Yeah, we was great together, lover. Had great times together. I always had big talents and Rodina was a gal with appreciation for big talents, wasn't you, baby? Now I guess maybe she likes little talents"—grinning, watching the tenseness of Theodore's face—"or maybe she *still* likes big talents, maybe you got big talents, too, never can tell. Let's show our talents, lover— you show yours and I'll show mine. How's that lover? We'll make it fair and square, the gang'll be the judge who's got the biggest talents. You stand up on the table and show your talents and I'll stand up there and show mine. How's that? The women'll be the judges, since they know something about talents. Or maybe just you ought to show your talents, how's that, because all these women've already seen mine. *All* of 'em have, lover. Not just your little lover girl. Just you show yours, how's that? Can I help you, lover? Can I help you show your talents?"

Still grinning, he looked at Theodore. Everyone looked at Theodore. Theodore met Hucks' eyes but said nothing, because he could not think of anything bitter enough to say or anything that was not too ridiculous to do. He could only stare at the man, hating his grin and loud laugh and loud voice, while Mrs. Houston's eyes darted eagerly from face to face, in exaggerated arcs, provocatively. All stared. Hucks would say nothing; he simply grinned. Deliberately, for about two minutes, he allowed the room to lapse into complete silence.

175

Theodore felt his muscles freeze into that rigidity of self-consciousness that made a mask of his face and permitted not one part of his body a movement that was without awkwardness; he sat there, staring, and then felt the horror of horrors—tears began to form in his eyes. He was determined not to waver before Hucks' gaze; he was determined not to close his eyes or blink; and yet, he knew that if he continued to stare the tears must assuredly flow. Hucks saw the tears collecting; grinning, he watched them, prolonging the stillness, beckoning them onward—and the eyes filled up, up, up. Theodore, enraged, wanted to shout loudly, wanted to punch in Hucks' leering face: the tear drops hung precariously a moment, and then they came, rolling in a sudden rapid stream down his face.

Hucks sighed. "Well, folks" (turning back to the game) "that's that. We've seen the lover cryin'. Now let's get back to the masculine part of the night's activities—"

With a faint cry Theodore charged savagely around the table, both fists swinging wildly. But Hucks was faster; he rose swiftly and seized Theodore's wrists; he stood with his face close to Theodore's, holding the older man in a grip of steel, and said, "Well, well, we got spirit, ain't we, though." The others watched; Mrs. Houston was tremendously excited. Hucks shoved Theodore from him. In the instant Theodore had charged in again, feeling an urge to kill; but again Hucks had seized him, held him harmlessly.

"Why not give up, lover?" he asked, laughing.

"You son of a bitch!" Theodore shouted into his face.

"That ain't nice language. Little boys get hurt for using language like that. Now go back to your mommy."

He shoved Theodore over to where Rodina stood. Theodore was about to charge again when Glenn seized him and held him tight. "Don't pay no attention to him, Ted," Glenn said. "He's crazy. Forget him. He's a son of a bitch."

176

Theodore stared, filled with hatred. He could feel the rage, an indigestion inside of him; he could feel it rise, rise, rise, driving him close to insanity. He could only stare; he could only struggle to free himself, to tear into the leering face, to rip out the eyes and smash in the nose and teeth of this man—to rip open his heart, if possible, and laugh as the face stiffened at the coming of death!

"Sure," Hucks said, laughing, "I'm a sonofabitch, just like Glenn says. Let's shake and forget the whole thing, eh?"

Still, Theodore had not found words. Still, he could only stare his hatred.

Something shot with terrific speed across the room toward Hucks—a jug of wine, thrown by the enraged Rodina. Hucks dodged and the jug sailed past him to smash itself against a wall. Rodina picked up another jug and charged toward Hucks. She was halted by Mrs. Houston, who, like a football player, threw a block.

"Just a second sweetheart," Mrs. Houston said, "that wine costs money, you know."

"F—— you and your wine!" Rodina shouted. "I'll kill that son of a bitch!"

"Now, that ain't nice language, baby," Hucks said, smiling.

Upstairs, in bed, Theodore listened to the epithets pouring endlessly from Rodina. He lay quietly, hating. But as strong as the hatred was his shame.

CHAPTER SIXTEEN

Dear Theodore:

Just a post-Christmas line or two to say hello, and wish you, in advance, a Happy New Year. I hope you spent a pleasant Christmas. Did you have a tree? I didn't bother to get one—weren't they expensive this year?—but I had some holly and they cheered up the place, giving it something of the holiday mood. I had a pleasant time Christmas evening reading over some of the poetry you wrote long ago. A lot of it is still here, you know, in the rolltop desk; someday you must stop by and pick it up. I particularly liked the untitled poem, which you wrote about husbands and wives. (Do you remember it? About how lonely each of the married couple can be, concealing a part of himself from the other, until, at last, they lose contact completely?) . . ."

Two days after Christmas this was shoved under the door by Mrs. Davis, read by Theodore and handed, without comment, to Rodina. She read it and said nothing, but tried to see what was in his eyes. He saw her searching; by his actions, he sought to reassure her. It was morning, so he washed and dressed and then went to work.

When he returned in the evening Rodina looked at him and he smiled, not meeting her eyes.

"My, that food smells good," he said.

She prepared the small table and they sat down. She said, "Are you tired, darling?"

"No," he said. Now he looked at her. "My work isn't very hard. Time drags sometimes, but that's nothing." He smiled. "Time used to drag when I was a night watchman."

"Yes," she said. "Perhaps you were anxious to hurry home."

"No." He tasted the food. "No, I wasn't particularly anxious to do anything. Perhaps I was anxious to get some sleep. That's all."

"I remember you that first night I saw you," she said. "Moving slowly in the rain." She looked at him and asked, "Did you ever steal, Ted?"

He smiled, almost embarrassed. "No. That used to lower you in the eyes of the kids in the neighborhod." But he did not like to talk about this, so he was silent.

After awhile, Rodina said, "You were married eighteen years, Ted?"

"Yes."

"Did you ever . . . did you ever . . . cheat?"

He looked up at her and smiled again, trying to see what she was after. He said, "No."

"No," she said, "you wouldn't cheat."

"Except with you," he said. He was happy he could say that. Somehow, that seemed his vindication. Somehow, that made him feel at least a little like other men.

"No," she said, "not even with me. You didn't even make one pass at me, or even try to kiss me. You just talked."

He protested, "But I cheated in my mind, Rodina. I wanted you in my mind. That's cheating."

"Did you want me?" she asked. "Did you really want me, the way other men would want me? Do you want me even now?"

"Of course," he said uneasily.

"Is that true? Then why haven't you touched me all these

180

months? Why haven't you done what anybody else would do?"

"I've explained . . ."

"Yes," she said, "yes, you have."

It was fantastic, she thought. All these months sleeping together in such purity. It was fantastic. He was inhumanly good. He was an angel. But he had left his wife. That was the one evil thing that he had done, and it haunted him. She had done many evil things and they had not, really, haunted her. That was the difference between them. That was the wall, as Juarez said.

"Ted," she asked, "did you ever lie when you were a kid?"

"Oh, yes," he said. "Many times."

She nodded. That was good. That was some satisfaction. He had lied, and he had left his wife.

They finished eating and she washed the dishes. Afterward, he lay across the bed and she sat beside him, stroking his hair. Such a soft, kind face, she thought. Then her eyes fell on the dressing table and she saw the letter.

"What happens when you read letters from your wife?" Rodina asked. "What do you feel inside?"

He had not wanted to discuss this. He had been happy, in the morning, to get out of the house, away from her questioning eyes. Home, he had been glad they talked of other things.

"I don't know," he said. He paused. "The letters make me feel sad for her. Eighteen years is a long time. She couldn't afford a tree this year; that's my fault. She spent Christmas alone, reading, because she's got so few friends now and I was her only companion. She can't help being the way she is, you know. I think of that. And then her letters seem so tender, so warm and so considerate of my feelings. I can't help thinking that somehow I failed her. If this warmth was always in her, then I should have been able to bring it out. The failure of our marriage was my fault as well as hers. Primarily mine, I

181

imagine, because I had the ability to help her, while she had no ability to help herself."

"And who was to help you?"

"If I had helped her, if I had brought out the warmth in her, then I should not have been in need of help. It was action and reaction. I'm the passive one, who reacts to the moods of the other."

"From her letters, she seems like a good woman."

"Yes," Theodore said. "She's a good woman. She was very loyal, trustworthy and dutiful. I know she didn't cheat, for instance; I'm absolutely positive of that. I know she didn't lie to me, or do one dishonest thing. I'm certain of those things."

Rodina nodded. She tried to stifle the growing hatred of his wife.

"Do you ever want to go back to her?" Rodina asked. The question left her only after great effort. Her voice was calm, but she was full of many confused fears as she waited for his answer.

He said, "No. It is like a revolution, Rodina. It is a harsh thing, but it is necessary. People are hurt. But the pain of some must be measured against the pain of others."

He had not thought of this in such a clear-cut way before. But even though he knew that what he said was correct intellectually, he was not sure that he accepted it emotionally. Nor could Rodina quite believe him. She wanted to, but was assailed by doubts. Of course, Theodore would try to reassure her. He would always be kind. He would always seek her happiness, and the happiness of every one else.

"Then you must be strong," she said.

He nodded, and looked away. "Yes," he said softly. Yes, he must be strong. But strength, he thought, was precisely what he had always lacked. All his life he had been one of those men who wavered between this decision and that decision, ending by making no decision at all; like Hamlet. Had he stayed with his wife, perhaps she could have known happiness of some sort, or at least an absence of the present unhappiness he saw between the lines of her letters. Having left her, he had now the opportunity of making both Rodina and himself happy —as they had been that first month. But now, as ever, he wavered; and he knew in his vacillation there was no peace for Rodina.

He said, "Rodina, do you think I am a man who can be strong?"

She said, "I think because you're gentle and loving and sympathetic with everyone, it's hard for you not to be sorry for hurting your wife, and it's hard for you to just forget the past." A kind of distress was in her eyes. "But I love you so much. I can't be happy if you're not happy. And you can't fool me. I always know when you're not happy. You left your wife and we're going to live together for the rest of our lives. That's what you've got to make up your mind about. For the rest of our life we'll be together, and we won't be happy if you worry always about the past. You *have* to be strong."

"Yes," he said again. He pondered the ceiling. "It's hard to be strong, though, when these letters keep coming. They keep reminding me."

"Oh, if only we could—" She cut herself short.

He looked at her. "What were you going to say?"

"Nothing," she said. "Nothing important."

She had been about to say: If only we could move! But the thought of her mother had stopped her. Always she thought of her mother. There could be no escape so long as her mother lived. But then she was old . . . Rodina closed her eyes tightly. She was evil, evil, evil! to think such things.

Strong, Theodore was thinking. One must be strong, must make decisions.

183

"Strong," he said aloud.

"What, darling?"

"I was thinking of Christmas night, during the poker game," he said, almost bitterly. "Did I seem strong then? Did I seem to have the makings of a strong man?"

"Why do you ask that?"

"I was a coward," he said.

"You were a gentleman," she said. "You took as much as you could stand, and then you jumped up and tried to beat the hell out of him."

"Is that really what you think?"

"Yes."

He said nothing. Well, she would be kind. Even though all the others knew, and showed that they knew. The tears. She would be kind. "Go to your momma," Hucks had said contemptuously. Theodore felt the rise of hatred again.

But it was never too late. Or, at least, it was not yet too late. He could be strong. Rodina said he could be strong.

2

But, afterwards, when the New Year had rounded the corner, and the windless cold of January affixed itself to the people, to the street, and to the red brick houses, both of them knew that he was not strong.

Dear Theodore. . . .

The letters came, one after another, laden with the melancholy and loneliness and brave sadness of the woman who lived now alone. Each time a letter came Theodore saw Rodina watching his eyes; each time he turned his eyes away and smiled and tried to cheer her up; each time he knew she saw easily behind the effort, and saw that he was not strong.

He was not strong when he received her letters, nor was he

184

strong in writing his replies. What could one say to a deserted wife? He could write about some of his activities; he could assure her that he was continuing with his writing; he could ask, again and again, that she forgive him. But could he press for a divorce? Could he say that he loved another? Could he demand that she write no more, remind him no more that she had belonged to him and served him and loved him and received his cruel parting as her reward?

Nor was he strong as regarded Hucks. For would a strong man hope upon hope, when coming home from work, that Hucks would not be in the hall, or in the tea room, or on the street near the door? Would a strong man, when he saw Hucks, become so full of fears and hates and trepidations? Would a strong man react with such silent hatred to the other's every smile or word? And would a strong man decline all further invitations to come down to Mrs. Houston's room, knowing that the others expected him to decline, knowing that they laughed at his every refusal, knowing that he was the object of their contempt and ridicule?

What must Rodina think of him—regardless of what she said? What went through her mind as she watched his eyes, as she listened to his silences, as she moved alone among the objects in this room, or in her mother's room, while he was at work? She was no ordinary genteel girl. She had been born in this neighborhood, known only the Huckses and the Glenns, known only the primitive creatures who traveled in gangs, fought at the drop of a hat, and knew only their own code of love-making. Compared to these, what was he? A foreigner. A weakling. To be contemptuously dismissed as a "poet." Could Rodina really respect him?

Because now he went to work early each morning, Rodina took her regular walks alone. Rarely did she travel the old routes; rarely did she wave so flippantly as before to the kids

185

who played on the street before going to school. She walked aimlessly, not noticing much. She thought of Theodore and his wife and of her mother and of Hucks and of herself.

He was not strong, she thought. Or, rather, perhaps he was not ruthless. He could not cause pain and forget it. She wondered what was to be done. She would not send him home to his wife—no, she would not do that. No, because if he went home he would not be happy, because really he did not want to be back with his wife, because if he had he would not have left in the first place—because, Juarez had said so. And Juarez was smart. If he went home to his wife he would be unhappy and she, Rodina, would be unhappy and even the wife would probably be unhappy. If he stayed with her perhaps Rodina could make him happy, and then she too would be happy and they could be happy always. Juarez had said so. And Juarez had told her how.

"Hello, Rodina," Juarez said pleasantly. "Can you have a cup of tea with me?"

"Sure, Juarez."

"We don't get a chance to talk alone like we used to," he said.

"No. I miss that."

Small talk. Glenn came, and then he brought their tea, and then they drank their tea and talked.

Finally, Juarez asked, "Is everything all right now, Rodina?"

She shook her head. He said nothing, but she knew what he must be thinking. Yes, she had been weak. Yes, he had been right: she and Theodore could not be happy unless he changed somehow. But he could not change. He had tried, and could not. And she could make no effort to change him.

"Juarez, I love him so much," she said suddenly and passionately.

"Yes," he said. He looked at her. What could one believe?

He felt pity rise up inside of him, but he pushed it ruthlessly away. He had felt pity before. But who pitied Juarez?

"How I wish we could run away!" she whispered. "Oh, Juarez, if we could only run away someplace, to someplace where nobody knew us. And nobody would know where we were."

He throttled compassion. "And would that be the solution?" he asked. "Would that break down the wall? I've told you what must be done. Every day that passes you must see that I am right. A little strength, a little courage is all that's necessary. Running away would solve nothing."

"It would! It would!" she insisted. "Then there would be no more letters from his wife. He wouldn't always be reminded. He wouldn't always have to feel so guilty about it."

Juarez regarded her. He said, "But you can't run away. You can't leave your mother."

Rodina looked at the tablecloth. She said nothing.

"Even you could not be so cruel," he said, and she did not notice the innuendo. He looked at her. "I wonder if I can tell what's going on in your mind."

She looked up at him, and he said, "Can it be that you wish your mother did not stand in your way? Can it be that you wish she were dead?"

"No!" Rodina said, horrified.

"No? Are you certain, Rodina? Are you certain that you do not, really, long for her to die? Don't you think, sometimes, about the fact that she is old? Don't you wonder sometimes just how much longer she has to live, and hope that it is not long?"

"No!" she almost shouted. "That's not true, Juarez!"

"I'm sorry," he said softly. "I hoped not. Still, I wondered." He looked at her closely. He said, "But running away will do no good. The wall remains. You will drift farther and farther

187

apart, until you lose contact completely. Then he won't love you."

"I'd rather lose him," she said.

"Yes? And you will. As sure as the sun rises."

3

When February came and the city was engulfed in bitter cold, they slept embraced. Then, awake or asleep, she felt his nearness and loved him and hated the vow, the wall, and the wife who kept them apart.

Sometimes she awoke in the middle of the night and kissed him hard until he awakened. "I love you, Ted, I love you!" she whispered desperately, unrestrained, clinging to him, her nails pressing into his skin, feeling desire and frustration and confusion, the flywheel's spinning. "Ted, we'll be so happy together," she said, hardly believing it anymore but wanting to believe it, needing so terribly to believe it.

They would lie there in the dark room where leaves danced on the wall when the moon was out, and hear the faint murmur of voices from the tearoom downstairs. "I love the tearoom," Rodina said. The tearoom was warmth. Their dull window was raised and the cold came in, but they slept without clothes—Theodore allowed her this, at least. She slept feeling him close, wrapped around her back, conscious of him even in her dreams.

"I love you! I love you!" she would whisper savagely, striving, by sheer passion, to tear him away from the doubts and guilts and fears which comprised the wall.

"Theodore," she said one evening, "has your wife written anything about the divorce?"

"No," Theodore said. "She never mentions it."

188

Rodina paused. "Then what will you do about it?"

He said, "I don't know. I haven't made up my mind."

"It's been a long time," Rodina said. She felt strange, because she did not want to seem to press him. "Perhaps she doesn't think of it."

"I know," Theodore said wearily. "Of course, this can't go on. Perhaps I'll have to start action, if she doesn't. Next time I write I'll ask her about it."

He did. It was two weeks before her reply came.

She was sorry for the delay, Sylvia said. She had been inconsiderate. However, she could not institute the proceedings; she could not bear to make the many charges against him—adultery, cruelty, perversion—which would be required. In addition, she had been ill for the past ten days. "Chiefly, the doctor said, it's my nerves. I'm easily upset—I cry easily." She could not, at present, stand the rigors involved in court action against him. However, if *he* wanted to go ahead and institute divorce action against *her* . . .

Rodina read the letter. "What will you do?" she asked Theodore.

"Nothing, for now," Theodore said. "She's ill. I didn't know that. Of course, I can't take action while she isn't well."

"No," Rodina said. "Of course not."

She went downstairs to the tearoom. Hucks was there. He started to call out to her, so she turned abruptly and went out of the front door into the street. The street was empty and cold; she had on only a sweater. She walked slowly, smelling the cold, clear air; thinking. As always lately, she was inwardly anxious and mentally confused: the flywheel spun.

At the corner, she saw the old taproom where the men used to dance with her sometimes. She smiled, and peered inside. One of the men, Bill, looked up and saw her.

189

"Say, baby," he shouted, "come on in. Don't stay out there and freeze."

She went inside. "Well, baby, how you doin'?" Bill asked her.

"Not so hot," she said. "How's life with you?"

"Same, baby," Bill said. "Same as usual. How 'bout a drink?"

"You're talking," she said.

The dour bartender set the drink in front of her. She drank it, and immediately Bill ordered another. She drank this, and Bill ordered a third.

"You must of got the blues," Bill said, grinning.

"You've hit it there, all right."

This is the old Rodina, she thought. This is the real Rodina. Without a whole lot of mix-up inside.

"You still dance, Bill?" she asked.

"Dance *at it*," he said.

"Then let's have at it," she said.

He shoved a nickel in the juke box and they danced, jitterbugging. The others watched her. She was very much different from the others in here: she was youth, freshness, in a sweater and skirt and low-heeled shoes and long, thick black hair. Everybody watched.

They danced again, and then she had another drink. But the whiskey did not make her feel gay; she felt unhappy. She stood at the bar near Bill, and eventually a man sidled up beside her and offered to buy her a drink.

"No thanks," she said pleasantly.

The man waited. After awhile, he said, "You sellin'?"

She looked at him without anger. Faintly, she smiled. "Do I look like the kind?" she asked finally, with curiosity rather than coldness.

"Can't never tell," the man said. "Gals in the trade look all kinds of ways."

He had a point, no doubt. "No," she said, "I don't sell."

"Okay," the man said. "No hard feelin's."

"No."

"Let's drink on that."

"Okay," she said.

They touched glasses and drank. Then the man left. Bill laughed and said, "He try to make you, baby?"

"Yeah," Rodina said.

"All in a lifetime, baby. You sure do look good, you know."

"Well, thanks Bill."

When she left the taproom, Rodina thought: Sure, that's the real Rodina. That's Rodina all right. "You sellin'?" Sure, she looked like that. That was Rodina. That was Rodina.

Upstairs, Ted said, "Rodina, I looked for you downstairs. Were you out in the cold, with no coat on?"

"Yes," she said. He did not question her further, so she said, "I was down to the taproom, in case you want to ask. I had several drinks."

He was hurt. "I didn't ask that," he said. "Have I ever questioned you?"

"No. I'm sorry," she said.

As she was getting in bed, she noticed that the letter was not on the dressing table. So he had moved it. He did not want it in sight to disturb her.

She climbed in bed. He turned out the light and joined her. He leaned over to kiss her and she seized him suddenly, hard, saying, "Ted, Ted, I love you," not letting him go, letting passion flow unrestrained. "Don't wait," she whispered harshly, "let's don't wait! If you love me, don't wait! If you love me, prove it; don't wait!"

He did not wait; he was, after all, a man. His resolution was caught up, engulfed, and then vanished in flames.

191

CHAPTER SEVENTEEN

"TED," SHE CALLED gently, tremulously, in the sleepless morning.

He moaned and stirred.

"Ted . . . darling . . . it's time to get up," she said.

He opened his eyes; she searched them. He looked at her sleepily a moment, and then remembered. His eyes softened in a smile and he reached out for her, pulled her down to him, and kissed her.

"Ted, Ted," she said. She lay kissing him. Then she sat up and again searched his eyes, and asked, "How do you feel?"

"I feel fine," he said.

So now it had been done, she thought joyously. So now this wall between them had been broken; he had come willingly and without regret into sin! Now there need be no more tenseness, no more lying, no more deceit, no more worrying. Now there need be no more fear or guilt. She kissed him again, held him tight. And it had been so easy! she thought. So easy!

He knew he was glad it had happened; he was happy, lying now in bed with the girl beside him. They had waited; they had been strong. Who now would indict them for having, after all these months, done what humans do?

He thought: I am a man. He had proven it. He was a man.

He thought now, as he had many times, of the image of the ideal man which had been implanted into him in childhood on the South Philadelphia Streets—the vision of a man large in size, brutal, violent and unrestrained—an avatar of the cave man. This, he had heard, was the type of man women longed for. And all of his life he had known he was not that man.

He thought of his wife. For eighteen years she alone had lain in his arms, and before her there had been no woman, for he doubted himself and was afraid to try it. And after the first year or so, his wife had lost interest, submitting occasionally out of duty, not pleasure. She had been bored; she had been contemptuous; often she had refused him.

And all through these years, as through the years before, he was haunted by the legend, by the image, painted on the street corners, of joys, of wild climbings through the heaven's roof. This he had never achieved. And so he had not been a man.

Now, in the morning in the red brick house, he looked into Rodina's eyes and saw joy. For the first time in his life, he felt like a man.

"Ted," she whispered in his ear, "you know, we may have a child."

A child? "Yes," he said.

A child, children. For eighteen years he had been married to a woman who was unable to bear children, and gradually the connection between children and the bed had left his mind. Children. Yes, now, in truth, they would have to hasten the divorce. Children.

"I'm so happy you're not angry," she said.

"Why should I be angry?"

"You know. You said you didn't want to. Not until we got married."

Yes. Had he really said that? "We are married," he said.

2

Juarez, lying across the bed in his room, the door, as always, slightly ajar, the room dark and shadow-filled and filled with that mustiness that comes from lack of light or lack of frequent use, could hear them in the hall, early in the morning. They stood near the stair, Rodina and Theodore, saying the last few words before he went off to work.

"I'm so happy, Ted. I love you so much."

"I'm happy, too," Theodore said.

Juarez had been long awake, lying in the bed, his mind wandering slowly and deliberately over those things which concerned it: Juanita, whom he had dropped from his life; being a Mexican, people he disliked, things he disliked, explanations—psychological and sociological—for these dislikes . . . and Rodina, the dual nature of Rodina. Now he did not stir, listening to them, hating them, yet realizing that this hatred was unreasonable, that he had no just cause for hating them, since neither had done anything to him. But emotion versus intellect, the primitive versus the civilized; the emotion, the primitive, was always victorious in the end.

"Will you be home right after work?" Rodina asked.

"Yes."

"Good. Then let's go out someplace, if you feel like it."

"All right. That would be fine."

"Wait. I'll go downstairs with you."

Juarez could see, in his mind's eye, their kiss, and then he heard the man and girl descend the stairs and go out the door. Juarez lay without movement, staring at the ceiling, watching the pictures in his mind. He saw Rodina and Theodore and Hucks. He felt the blind, emotional stirring inside of him. He compelled hatred to rise.

It was an effort to hate, as it was not to hate, he noted idly, lazily, closing his eyes. Before, in the days of newborn understanding, his intellect had tried in vain, but tried, to control his emotions, keep them in check, make them subject to the understanding of causes and effects in his mind. He knew that a man, born into a certain world, was carved inexorably and innocently into the thing he was. Why hate him then? Thus had spoken his intellect, drowning out the emotion, keeping hatred on a leash. Now, desiring hatred, he must not let the intellect be heard. The emotions must be given reign. They strove, at his command, to stifle the voices within him which told him to desist, to remove this hatred, to look at Rodina with sympathy, understanding and pity. But the ceaseless struggle was difficult.

What was left but to hate? he wondered, moving his arm lazily to the package of cigarettes on the radiator, extracting one, lighting it and watching the smoke rise up in the room, ghostlike in the semidarkness, silent, warm and companionable. What else was there—job gone, in a moment of bitterness and anger; his thoughts on the Rodina who walked through halls in the nighttime and came in the daytime, in the light, to sit in the tearoom with innocent eyes and innocent smile and innocent face and innocent voice to tell of innocence and fear of evil, to unroll the sympathy like twine from the last-unwinding spool in his heart? Now there was loneliness, the darkened room, the tenement. There was not knowing where the next month's rent was coming from, not caring, willing to drift, being tired. There were the noisy kids on the street dirty and reminding you of childhood, the restaurants where they did not really want to serve you, the Mexican quarter, being ugly with pockmarks and oily skin and a scrawny body, hating the restaurant manager and the people who came to the restaurant and the waitress, the cute waitress, named Jean. Now there were years ahead about which he cared nothing, knew nothing, except that they could not bring renewed hope or trust or faith or love.

What were there now except brooding and hatred and hunger and filth, which were unhealthy but strong, some exercise for the emotions and body, giving some distorted but intense satisfaction? (He saw the man, Theodore, departed, sent home to his wife, discovering now that he had not really loved Rodina, but had loved his wife, because she was his kind, his sort, gentle, saccharine, making few demands on the emotions; and Rodina, now without the always-present man, discovering that she had not really loved Theodore, but had only convinced herself that she had, her old self again: picking pockets, happy, winking at the men, in bed with Hucks again, carefree, her skirts swinging wildly, her eyes bright, going out again with Hucks and Tom and John and Cohn.) Now there was confusion and anxiety and fear, Theodore remaining, Rodina still under the hypnosis of the illusion of love, (though still a deceit! though still a lie!), and Juarez could lead them further down the path, emotion quelling intellect, the primitive conquering the civilized. Now he could go down the path inexorably, leading these three, hating them.

3

"Juarez!" she cried, late that afternoon, coming into the tearoom, "Juarez, you were so right. I'm so happy. You're wonderful, Juarez; I could kiss you."

He smiled and she sat down, exuberant, opposite him.

"Oh, you're just the smartest man on earth," she said to him, her eyes dancing and her face lighted. "You were so right. I was scared to do what you told me, and then suddenly I did and everything turned out fine."

"Whoa," Juarez said gently, "hold up a moment, Rodina. What did I tell you, and just what is it that's turned out all right?"

"About Ted," she said. "You remember what you told me? To make him do something—well, bad, and then everything would be all right, we'd be happy from then on. Well, I did it, and it worked. Now I won't have to worry much anymore about his being so good. And it was so easy. He didn't even mind. I just asked and he did it and he's happy about it."

Juarez lifted the tea cup and avoided the eyes of the girl. He said, "What did you have him do?"

She opened her mouth, then looked at the tablecloth and said, "Well, I can't tell you that, Juarez. It's kind of private, you know."

Juarez looked at her and nodded. He said, "And now everything's all right?"

"Yes."

"And Theodore did not mind?"

"No, Juarez. He was happy about it."

Juarez shook his head. Rodina looked at him and said, "Juarez, what's wrong?"

"Well," he said, "well, I'm happy about it, but I'm a little wary. I'm just suspicious, you know. I want things to turn out right."

"Sure," she said. "So do I. But I did what you said."

He stirred his tea. "Tell me," he said, "was the thing you had Theodore do *very* bad?"

"No," she said, after hesitating.

He nodded thoughtfully. Then he said, "I don't doubt that you've helped him along, Rodina. But you mustn't think the whole job is finished. I don't want you to be disappointed, you see. You mustn't think that everything will be utopia from now on. It won't. No doubt you've succeeded in easing your

198

relationship a little, whatever you did. But don't think it's permanent or complete. It isn't."

"Oh," she said, "but it worked, Juarez. I can tell you. He acted different afterwards. He feels good about it."

"Then he must not, originally, have been too averse to it," Juarez commented.

Rodina had not thought of that.

"And whatever he did must not," Juarez went on, "have required any significant basic change in his thinking or morals. You can see that, can't you?"

Rodina nodded.

"Don't feel disheartened by what I say," Juarez said. "I'm just trying to warn you in advance, so that nothing comes as a shock later. If you got him to do something he would not have done before, then you've made some progress. But the change in him, really, must be complete. I'm sure you'll be able to manage it."

Rodina pouted. She thought a moment, still pouting. "I don't know whether I'll be able to do anything else. I hope I won't have to. But he's so sweet, Juarez, and he seemed so happy this morning when he went to work. He told me he loves me. It's the first time he told me so I really believed it for a long time."

Juarez said nothing.

"Can you see us married, Juarez?"

"Yes," Juarez said.

"I can," Rodina said. "I can see us married and living off someplace where nobody knows us, and being happy. I can see us in a nice house with a lawn, and with children. Can you picture that?"

"Yes," Juarez said.

She thought a moment. "Things seem to happen, though," she said finally, a little of the lilt gone from her voice. "Sometimes I feel like we're surrounded by things we're not bothered about, but that keep us from being happy anyway. Evil spirits, almost. Things surrounding us, and no matter what we do they close in on us and keep us from being happy." She smiled then, looking at him. "But you don't believe in spirits," she laughed.

"No," he said. "I don't believe in spirits. Although I do believe in good and evil."

Again, she nodded. He had taken the edge off of her excitement. After awhile, she said more softly, "Juarez, do you *really* think everything's going to turn out all right?"

"I believe in justice," Juarez said. "I believe that justice has a way of winning out in the end." He paused and then said, "But you've got to help justice along."

4

At the back of the basement café three Negroes played piano, bass fiddle and drum and a Negro woman in a long, sleek black dress sang low and soft as the veiled lights shone over the tables and against the blue smoke which rose, floated and twisted in the room. Smoke of all kinds rose in the room from cigars, cigarettes, pipes, twisting together, curling thickly, filling the lungs, at once acrid and sweet. Shaded colored lights and pencil drawings of naked women adorned the walls, and linoleum covered the cement floor. White men and women and Negroes and Mexicans sat at the wooden tables with cracks straight across them as men in white aprons and shirts walked around the room with trays bearing drinks at high prices. The woman sang softly the blues. Theodore looked across the table and saw Rodina's happy black eyes shining toward the singer. She saw him look, and smiled.

"Glad you came?" she asked.

200

"Yes."

"I'm glad we decided to go out tonight. We need to get out once in a while."

Across the room Theodore saw a woman leap to her feet and slap the man who had sat beside her; and the man said hastily, "Okay, baby, okay, okay, you got it all." In the corner behind these two, a man was smoking a cigarette, only, he seemed to be sipping rather than inhaling its smoke.

"What's that fellow doing?" Theodore asked Rodina.

"Smoking a reefer," Rodina laughed. "You know—dope."

"Oh," Theodore said.

Rodina asked, "Want a drink, Ted?"

"All right."

The waiter came and Theodore ordered the drinks. It had been a long time, he thought, since he had tasted liquor. He watched the singer and the antics of the customers. The glasses were placed in front of them, and Theodore tasted the bitter-strong whiskey. A long time.

"I like this place," Rodina said. "I like this street—South Street. You can't imagine what goes on here, on this street. You see everything. People are poor, but they've got hearts, and they've got brains, some of them. I used to walk on this street all the time, and I'd go in a saloon and talk to some of the people. Some of them speak a lot of languages, and a lot of them went to college. They're smart, but nobody cares anything about them. They live in dirty houses and have a bunch of kids. Who's happy, Ted, when so many people are poor and forgotten? And when all the kids want to do is go out and steal, and get a lot of money without working, and buy a sharp Cadillac? All kinds of people, look at them here, and people call them bums. They're not bums."

He stared at her, and wondered whether the drink had had some effect on her already. He saw it had not. He sipped his own drink, feeling the sincerity and the truth of her assertion. She had never spoken like that before. But what did one person ever know about the heart of another?

"All my life," Theodore said now, "I think I've been trying to be like these people; honest with myself, and without inhibition. But I can't be like them. I've been ruined, already." He sipped the drink. "When I was young, a kid, I lived in South Philadelphia among people like these. But I never really got to know them, and they never got to know me. They could do what they wanted, say what they wanted—they stole, cursed and fought and swore. I wanted to be able to do the same, but I never could. I was always quiet, I liked to read, to go to school, to study. I wanted to be like these people, but there was some kind of wall between me and them, which kept us apart, and I never felt right, I felt like a foreigner, a sissy."

The word came out with difficulty. "I never got over it," he said. "I still feel the wall—between people like me and Hucks, for instance. A wall of different rules, and different values." He smiled and said, "Why do you stare at me so strangely, Rodina? Do I sound drunk?"

"No," she said hastily, "no."

"I probably am," he said. "It takes only a few sips to make me drunk."

They walked home, swinging their arms like school children. As they approached the tenement, Theodore saw Hucks coming from the opposite corner.

"There's your boy friend," he said jokingly to Rodina. He noticed that her head shot up and she looked at him strangely.

They went inside and past the tearoom door. Juarez, who was sitting at one of the tables, called, "Hello, come on in," and they went inside and sat down beside him.

"How about a cup of tea?" Juarez asked.

"No, thanks," Theodore said. "We've just come from a night club."

Juarez felt a chill gust of air, and, looking up, said, "You left the front door open."

Theodore said, "For your friend, Hucks. He's on his way."

"Oh. Well, how did you like our South Philadelphia joint?" Juarez asked.

"Fine."

Hucks came in and closed the door behind him. He was wearing the brown lumber jacket. Juarez saw him and yelled, "Hucks."

Hucks paused and stared into the room. He saw Rodina and Theodore. He said to Juarez, "Yeah?"

"Come on over. Join the party."

Hucks looked at all of them. What the hell was this? For a moment, it seemed he would ignore the invitation, but finally he walked over to the table.

"What party?" he asked suspiciously.

"Us," Juarez said. "Pull up a chair and sit down. Have some coffee or tea. Theodore was just talking about you."

Hucks looked at him. "No thanks," he said. He turned and looked at Theodore but said nothing.

"Then how about something stronger, a little brandy or bourbon?"

"You treatin'?" Hucks could not make this out.

"Yes."

"Gettin' mighty generous."

"I won at the races," Juarez said softly, smiling, his watery eyes on Hucks' face."

Hucks sat down. Glenn came to the table and Hucks ordered some bourbon "on him." He sat without talking at the table, glancing at Theodore every once in a while. Neither Theodore nor Rodina would say anything. Juarez chatted cheerfully.

"Well, Hucks, how have you been?"

"I been all right," Hucks said. Damned if he could figure this one out.

"Pretty cold outside. And you just wearing a lumber jacket, working on an open truck. Pretty rough, eh?"

"I can take it, all right," Hucks declared. "I ain't no poet." He was thinking: Talkin' about me. What the hell he doin' talkin' about me? I oughta punch that sissified sonofabitch in the mouth. He better watch hisself.

"You're goddamned right you're not any poet!" Rodina said angrily, furious at the thought that Hucks was again, apparently, about to pick a quarrel.

"Relax, Rodina," Theodore said. "Ignore it."

And this, I suppose, will go on forever, Theodore thought. Forever, whenever I come into contact with him, this thing will appear, again and again, without the possibility of peace for either him or me? Sad. He's big, but he has an inferiority complex as far as brains are concerned, and he tries to overpower it by noise and brute strength. Like the kids on the street who used to throw rocks, and dirty words. I hate his guts.

"How come you're so gay tonight?" Hucks asked Juarez. "How come you buyin' me a drink? You ain't lovin' me."

"Oh, I don't know about that, Hucks. Maybe I am loving you, eh? Maybe I'm trying to win you over."

"Is that supposed to be makin' fun of me?" Hucks wanted to know.

"Not at all. To tell the truth, Hucks, I just feel convivial tonight. All night I've had an overpowering desire to be surrounded by friends brave and true, and to spend some money on them. Rodina and Theodore, here, don't care to drink,

204

since they've just come from a nightclub. So I called you. Simple."

"Simple as hell," Hucks said.

"You seem sullen," Juarez said. "Anything wrong?"

"Ain't nothin' wrong," Hucks said.

"Sure one of your flock of girl friends didn't pick this particular night to give you the cold air?"

"Hell, no," Hucks said. He glanced at Theodore with animosity. He looked at his drink. "Ain't no girl givin' Hucks the air," he said.

"Oh, come now," Juarez said, extremely cheerful, "do you mean to say no girl has ever given you the air?"

"Not a one!" Hucks said, as though angered that Juarez should doubt his word.

Rodina laughed and Hucks turned to her quickly. "What's troubling you, baby?"

"You," Rodina replied.

"Yeah. Well, watch yourself, baby. You know, I could spill a few things 'ud upset your cute little applecart."

Rodina's mouth closed in a straight line, she stared at Hucks hotly. Theodore looked at her, and at Hucks.

"That's right," Hucks said, "I could tell some thing that might disillusion your boy friend here about his sweet, lovin' baby, ain-at right?"

She stared at him and her eyes looked as though they were swollen by sleep. She said nothing.

Hucks leaned back and finished his drink. "Well, thanks," he said to Juarez. "Something seems fishy about this, but I got a drink free. I'm cuttin' out." He rose, but before leaving pointed a finger at Theodore. "And as for you, don't go around talkin' about me behind my back no more, either!"

Juarez said quickly, "But he didn't say anything out of the way, Hucks."

"Yeah, I know," Hucks said. "Well, just see that it don't happen no more. Else somebody'll be walkin' around here toothless."

He walked off. Juarez turned to Theodore, his face filled with bafflement. "Well, something certainly was eating *him!*"

Theodore smiled without mirth and looked into Juarez's eyes. "Yes," he said, slowly and insinuatingly, "something certainly was, wasn't it?"

Juarez heard the insinuation and saw what was in Theodore's eyes. He returned the other's smile.

5

Upstairs now, in their room, Rodina was upset. She wondered what Theodore was thinking. In the tearoom, Hucks had come closer than ever before to telling Theodore about the wallet, and perhaps about that night in his room. She trembled and was afraid Theodore would see her. She felt again the fear which had, for this day at least, left her in peace. She wanted to be out of the room; she wanted to be forever rid of this destructive tension.

"I've got to go in to see momma," she told Theodore.

She left the room and walked along the hall to her mother's room. It was peace to be away from Theodore now. Later, she would be all right. Hucks was bluffing. Sure, he was bluffing. Else, why didn't he just go ahead and tell?

She was surprised to find Juarez in her mother's room. He got up when she entered.

"Oh, hello, Rodina. I wasn't sure you'd be in here tonight."

Mrs. Baleza said, "Well, how's the night owl?"

Juarez, along with others in the tenement, sometimes visited Mrs. Baleza to help dispel the loneliness of the room. Rodina went into the kitchen and made some tea; her mother liked tea at night. She returned to the room and served a cup to Juarez and to her mother.

"Tea downstairs and upstairs," Juarez said wryly.

"Yeah," Mrs. Baleza said. "I can't get downstairs like you others."

"No," Juarez said, "you get curb service, Mrs. Baleza."

Rodina asked, "How do you feel, momma?"

"Oh, fair," Mrs. Baleza said, "pretty fair, Rodina. Felt better today than in a long time. Dr. Jamison says I'm gettin' along mighty fine. Little trouble with my legs, though. Dr. Jamison asked for you. He come in right after you went out this evenin'."

Rodina got more tea from the kitchen. Nearly every night she performed the brewing ritual. Juarez watched her go into the kitchen and come out again; he saw her long, thick black hair and careless walk.

"You have a marvelous daughter," he said to Mrs. Baleza.

"Yeah," Mrs. Baleza said. "Didn't useta think so. Useta think she was the daughter of Satan, 'steada me. Useta think she was hell's own maiden. She ain't so bad, though. Ain't like some other people I know."

Rodina looked at her mother apprehensively. Mrs. Baleza said, "Was tellin' Rodina about some a the people I know. Regular prostitutes, you know. Sleep with any old man. Don't care nothin' about God, or the Commandments, or nothin' else. Just do t'suit themselves. Them's the kinda people goin' t'hell, sure as you're born."

Juarez nodded.

"You're a good man, Juarez. Believe in God. You're a Mexican, and I ain't never had much to do for Mexicans, but you're different, Juarez. Damned if you ain't just about the same as any regular white man I ever seen. You're a good man. A fine man."

"Thank you," Juarez said.

Mrs. Baleza looked at him and at Rodina. She felt tired, old and bitter. With Juarez, she felt a kind of rapport: he was shriveled, ugly, and he was a Mexican. She looked at Rodina's youth.

She said, "I'm gettin' old, Juarez. Old and weak. Can feel death comin' closer all the time."

Neither Juarez nor Rodina knew what to say to this.

"Can see old death comin'," Mrs. Baleza said. "I hate it!" she said with sudden vehemence. Her eyes were afire a moment, but swiftly they lost their brightness. Quiet again, she said, "You're a good man, Juarez. Fine man. Always been nice to a old woman. Want you to look after my daughter after I'm gone."

Juarez said, "You won't be going any place for a long while, Mrs. Baleza."

"May be. But want you to look after Rodina, when I do go. Want to make sure she grows up to be a fine woman. Don't want her to be a sinner, go to hell. Want her to be fine. Not like them other women."

"Like what other women, Mrs. Baleza?"

"Lania and Sarah and Bertie and the rest. You seen em, Juarez. Ain't got no decency. Husband stealers. Go to bed with anybody for a price. Live with anybody. Don't want my daughter to be like that."

Rodina glanced at Juarez, who did not look at her. She stood up and started toward the kitchen.

"Where you goin'?" Mrs. Baleza asked.

"To get more tea, momma."

"Stay here. Want you to hear."

"But momma, I've heard it all before."

"Stay here," Mrs. Baleza commanded. Rodina sat down. Mrs. Baleza smiled. "I want Juarez to take care of you. Juarez is a

208

good man, known you a long time. I want him to take care of you."

"Oh, momma, you'll live a long time yet."

"May be, may be," the woman said impatiently. "But I want to say this. Don't want you to grow up wrong. Like Lania and Sarah—"

"Momma, you've said this a million times," Rodina interrupted. "Why do you have to keep saying it? I heard it before. I know by now what you want. There's no need to say it over and over and over again, day after day, every day of my life. I can hear, momma. I can understand. I'm not like you want me to be, but I get tired of hearing it. I get tired!"

Mrs. Baleza stared at her with wide eyes. "Do you get tired of the word of God?"

"Yes," Rodina cried, "I get tired of all of it. I get tired of everything."

"Do you want to be like them others? Do you want to be like Sarah and Lania and them? Do you want people talkin' about you?"

"I don't care. I don't care anymore."

"Do you want to burn forever in hell? Do you want that? Do you want to beg for mercy through eternity? Do you want that?"

She shuddered. Softly, she said, "No."

"Then listen," Mrs. Baleza said. "Listen to what I got to say. Your father would be ashamed of you, talkin' like that to me. What I tell you is for your own good. I think about your salvation. I want you to be a good girl. Can't you understand that?"

"I'm not a good girl," Rodina said.

"You could try to be. A person could try."

"I don't want to try," Rodina said. "Not any more."

"What's that?"

"All my life I tried and I just can't. You said you're born the way you are. Well, I'm born my way. I can't change. I'm tired of trying."

"Tired, are you?" her mother said, her eyes blazing.

"Yes," Rodina almost shouted. "Yes, I'm tired. *I* live with a man, momma! *I* sleep with a man every night! A *married* man! And I'm happy about it! I don't want to change. I don't want to be good. I want to live with him for the rest of my life, and to hell with everything else."

"You talk to me like that?"

"It's time I did!"

"You want to go to hell?"

"Yes!" Rodina cried. "I want to go wherever I'm going. I don't care."

"You're evil!" her mother hissed, but her eyes glowed with happiness. "You're evil! You're the daughter of Satan!"

"I am," Rodina said, feeling the tremendous thrill of catharsis, glad that this deception could be ended.

Mrs. Baleza stared at her daughter, who was breathing heavily. She lay back against the pillows, her eyes bright. Juarez said nothing. After what seemed a long, long time, Rodina rose and fixed her mother's pillows for her sleep during the night. Her mother did not talk to her. Rodina asked, "Are you comfortable, momma?" but Mrs. Baleza did not reply.

As she and Juarez left the room, both of them said, "Good night," but Mrs. Baleza said nothing.

"Do you think you should have talked to her like that?" Juarez asked in the hallway. "She's an old woman, and pretty weak."

"Oh, shut up!" Rodina shot at him. Immediately she was sorry. "I'm sorry, Juarez," she said. "I guess I shouldn't have said those things that way. But I was going crazy. All the

210

time, *all the time*, she says those things, over and over. I had to tell her."

Juarez said nothing. Rodina looked at him and said, "Juarez, I really *am* bad, just as she said. I really *will* go to hell when I die." She said it plaintively.

Juarez said softly, "I never have believed in things like that, I told you so before." He paused, then said, "But who can tell? Who can tell anything about the power and presence of evil?"

CHAPTER EIGHTEEN

Yes, who could tell?

She lay awake in the bed, staring at the dancing leaves. She was so warm! Theodore was asleep beside her. Theodore. Wonderful Theodore. Theodore was like God, so good; he loved her, he said he did, but there was the wall. Even he had admitted that there was a wall.

Who could tell? Yes, she had been right all these years, and her mother had been right. If poppa had lived maybe he would have been able to help her. He was a minister and good. As Ted was good. As Juarez was good. But not her. All of her life, from when she was a little girl, she had been sinful.

Hell! She had seen pictures, illustrations, painted for books and Bibles. She had seen the dark, jagged twisting body-souls with fiery red eyes and arms and legs like twigs screaming in Satan's cauldron. What was that her mother had used to tell her about the man who sinned and went into hell and then begged a man in heaven for a drop of water for his tongue, just a drop, just one drop? Burning forever. Not for seventy years, or for one hundred years, or for one thousand years, but forever—for millions and millions and millions of years. So that a lifetime was a second. Always burning.

You were born to this, like Judas. You had to be. God saw all, the past and the future, and when you were born He knew whether you would be good or evil. He knew, and so, knowing, there would be no point in allowing you to be born unless

213

for some reason He intended for you to go to hell. God was too good just to permit you to be born, knowing you were going to hell, unless He intended for you to go there. He intended for her to go there. There was some reason, although she could not know it. Better not to wonder—no one could question God.

She wanted to be happy here on earth and so she did the things that made her happy. She worked at home and liked it, because she worked not for money but for her mother and for Theodore whom she loved. But she hated the jobs outside. You worked just for money, for yourself and your boss, and she did not like that. And the boss could order you around, or fire you, or get fresh with you, and she did not like that. So she stole, she picked pockets. That was fun. But it was wrong; she knew it was wrong. And men. She was wrong with men. She went to bed with men and was not married—that was fornication. She had met no one she wanted to marry, but she was growing up and needed to go to bed. So she went to bed without marriage. But it was evil. It was fornication.

Theodore stirred in the bed. She looked at him. Dear Ted, darling Ted, lovely Ted! In all her life before she had never met a man she loved, but she loved him. She loved his soft face and his soft, gentle smile and his soft way of talking and that he was smart but did not show off that he was smart. Yes, she loved these things and a thousand other things, tiny things. How shy he was about some things. How good he was.

But he had done some evil. It was funny, but he had been happy only after he had done the evil. He left his wife, which was evil, and then he was happy with her. Then he was unhappy for awhile, getting her letters, getting picked on by Hucks. Then that night in bed, oh, that night in bed, and afterwards for awhile he had been happy again; and this had been evil, for he was married to another woman and besides

214

they, Theodore and she, were not married. Then he was unhappy again, because of Hucks. Hucks and the wife who sent the letters. Rodina hated both of them.

It was good that she had told her mother about Theodore tonight. Now she would not have to pretend anymore, or listen to that talk anymore. The talk drove her crazy. Now she would not have to worry about it; saying what she had said had taken a load off her mind. Why pretend and stay nervous all the time and afraid?

And why pretend with Theodore? With him she did not like to pretend anything. If only he had not been good. If only he had been born down here and grew up like the others and like Hucks, and then was still the way he was in other things. Then she could tell him all the truth, and not worry. And then she wouldn't have to be afraid of Hucks. That goddamned Hucks! And Theodore wouldn't have to be afraid of the letters from his wife.

She trembled with a thought. No, she said to herself, no! But the thought persisted. She lay staring at the shadows of the branches on the wall. For half an hour she stared and thought.

She climbed out of bed and turned on the light. Theodore still slept. She put coffee into the pot and lit the gas on the little stove. The coffee began to percolate. She walked over to the bed again and shook Theodore gently.

"Ted," she said, Ted."

He opened his eyes. He stared at her sleepily, then came to a sitting position. The light shone brightly; through the window he could see that it was still dark outside. He looked at Rodina, puzzled.

"Ted, are you awake? I'm making some coffee. I want you to listen carefully. I have something important to tell you, and I can't wait until morning."

He sat up and drank the coffee. Rodina watched him, trembling. He was worried, looking at her. "What is it, darling?"

First, she turned out the flame under the coffee pot. Then she sat on the edge of the bed and could not meet his eyes as she said, "I just came in a little while ago from momma's room. You were asleep. She told me the doctor was there today and said she had to have an operation in a couple of days, or else she might die. It costs a hundred and fifty dollars."

She waited and said, "I have to get the money tomorrow, Ted. Or at least by the next day. I know how to get it. I just want your permission."

His eyes widened. "You mean—?"

She turned her head. "What other way is there? I have to get the money."

Theodore looked at the ceiling. "An operation—One hundred and fifty dollars." He looked at Rodina, touched her arm. "We'll have to get the money somehow, darling," he said. "But not the way you're thinking. I won't have you picking any pockets."

"How else?" she cried, still not looking at him, not daring to look at him. "How else can I get it?"

"We might be able to borrow it."

"We don't know anyone who has that much money."

No, Theodore was thinking, we don't. The room seemed very quiet. He said, "No, we don't know anyone with that much money. But you can't steal. I won't have that, Rodina. I'll think of a way to get the money, somehow."

Rodina trembled and said softly, "You can't get the money, Ted, unless—"

"Unless what?"

"Oh, Ted!" she cried suddenly, "I just can't let her die!"

"No," he said tenderly, "you can't. Unless what, Rodina?"

216

Now she could look at him. Now she felt repugnance but felt too that this was perhaps the last gamble, the last chance; she had gone too far to turn back now. "Unless you could get a couple of those expensive cameras where you work."

She could not look at his shocked eyes. She closed her own and pressed her head into the blanket and sobbed. Theodore's eyes rested on her for a moment, and then his hand went out to pat her back. He said, "I certainly wouldn't like that. But I can understand; I feel the same way."

He was silent, feeling her sobs as they shook his arm. "Come on and get in bed," he said. "I'll sleep on it, and by morning I should think of something. I think I know how to get the money without stealing. Maybe so, maybe not. Anyway, I'll get the money somehow."

She lay sobbing, despising herself. Pity flooded Theodore.

"Come, get in bed, darling," he said. "I'll think of something. Trust me."

2

The following morning, she did not mention their conversation of the night before. Nor did Theodore. As he ate, they spoke of how cold it was and how nice it had been to go to the nightclub. She felt guilt and shame; but this was the trial, this was the test. This was necessary.

As he passed Mrs. Baleza's door, Theodore thought of the sick old woman in the bed and her sickness and need for an operation. One hundred and fifty dollars. And he had promised to get it. Rodina kissed him, leaning over the bannister, and he went out into the cold. He would walk to work. He walked, thinking. He did not want to go to work today; he did not want to go into the office and smile at the smiling people, feeling as he did. Perhaps he could borrow the money, perhaps from Mr. Davidson. The thought cheered him.

"Good morning, Theodore," Mr. Davidson said. The manager was short and cherubic; his cheeks were red, and his head partially bald. "Lovely weather we're having. Cold, but dry; not at all that fogginess that seeped into your bones."

"Yes," Theodore said.

Mr. Davidson grinned. "Now, if we have a little snow, you'll see business pick up. People like to take pictures in the snow."

Theodore hung up his coat and went behind the counter. The two girls were not yet in the store. The stock boy (the one who fetched the things from the basement and wrapped cameras for mailing) was mopping the floor. Across from the counter Theodore saw the glass showcase filled with cameras—box cameras, Speed Graphics and Graflexes, Voigtlanders, Contaxes, Leicas.

"Brother!" DeWitt exclaimed, "feels good to get inside the office."

"Wonderful," Theodore said.

"Davidson likes this kind of weather, but not old DeWitt. Winter hath no charms to soothe this savage beast—I cried like hell when I came out of the womb." Theodore grinned. DeWitt looked at him a moment and then said, "I been thinking—the Socialists are having a meeting Friday; how'd you like to come?"

"I don't think I can make it," Theodore said.

"You ought to come, really. You'd learn a lot, and there's a lot to learn. People are having a lot of troubles these days, all kinds, and they ascribe them to a lot of reasons—most of which are bunk. That's the viciousness of this world. People blame certain things for their troubles—mostly they blame some crazy abstraction—when really, if they could see behind the scenes, they'd find their troubles lay elsewhere, in the sys-

218

tem itself with all its accompanying symptoms, mainly. You ought to come."

"I don't think so," Theodore said, amused at DeWitt's headlong enthusiasm.

DeWitt shook his head. "Okay," he said, "but it's the people like us who get hurt in the end, you know. We get the troubles."

"I don't have any troubles," Theodore said with a smile.

The two girls came in. Rosalie said, "Whooosh, it's *c-o-l-d* out there!" She rubbed her hands and patted her cheeks and ears. Miss Lewis, the other one, said, "Good morning," rather primly but pleasantly, and proceeded directly to the cloakroom. In a moment she was back.

"One big happy, grinning, mercenary family," Rosalie said.

On the wall opposite the counter was the showcase, with the Contaxes and Leicas. Theodore would have to ask Mr. Davidson for a loan. He did not believe he could get it; still, he might as well try. He noticed that his stomach seemed a little queasy and that his hand trembled slightly. He felt very tired.

Customers came in from time to time. At twelve Theodore went out to lunch, and when he returned a customer was waiting for him.

"How do you do, Mrs. Bannister?" Theodore said.

"Oh, Mr. Hall, I waited for you. Especially for you." The woman was of medium height, middle-age, stout and a bit silly.

Theodore said, "I feel flattered, Mrs. Bannister."

She took some prints from her purse and handed them to Theodore. "Some pictures I took last summer, while I was on vacation," she said in her high, inflected voice, smiling sweetly. "I'd like to have them enlarged. I lost the negatives."

The pictures were of the woman, on the beach, wearing a rather revealing bathing suit.

219

"I suppose I can really be accused of trying to be younger than I am," she said, laughing on a high, false, note.

Theodore said, "Not at all. You're very attractive in a bathing suit, if I may say so, Mrs. Bannister."

She smiled and looked at him coyly and said, "Well, thank you very much."

When she was gone, DeWitt laughed. "She's a widow, Theodore," he said. "You'd better watch out."

Theodore smiled; his eyes wandered to the showcase.

In the afternoon Theodore went to Mr. Davidson. "Mr. Davidson, I'd like to talk to you if I may. It's pretty important. I hardly feel justified in asking this. I feel I'm imposing, but I wonder if I might get a loan from the store. I'd pay it back out of each week's pay."

Mr. Davidson thought a moment, and said, "How much would you want?"

"A hundred and fifty dollars," Theodore said.

Mr. Davidson ran his hand over his balding head. He shook his head sadly. "It's not my store, you know, Theodore. I'd have to get the money from the owner, and that'd be pretty hard. He doesn't know you. I doubt if he'd do it." He thought a moment more. "How soon would you need this money?"

"Today," Theodore said. "Or tomorrow, at the latest."

"I'll see," Mr. Davidson said. "I'll call Mr. Timms, and let you know what he says."

Later Mr. Davidson called Theodore over to him, and Theodore could see by his face that the loan had been refused. Well, what had he expected? How could these people know that he would not suddenly quit work, without repaying the loan?

"I'm sorry," Mr. Davidson said. "Mr. Timms says no, Theodore."

"I thought as much."

220

"I'm sorry."

"Sure."

When he had reason to open the showcase near closing time, Theodore took out two Leica cameras and carried them behind the counter with him. He shoved them far back under the counter, his heart beating violently. When he glanced up, DeWitt was looking at him and smiling. In Theodore's mind the question flashed: *Did he see me?*

Well, he thought, it's come to this. Throughout his youth, when the other boys stole, he had wished he could somehow be like them—that he too could steal and curse and fight like they, and be a part of their lives, their friend. They would have accepted him then, had he had the courage to do the things they did. Well, here it was; he was stealing now. He was sneaking around guiltily in a store, stealing from a manager who had given him a break, betraying employees who from the first had been kind to him. The boyhood wish come true, he thought bitterly.

But it was for Mrs. Baleza, he thought. If it was a choice between the saving of her life and his "moral code," the code must go. She was Rodina's mother.

"You look positively gloomy today," Rosalie said. "Indigestion?"

"No," Theodore tried to laugh. I'm a novice, he thought. I was always a novice at things requiring courage. They'll miss these cameras soon. How should I act if they question me? Won't I give myself away? Won't they suspect me first, since I'm the newest employee? How will I get the cameras out of here? In my coat pocket? I can see myself brushing against the door, the sound of the hard cameras audible to everyone. Or the cameras falling out of my pocket. This is silly. I've got to think about other things now.

Even if they did not find out about the theft, how could he face these people through all the days to come? Every day when he came into the store he would be apprehensive, wondering whether they had found out yet. And if they hadn't, how could he accept their cheerful, pleasant greetings, and return them in kind, knowing in his heart that he was a fraud? The pretense, the continued role he would have to play!

"Ready, Theodore?" Mr. Davidson asked.

He started. He stared at Mr. Davidson wide-eyed. "What's wrong, Mr. Davidson?" he asked.

"Closing up. Ready?"

"Oh." Theodore looked away. He was acting like a fool. "In a moment."

He wanted to take the cameras back to the dressing room with him; there would be no excuse for returning behind the counter once he put on his coat. But Mr. Davidson was standing nearby. The others had put on their coats already. They stood near the door. Mr. Davidson said, "We're ready to take off."

What could he do? He stood still, ridiculous in his own eyes, the others waiting for him. What could he do? He knew a wild panic. His muscles seemed paralyzed.

"I have to get my coat," he said finally.

He moved off to the cloakroom and put on the heavy coat. When he came back into the room the others stood near the door, talking and laughing. He went behind the counter, looking at the others, his heart beating wildly. He reached down and felt one of the cameras, lifted it swiftly and placed it in his pocket. He reached down and felt for the other . . .

"What's up, Theodore?" Mr. Davidson asked. "Good receipts today. Leave whatever you're doing for tomorrow; let's take off, eh?"

"Yes sir," Theodore said. He grasped the other camera. The

others were looking at him and there was no chance to put it in his pocket; the movement would be observed. He pulled his arm up into his sleeve.

"You seem reluctant to leave the old homestead," Mr. Davidson said to him as he came to the door. "Don't worry, you're invited back tomorrow."

Theodore smiled. He said goodbye. Outside, he walked rapidly toward home, still trembling, still weak.

CHAPTER NINETEEN

WHEN THEODORE WENT to work in the following days he was greeted with the usual good cheer, the usual smiles. He returned them, and did his work. He was quieter than usual, and the others noticed it.

"You must not love us any more," DeWitt said.

"Why do you say that?" Theodore asked.

"That long face you wear to work. And the gloomy silence you carry around. You really look like you've got troubles."

Theodore said, "Nothing's wrong."

"I'd think your mother-in-law was visiting you, if you were married," DeWitt said.

Vaguely, Theodore smiled. When applying for the job, he had told them he was single.

Every evening, Rodina greeted him with smiles; every night, she prepared something special for his supper. The room was immaculately clean; she turned the bed down for him, and when he came into the room he noticed always that she had changed her clothes for him.

"The little bee," he would say as he kissed her. "My, you must have been working hard all day, in here and in your mother's room."

"I aim to please," she would say.

She smiled always and she was cheerful always, but she searched his eyes. He should be a new person now; he should be happy now. She searched his eyes to see if she could perceive the change. She saw little that was different. Sometimes, she thought she saw the slightest hint of sadness or worry; at other times, she thought she saw the pinpoint gleam of evil. She could not be sure. She could not be sure.

"Are you happy? Do you love me?" she would ask him, holding him.

"Yes, twice."

"Really? Are you glad you're with me? Are you glad you left your wife for me?"

"I love you and I'm glad for anything I did."

"And will you always love me? Always? Till I die?"

"Always," he answered.

She wanted to ask him: Aren't you glad you stole the cameras? Don't you feel like a changed man now? Don't you feel closer to me, more like me, less like an Angel or like God? Aren't you happy now that we can go to Hell together?

She wanted to ask him these questions, but she never could.

"Oh, hello, Theodore," Mr. Davidson said, and Theodore knew that this was the day, this was it.

He knew by the tone of Mr. Davidson's voice as he walked into the store, and by the looks on the faces of the employees who stood in front of the counter. Theodore felt his hands tremble. He went into the cloak room; when he returned, Mr. Davidson had closed the front door and locked it.

"Well, I guess we're all here now, except Jimmy, the stock boy," Mr. Davidson said to them. "Now, as I was saying, two cameras are missing—Leicas, pretty expensive as you know. Of course, I'm responsible for them. There's no record of their sale, and our records show that they were delivered here. As a matter of fact, I saw them in the showcase myself. When we found out about it, we called in police and they say that

226

no burglar has come into the place. You can imagine, therefore, what they think about it."

Mr. Davidson paused. He seemed sad. It was obvious that he did not like talking like this. He looked at each of the employees. The room was silent. Theodore was filled with loathing of himself. But he kept his eyes on Mr. Davidson. His throat and lungs were clogged with fear.

"Now, we've checked everything that could possibly have happened to the cameras. We know that they weren't just mislaid. We're positive the cameras were stolen. I'd give my right arm not to have to say this"—his eyes, it seemed to Theodore, were moist—"but we're almost positive that this was an inside job."

Theodore had known this day would come. And who was to be suspected by the police, and by Mr. Davidson? Would they suspect Ro, her sister, or DeWitt? Hardly, after so many years of working here. No, he himself would be the suspect; hadn't he tried, on the very day of the theft, to borrow one hundred and fifty dollars?

"We'll check everything again," Mr. Davidson said. "I'm hoping against hope that what we think isn't true. But I want you to know what the score is. Until we find out what happened to the cameras, all of you must of necessity be suspect. That's about all I have to say."

They moved back to their work. The front door was again opened. In a few moments, Jimmy, the stock boy, came in. He said hello, and noticing the silence, said, "Hey, what's the matter with everybody? Somebody die?" Mr. Davidson called him over and talked. The boy nodded several times, and his eyes widened. Theodore looked at his work.

It was sad, he thought all through the day, looking at the others. This was a wonderful place to work; these were wonderful people. Now it would begin again—the search for a job, the worry, the borrowing, the doing without. Failure again. And how many more times would failure greet his efforts? Well, it was all right. One became accustomed to oneself. One learned to accept oneself. Sad, leaving these people though. They had liked him. He was sure of that.

At the end of the day, Theodore went to Mr. Davidson and said, "You know, of course, that I won't be coming back, Mr. Davidson."

The manager looked at him reflectively. "No," he said, "I didn't know that."

"Of course you did," Theodore said. He managed a wan smile. "I won't be back. But I've enjoyed working here, and you've been a fine boss." He hesitated. "You'll be getting money from me from time to time," Theodore said. "And of course you can keep this week's wages, and count it toward the debt. I'll pay it all off." He stopped again. "I feel very sad. I needed the money desperately. It was, literally, a matter of life or death. Goodbye, Mr. Davidson."

"Theodore—" Mr. Davidson began, and again Theodore saw tears gather in his eyes.

"No, don't say anything, Mr. Davidson." He smiled again. "Tell the others goodbye for me tomorrow. I'm too much of a coward to tell them that myself."

And he left the store.

2

"Of course, they knew I stole the cameras," Theodore said.

"How could they know?" Rodina asked.

"Whom else could they suspect? I had tried to borrow the money. I was the last employee hired, and they knew the theft was committed by someone who worked there. I was the only logical person to suspect."

228

"But they couldn't prove it."

"No," he said, tired of talking about it now. "They could not prove it. But even so, and even if they did not suspect me, I knew I was guilty. Everybody there, especially that little kid, the stockboy, would have been suspected while I was the guilty person. I had to let them know who did it. Now the rest of them can breathe."

That was right, she knew, the right thing to do. But she did not want him to do the right thing. This was something new, this was something different from what she had expected. Had he really changed then? If not, why not? What had gone wrong? What had she done wrong? *It could not be* that this evil she had had him do had gone for nothing. She could not accept that and continue to accept his love. What had gone wrong?

Rodina was anxious and nervous. Because he had stolen, and because she felt guilty that he had stolen, she was like this, he thought. He wanted to comfort her. He was sure she felt guilt and sadness even more acutely than he. He wanted to reassure her.

"Rodina," he said one night, "you feel bad because I stole the cameras, don't you?"

"Yes," she said, in a small voice.

"But you shouldn't, darling; I don't want you to. The reason was a good one—that's the important thing. You sold the cameras and got enough money to save your mother's life— that's all that matters. I tried to borrow the money. We had to have it, no matter how we got it. You mustn't feel bad. I'll get another job pretty soon, and everything will be fine again."

She held on to him. Everything was confused inside her. This was not what she had expected. This was not supposed to have happened. What was wrong, what had she done wrong? What was she to do now? What would become of them?

Every day he looked for a job, without success. "We're tightening up," the managers would tell him. "No room for unskilled labor." The war boom was over now. A lot of people were looking for jobs.

In the evenings after both had been out all day looking for jobs, they would meet in the room and look at each other and know that for both the search had been fruitless. Theodore worried about Sylvia, though he did not mention this to Rodina. He could not send her money; how was she paying the rent, eating, paying doctor's bills? He had written her a letter, explaining that he had lost his job. He was looking for another, he said, and would send her money as soon as he found one. So far, she had not answered.

"Ted," Rodina told him one day, "there's a way I can get money."

"How?"

"You know how."

He shook his head. "There'll be none of that, Rodina."

"Darling," she said impatiently, "darling, why not? We have to eat. We have to pay the rent. We have to pay mamma's doctor bills, even after the operation. Why shouldn't I get the money any way I can? You said yourself that it was justified."

"I'll find a job," he said, helplessly.

"But until then?"

"Until then we'll eat canned goods. And the doctor can look after your mother on credit."

"But what if the doctor won't do it?"

"He will, he will Rodina," Theodore said, feeling the pressure mount.

"And what if the canned goods run out?" she said, needing his assent, seeking desperately for some reassurance that all that had gone before had not been in vain.

"Then we'll starve, Rodina. There'll be no picking of pockets, and that's that." He felt that panic which comes when logic runs out and only emotion remains.

"Why not?" she almost cried. "Why not? You shouldn't object now, darling. Not *now*, Ted."

Immediately she knew, by the way he looked at her, by the way silence burst upon the room, that she had made a mistake. She was so confused. She did not want to offend him. She did not want to hurt him, or make him angry.

"Ted," she said, "don't look at me like that. Ted, I'm sorry." After a moment, he said, "It's all right, darling."

He had not changed. It had all been a mistake, and now he was unhappy and without a job and angry with her. She felt frightened, panicky. She was sad, and wanted to lay her head on his shoulder. But he was far away from her, miles away. What was there left for her to do?

3

Dear Theodore:

In view of the circumstances, the doctor told me it would be all right for me to get out of bed and take a job, at least until you find another . . . Theodore, I was so sorry to get your letter saying you were out of work. Of course I understand that it's not your fault. I've found a part-time job, as a waitress at the self-service restaurant on Sixteenth Street. They pay almost nothing, but then . . . I imagine you're finding it hard to make ends meet. If I can send you part of my pay to help you out of your difficulties, just let me know. I'd be happy to. Don't worry about me, dear. I'll make out all right . . .

How I misjudged Sylvia, Theodore thought wonderingly. Who would have suspected, a year ago, that she contained this

231

capacity for tenderness and mercy? Only Howard. Howard always admired her. He was closer to the truth than I.

Theodore said to Rodina, "She's a fine woman," feeling again that confusion of the emotions that accompanied his thinking of Sylvia.

"Why is she fine?" Rodina asked, a hint of scorn in her voice.

He looked at her, in something of surprise. "Why? Because she's so forgiving. Because she has so much courage."

"Does she really?"

He looked at her quizzically. "You can't be jealous, Rodina. That's not like you. Of course, she has courage. She doesn't feel sorry for herself, feel angry. Now, she's even offered to send me part of what little money she makes, if I want it."

"Why does she have to write to you? Why doesn't she leave you alone?"

"I *want* her to write. I want to know how she's getting along."

"I hate her!" Rodina said. "She's so sweet; such an angel."

It had to come out. Why pretend? She was tired of pretending.

"Why do you answer her letters?" she asked Theodore.

"What should I do?" he asked, his eyes softening. He knew that love of him motivated her outburst; so he could not be angry, he could understand and sympathize. "Should I ignore her? After all, she did nothing to me. It was I who did something to her. If she forgives me, why shouldn't I at least answer her letters? That's little enough."

"She did nothing to you? Then why did you leave her?" Rodina went on relentlessly.

For a second Theodore was silent; then he said, "For two reasons, Rodina. Because I couldn't bear to live with her any longer—which was my fault as well as hers; and because I loved you."

232

"Loved?"

"Still love, darling." He smiled. "Why are you so sensitive? I still love you, of course. With me it will always be the same."

"Then why can't you decide? If you love me, if you'll always love me, why can't you forget your wife completely. If you've chosen me, why not make a clean break. Forget her completely. Stop writing to her."

He shook his head. "It's not so easy, darling."

"No," she said, "nothing is easy. It takes strength. Don't you have the strength?"

His eyes held her own, firmly, gently. "I don't suppose I have," he said.

"Then you're not really a man," she said, "if you can't act like one." She looked down at her hands. "Why can't you act like a man, Ted?"

He stared: this time he felt real pain close like the cannibal leaf around his heart. He could only stare; feeling, thinking, that now perhaps the truth had come out. Had this been her thought all these weeks and months, even as he had suspected? Had this thought crossed her mind those months that he did not touch her in bed, that night at the poker game with Hucks, and those other days and nights, one after the other, during which he had shown his weakness and his fears? Had she thought this thing, hiding it even behind those expressive eyes, really despising him?

She saw the pain in his eyes. She was about to speak, to retract whatever she had said that had hurt him, when the knock came at the door.

"Rodina," Mrs. Davis, the landlady, called, "Rodina, yew in there?"

"Yes, ma'am," Rodina said.

"Come quick, Rodina. Yew're mother's real sick. I'm gonna call a doctor."

Rodina was gone from the room. Theodore stood near the bureau, tired, wondering whether he'd have better luck tomorrow when he went out to look for a job. The room seemed so empty when Rodina was not there. He looked at himself in the mirror: Theodore the Indecisive, he thought. He did not like being alone in the room. He decided he would go downstairs.

He sat down at a table in the tearoom and Glenn came over to take his order. Theodore leaned back, sipping the soft drink he had ordered, trying to straighten things out in his mind. She was an odd person, Rodina. A strange and wonderful person. Who knew what devious routes her thoughts took?

"Hello." It was Juarez. "Mind if I sit down?"

"No," Theodore said.

Juarez said, "I rarely see you down here alone."

Theodore smiled absently.

Juarez ordered, and the two men sat at the table in the tearoom which was filling up, saying nothing. It was pleasant here; people surrounded you in the room, but you felt secluded somehow, alone.

After awhile, Juarez said, "I'd like to ask you something."

"Go ahead."

"You don't like me very much, do you?"

Theodore shrugged. His thoughts were far away from this Mexican who sat opposite him. "I hadn't thought about it."

Juarez waited, and said, "But I like you. And that's strange, because there are not many people I like." He waited again, and when Theodore did not respond, he said, "It seems so strange to me . . . I've known Rodina a long time, and I can't quite understand why you should be attracted to her. But she's a fascinating creature."

234

Again, Theodore's only answer was silence, but this time a waiting silence. Juarez said, "It's too bad."

"Why is it too bad?"

Now Juarez shrugged. "I just think it is." He lifted the cup of tea, loving the hot, scented liquid that flowed into his mouth and warmed his throat and poured, comforting, into his stomach. "Where's Rodina, by the way?"

"With her mother. Mrs. Baleza just had a relapse, I think. She's very ill, Mrs. Davis says." Then Theodore said, "It's a pity. They'd thought the operation was successful, too."

Juarez said, "What operation?"

"She was operated on about a week or so ago. An emergency. They'd thought it would save her life."

Juarez looked at Theodore and lifted the cup again. He drank, then lowered his cup. He looked at Theodore.

"Mrs. Baleza had no operation," he said.

"Of course she did. Rodina told me. She had an emergency operation, nearly two weeks ago."

Juarez looked at him over the table. He said, "I visit Mrs. Baleza, everyday. If she'd had an operation, of course I'd know it." He watched Theodore's puzzled eyes. Then he repeated, "Mrs. Baleza had no operation."

CHAPTER TWENTY

THE NIGHT NOW GONE, the morning come, Rodina stood near the window in her mother's room and watched the blooming leaves of the tree sway gently in the wind. Behind her, the doctor administered an injection to Mrs. Baleza while Mrs. Davis and Juarez, as of half an hour ago, looked on. The mother talked senselessly. Rodina, near the window, heard the sounds of the room from a distance. She watched the just-budding leaves moved gently by the wind.

Everyone knew that this was the end. The doctor, before leaving, patted Rodina's shoulder. He said nothing. Mrs. Davis came over to her and said, "If there's anythin' I can do, Rodina, yew call me, hear?"

"Yes, ma'am," Rodina said.

Only Juarez remained, half asleep, seated on the stool near the bed. The room was quiet. The leaves sighed peacefully. Rest; sleep. The wind and the trees. At night there would be moonlight or light from the street lamp and the leaves would sigh and their shadows would sway and dance on the walls and she would be frightened. The leaves were so quiet, so alive. They were so shadowy, like ghosts, like black spirits dancing on the wall. All of her life she had lived with the leaves. They were peaceful in the daytime. At night they scared her.

They spoke to her, almost. Why did leaves dance so on her wall? Even when she was a little girl, a bad little girl, the leaves always danced on her wall when she had gone to bed. They told her she was bad; they did not talk out loud, but she could hear their words. They told her she was evil, as her mother had told her. They were evil, too, the shadows; they were like her. They were evil; like cats. Cats, with their shining eyes, with eyes that shone like her mother's, cats were soft and dark and silent and slinked around and meowed so strangely.

She lighted a cigarette. Even the smoke. Even the smoke rose without noise and curled, like a ghost. But smoke was white. Ghosts were white. But so were Angels. But Evil was dark. Smoke was not evil. She was dark. In the window she tried in vain to see her own reflection: but it was too dark, she was too black inside.

Dear, darling Theodore. She caught her breath in a sob, but her face did not change expression. Dear Theodore.

Now her mother would die. She would die, and then she and Theodore could go away. That was an evil thought. But it was true. Her mother would die and then they could go away. And they could be married and have children and a nice house and not be poor and sneaking around in a tenement and ashamed. Then Theodore could be happy. He could work at a job he liked and write and be happy. Then his face would light up like a little boy's, even if he was a grown-up man forty years old, and his eyes would light up and he would smile and she would feel so good. She liked to see him like that. Like he had been when first she met him. When they used to go to the diner and talk. And afterwards when he came to live with her, before he lost his job.

She sobbed again. Still, her face did not change its expression. That job, if only he had not lost it. Afterwards she had stolen and it had happened with Hucks. That sonofabitch Hucks. And then the letters and everything. Maybe if he

238

hadn't lost the job, everything would have been all right. Maybe. But Hucks was always bothering him, trying to show Ted how damn much of a man he was.

Now her mother was dying and they could go away and be happy. No, they could not go away and be happy. Theodore was too good. He was too good, and she was too evil, and later something else would happen. No matter where they went something else would happen. He was too good; he hadn't changed, not really. He had stolen but that was not enough. She couldn't change him. They would drift. She wouldn't let him go, wasn't good enough to let him go. They would drift and he would find out how she was soon enough, find out for sure. He wouldn't want to believe it the first time, but then he would find out again. It would be right there in front of his eyes, and he would have to believe it. He wouldn't leave right away, but the things would happen, little things, again and again and finally they would be apart, forever.

The cigarette burned her finger and she tossed it out of the window. She turned and looked at her mother. She was asleep. Her face was so strong; she was so right. People should listen to their mothers. "Honor thy father and thy mother." Her mother had read her that from the Bible. "Honor your mother and your father, who is dead," her mother used to say. "Honor and respect them. Admire them." The Bible was the word of God. Her mother was like God. She was always right. She was strict, but she was always right.

Her mother was asleep. Even asleep, she looked so stern. In that bed all the time. No fun in life. That was hard. And with a daughter who was not good. Rodina should have been good, but it was too late now.

Rodina kept staring at her mother. Mrs. Baleza did not move. Rodina went over to the bed and touched her mother. She was dead.

239

Juarez awoke. He saw Rodina standing over the bed. Rodina looked at him blankly.

"She's dead," Rodina said. "God has taken her away."

Juarez looked at her. "God?" he said. "Is God the one who willed your mother dead?"

2

Two days later Mrs. Baleza was buried. Everyone from the tenement house rode to the cemetery and heard the minister say the last words, and then saw the body lowered by the disinterested diggers into the grave. Rodina stared fascinated at the wooden casket.

Afterwards all of the people came over to her and said that they were sorry. Mrs. Houston cried. Rodina did not cry. She stared at the men as they began to shovel earth over the casket. Her eyes widened as the dirt went in, over, in, and the casket could be seen no more. She opened her mouth as though to scream but did not.

"We'd better go home," Theodore said tenderly.

They rode back to the house. Rodina went upstairs and into her mother's room. She stared at the bed, and at the furniture in the room. The bed was made up, and she rubbed her hand over the spread. She walked to the bureau and ran her hand wonderingly over the top. She looked out of the windows. She touched the glass of the panes; she was astonished, they were real. She looked at the walls with their dirty paper and at the floors with the worn linoleum. She stared, fascinated, in wonder. She walked through the door into the kitchen and looked at the stove, at the coffee percolator and at the pot in which, every night, she had made tea. She went back into the bedroom. On the little table she saw her mother's Bible. Her breath came hard; she opened the Bible and looked at the

240

print; she did not try to read it. She closed the Bible and went out of the room.

The light was on in Theodore's room; she could see it under the door. Maybe he wondered where she was. She went downstairs and past the tearoom and out of the door and down the street. She walked to Rittenhouse Square, sat on a bench, got up and walked some more. The trees were budding; it was now the beginning of spring. Spring. Baseball came with spring. When she was a little girl she used to play baseball with a rubber ball in the street, bouncing the rubber ball and hitting it and running to chalked bases. She was better than nearly all of the boys.

Boys used to act just like she was another boy. She could play anything as good as they could. They liked her, just as if she was a boy, but they didn't like the other girls. Rodina was different. Later they stopped liking her as though she were a boy, but she did not know it. She still played with them. Only, when they tagged her, it was always in certain places. She always laughed. It felt good, being tagged in those places. She wondered why it felt good. There was one special boy, Bobby, and he always tagged her in a special place. She liked to have him tag her. Later, when they used to sit on the steps at night, the whole gang of them, and play movies or tell stories, Bobby used to sit beside her and rub the place. She liked Bobby.

One night they went for a walk by themselves and ended up in the schoolyard, which was dark. Bobby said, Let's go in the schoolyard, Rodina; and she felt excited for some reason. They went in, and it was dark, and Bobby rubbed the place. It felt good. Then he did other things to her, and they did things together. She liked that. She asked Bobby to take her there again. Only, she did not understand why they had to be in the schoolyard, where it was dark. Something must be

241

wrong about it. Bobby told her nobody must know. She did not understand why, but if Bobby said so then it was necessary.

There was a man in the block who had always been nice to Rodina. He gave her pennies to buy candy and gave her cake or ice cream sometimes. He was nice to the boys, too; he bought baseball gloves for them, and gave them a football to play with. One day the man told her to come inside his house. When she was inside, he smiled and kissed her and touched her where Bobby and the other boys did. He breathed hard and made funny noises and lifted her dress and took off her panties and did the things Bobby had done to her. He hurt her and she cried. He told her that if she did not cry, and did not tell anyone, he would give her a whole cake. She promised, but she was frightened. Some of the boys peeped in through the window and saw her and the man, and they went and told her mother. Her mother gave Rodina hell; her mother said she was no good, that she was evil, and had always been evil, and would always be evil. Her mother never let her forget it.

3

Rodina walked slowly, circling the blocks, moving vaguely toward home. Why did she want to go home? What would she do when she got home? She asked the questions idly, absent-mindedly, seeking no answers, knowing peace in a sort of mental numbness. She passed a few people on the street; once, a fellow whistled at her. She did not hurry; she was not interested in anything that occurred around her; she was conscious only of walking, of feeling her legs move beneath her body and feeling her arms swing. Eventually she was passing the saloon on the corner of the street where the tenement was. She glanced inside, and one of the men called, "Come on in."

She went inside. The bartender, without asking, poured a scotch and water and shoved the glass in front of Rodina. She drank from it absently.

"How come you're wearin' black?" one of the men asked.

"My mother died," she said.

A couple of the men stared at her, embarrassed. Finally, the man who had questioned her said, tenderly, "I'm sorry, baby. I guess maybe I shouldna bothered you. You shouldn't be in here."

"It's all right," Rodina said.

She drank several of the whiskies and began to feel a bit high. The men talked loudly, laughed loudly, but not much was said to her. Nobody asked her to dance tonight. Funny; every other time they asked her to dance. Why not tonight?

"Why not tonight?" she asked.

"What, baby?"

"How come nobody asked me to dance?"

"Baby, you ain't supposed to dance when your mother's dead."

She stared at the man. Mother dead? Mother dead? Was her mother dead? Oh, yes, her mother was dead. She didn't have to die. Her daughter hadn't loved her enough and wasn't good enough and didn't make enough money to get the best kinds of doctors and give her the best kind of food and her daughter was selfish; she had wanted to go away, and her mother had died.

"I killed her," Rodina said.

The man stared at her. Awkwardly, he put an arm around her and she felt him pull her close to his chest. After a moment, the man said, "You better be gettin' home, baby." He said it tenderly.

She stood still, staring at herself in the mirror in back of the bar.

"Here, let me take you home," the man said.

She straightened up. "No, thanks," she said. "I can make it all right by myself."

She walked out. There was a tang to the air, although it was not cold. She did not glance into the tearoom when she entered the tenement. At the landing, she paused for a moment and looked unbelievingly at the door of her mother's room. She bit her lower lip and went into Theodore's room.

"Darling, I was worried," he said. He saw immediately that she had had a few drinks. Poor Rodina, he thought. "Lie down," he said, "let me undress you and put you to bed."

Obediently, without thinking, Rodina lay down. Theodore undressed her quickly, and slipped a nightgown over her head. He put the covers up to her chin.

"Now, go to sleep," he said softly.

She lay on her back with her eyes open, unfocused. Without looking at him, she asked, "What are you going to do?"

"I'm coming to bed in a moment," he said. "You go to sleep."

As though from a great distance, she asked, "Ted, would you kill someone for me?"

She was very much upset by her mother's death, Theodore thought. Who could have known the depth of feeling which evidently bound her to her mother, despite all the unpleasantness that had passed between them? One never knew. Outsiders did best not to try to gauge such things.

"Why don't you sleep, darling?" Theodore said.

"Would you? Would you kill for me, Ted?"

"I don't know," he said. "You can never tell about such things. It would depend on the circumstances, I imagine."

"You wouldn't do it," she said, distantly, without emotion. "I know you wouldn't."

He said, bowing now to her whim of the moment, "I don't suppose I'd ever think it necessary to kill anyone, regardless of the circumstances."

244

"You wouldn't do it," she said. "You don't love me enough."

"I love you very—"

"I'd kill for you," she said. "I'd kill your wife. I'd kill anybody."

Her eyes were turned toward the ceiling. She lay motionless, speaking slowly and distinctly, as though listening carefully to her own words. Theodore felt that she was not really talking to him. It had been a blow, her mother's death.

"There's a gun in the drawer," she said. "We made a wish on it. When we first came here. When you were happy. But now you wouldn't use it for me."

She closed her eyes now and turned toward the wall. "There's no hope," she said, "it's all over. All over."

He came over to her and pulled the covers up. "Go to sleep," he said. "We'll talk about it in the morning."

"It's all over," she said. "There's no hope."

CHAPTER TWENTY-ONE

Now BEGAN A SUCCESSION of, for Theodore, uneasy days, through which Rodina moved like one hypnotized. She ate little and spoke little, except in answer to statements or questions from him: her replies came from a great distance, in a monotone. He felt incapable of helping her.

He found a job—seasonal work, loading potatoes for a whiskey distillery—but even that seemed not to affect her. He would get up in the mornings to find her already dutifully awake, preparing breakfast for him. He would greet her with enthusiasm, hoping for a change, but her response remained pleasant, mechanical and subdued. Through the day there was the heavy labor and then would come evening again, the home-going and the exhaustion again, and the prompt dinner, the clean room, and the Rodina who was far away.

It was incredible, he thought, that her mother's death had affected her in this way. Gradually he realized that the mother's death alone was not responsible for this torpor through which she moved; that the death had merely been a culmination, a breaking point, perhaps, in some struggle which had, for a long time, been going on in her mind. He sought to bring her out of it; he felt lonely in this world outside her consciousness to which she had seemingly relegated him: but his efforts went for nought.

"Let's go to a movie," he would say. Or, "Let's go to a night club," or, "Let's eat out tonight. At Kugler's."

She would go, of course, but dutifully. And in these places her eyes would sometimes meet his, and she would smile, and look away. And afterward she would say she had enjoyed herself, and thank him for taking her. But all this was passive: all this was response to actions initiated by him. She had no suggestions to make; she seemed indeed to have no particular desires. She was lost, it appeared, in a world of her own construction, into which she would not permit him to pass.

He speculated: his mind tried to trace her own's devious paths to arrive at some conclusions as to what, precisely, disturbed her. In vain did he try to reach a conclusion as to the significance of what Rodina had said the evening of Mrs. Baleza's funeral. He imagined that somehow the question of whether or not he would kill for her was bound up with her mother's death—as though, now that her mother was dead, she was seeking someone else's death to complement the loss she felt. "There's no hope," she had said. No hope for what? For whom? He could not understand, and he feared to question her about it.

He was disturbed, too, from time to time, by his recollection of Juarez saying that her mother had not been operated upon. It was absurd, of course, there was no reason even to consider it seriously, and yet Juarez had seemed so positive, as though he knew things Theodore did not know. Theodore tried to push the questioning, the doubt, from his mind, but it remained, heavy, unabsorbed.

Eventually Rodina began to leave her private world, to smile and talk almost as before. Almost—for always there remained, as Theodore realized, the danger of swift and impervious withdrawal. But one day, when she was better than usual, Theodore put the question to her that was upon his mind.

248

"Darling," he said, "I want to ask you something about your mother's operation—she *did* have one, didn't she?"

Rodina's eyes were wide open and her lip trembled; she seemed to search his eyes before answering, "Yes."

He would perhaps have said nothing more, but she continued to stare, and in a moment asked, "Why did you ask me that?"

He shrugged; he felt embarrassed, and felt, too, that it might somehow be better not to pursue the question further. But he said, "Well, someone said that she had had no operation . . . implied that you had lied."

"Lie, Ted? Why would I lie?"

"I don't know," he said.

"Do you think I would lie?"

"No," he said. "No, darling. It's nothing, really. The person simply said that he often visited your mother, and that she had had no operation."

"I wouldn't lie to you, darling," she said. He could hear the hollowness, the distance, returning. "I love you. Why should I lie to you if I love you?"

"Of course you wouldn't. Let's forget it."

"I wouldn't lie to you," she said, still looking at him anxiously, but withdrawing still more into the shell where he could not reach her. "Why would I lie to you? I love you. Don't I love you? Don't you love me? Why would I lie, darling? Why? With you, I always tell the truth."

2

Sometimes, in the evenings after supper, Rodina would lie across the bed fully clothed and fall immediately into a deep, childlike sleep. On such evenings Theodore would turn out the lights and go outside for a short walk and then return to sit in the tearoom. At a table he would listen to the murmur of voices, nodding now and again to people who came in, chatting briefly with Glenn, the good-natured waiter.

Juarez would sometimes join him, talking in that voice always soft and mellow, prodding, deftly questioning, affirming—for reasons, Theodore thought, other than those of idle curiosity or casual neighborliness. In particular, Theodore noticed with resentment the way Juarez played subtly upon his dislike and fear of Hucks.

"Ah, there's Hucks," Juarez would say, "I'll call him over," and Theodore knew that Juarez knew that this would fill him with apprehension.

"You don't like Hucks very much, do you?" Juarez said, on another occasion.

Another time, with a mild smile, Juarez said, "You're Hucks' favorite dislike," and at another, "You won't like this, Theodore, but have you ever thought that Hucks is in love with Rodina?"

Theodore hesitated in the face of the unexpected question. Then he said, rather coldly, "No, I haven't."

"I'm sure of it," Juarez said. "Why has he taken such a violent dislike to you? Why does he keep beating his breast in front of you and Rodina, showing off his brawn, ridiculing you because you like poetry? Listen, have you noticed?—he never baits you when you're alone, or with me, like tonight. Only when you're with Rodina. Why is that?"

Theodore said, "I never thought about it."

"That night, at Christmas, during the poker game, and later, he kept referring to the fact that he and Rodina used to go together. He wants you to know that. Why?"

Theodore said softly, looking into Juarez' eyes, "As I recall it, you were the one, at the poker game, who first said that Hucks and Rodina went together."

250

"That night, perhaps, yes," Juarez said, a suggestion of amusement behind his eyes, "but what of the other nights? He always brings it up. Why is that?"

"I'm not interested in the least," Theodore said. But it was a thought.

"It interests me. The savage brute in love, not knowing how to express that love, except in obscenities and fist-swingings. Love in vain." He smiled. "Or is it love in vain?"

Theodore's eyes did not move from his.

"It's not in vain," Juarez said, with a smile. For all was in the open now. "I can see it clearly. When they first started going together, years ago, Hucks was still the tough man, the hard man, but you saw the hint of tenderness. He used to come in here whistling. Rodina would come downstairs and Hucks would say, 'Hi, baby.' They'd talk, and maybe go out. Hucks was happy; she was happy; neither had a care, a real care, in the world. Then something happened, I don't know what, and things changed. But is the emotion gone? I ask you. Is it gone?"

"Is it?" Theodore said, playing the game.

"I only know," Juarez said, "that now she says she hates him. I only know that she looks at him with hatred, that she shouts and swears at him, that she cannot tolerate him, that she hardly speaks to him. I know that when possible she avoids contact with him. Is that natural?"

"You're doing the talking," Theodore said.

"What reason has she to hate him? What has he done to her? Why shouldn't she treat him simply like she treats, say, me, or anyone else here? Why should she have to be so violent and outspoken in her dislike?" Theodore did not answer and Juarez said, "You know that hate is close to love. A cliché, but where men and women are concerned, it's generally true."

"What," Theodore said, "is your interest in this matter?"

251

Juarez smiled again. "Interest? I am simply interested in people. I am fascinated by emotions."

Theodore said, "You've been talking nonsense."

"Have I?" Juarez asked. "Have I, really?"

Juarez did not talk only to Theodore. He talked, too, with Rodina, who heard him from a distance, nodding now and again, not really knowing what he said. And he talked to Hucks, in the tearoom, when he saw him sitting alone.

"Mind if I sit down?" he would ask, and Hucks would usually shrug.

"You're gettin' mighty friendly lately," Hucks said.

"Why, that's because I admire you, Hucks."

Hucks looked at him suspiciously. "What the hell for?"

"Oh, because you're pure one-hundred-per cent American, good looking, and have plenty of girls."

Hucks looked at him and snorted and said nothing.

"How about a drink?" Juarez said.

"You treatin'?"

"As always."

Glenn brought the drinks. Juarez lifted his glass. He said, "I wanted to talk to you, Hucks."

"About what?"

"About Rodina."

Hucks said, "What about her?"

"Toast," Juarez said, and touched Hucks' glass. They drank the whiskey.

"What about Rodina?" Hucks asked.

The rush toward doom, Juarez thought, with the dark joy which came from awareness of intellectual superiority. Speed without direction; force without meaning.

Juarez said, "You're always riding me, Hucks. About Rodina. As though you think I'm interested in her. I'm not—but you are."

"What the hell you talkin' about?" Hucks said, moving toward anger.

"Relax," Juarez said softly. "She loves you, Hucks."

For a moment Hucks could think of no response; he seemed stunned into speechlessness. Then he said, "You're crazy as hell, Mex."

"It's true."

"You're crazy as hell!" But he watched Juarez' eyes.

Juarez leaned forward. "Listen," he said, "do you think she could love that weakling she sleeps with? Do you think a woman like Rodina can be satisfied with a puny crybaby who spends all his time mooning about poetry and art? Do you think she really wants some bookish sissy who probably can't do any more than tickle her in bed?

"Not on your life, Hucks. Do you notice they don't go for walks anymore? Do you notice they don't go holding hands like they did at first? Can't you see that both of them are unhappy? Can't you see it in their eyes? She doesn't love him. She despises him. Listen, you know she likes to talk to me, to tell me things. She told me she doesn't love him. She thought she did at first, but now she knows she doesn't. But what can she do? He hangs around. She got herself into something she can't get out of. She loves you Hucks; she can't help herself. She even told me she's been to bed with you since he came here to live, and how much she enjoyed it."

Hucks stared at him. "You're crazy," he said, but he said it weakly.

"You know I'm telling the truth. Why should I lie? What are you going to do about it?"

"What are you gettin' out of this?"

"Nothing. What could I possibly gain?"

"I dunno. I figure you got somethin' against him. I think you're full of bull. Anyway, it ever occur to you that maybe I ain't a damn bit interested in Rodina? It ever occur to you that maybe I got enough girls of my own, without her? You ever think of that?"

"Certainly," Juarez said, leaning back. "I know you have a lot of girls. But I think you love Rodina. I think maybe you still remember the old days, the way you two used to be together."

"Well, maybe you're wrong," Hucks said. He stood up. "I never did like a goddamn stool pigeon. Besides, I don't give a damn what the hell that goddamn bitch thinks of me. If she got in something she don't like, let her get the hell out by herself."

"She loves you," Juarez said, leaning back in the chair, watching his eyes closely.

"Go to hell!" Hucks said. "And keep your goddamn nose out of people's business!"

He turned and walked off. Juarez watched him disappear into the hall.

CHAPTER TWENTY-TWO

HUCKS ONCE WANTED to be a lawyer. This had not always or consistently been true: at varying stages of his life he had wanted to be a doctor, an engineer, a prize fighter. But primarily he had wanted to be a lawyer.

When he was in his teens, Hucks used to talk to his two brothers—one older, one younger than he—about Law, and how one day he was going to be as famous as Old John Johnson, whose magnificent house still stood as his monument on South Broad Street.

"I ever tell you about Old Johnson?" he used to ask his brothers. "He was the greatest goddamned constitutional lawyer this town ever saw; the best this country ever saw. And he never went to any damned law school, either. Made it on his own. A damned self-made man. I ever tell you about Old Johnson and J. P. Morgan?"

He had told them many times. But his brothers were good-natured, and let him go ahead and repeat his story. "Old J. P. and some of his financial buddies were settin' up the biggest corporation in the world, you know—the United States Steel Corporation. Everybody was real excited about it, and everybody in the country was trying to sop up a little bit of the gravy. This here corporation was gonna raise sand, and everybody wanted to be in on the ground floor.

"Well, sir, Old J. P. needed himself a damned good lawyer to set this corporation goin' right, and so naturally him and

255

his buddies picked out Old John Johnson. In the middle of a board meetin', J. P. got on the phone and called Old Johnson —right there at 510 South Broad—and asked if he could come over to New York to take over the law part of the shindig.

"Now, Old J. P. was just about the most powerful man in this country, not barrin' the President, and people usually jumped whenever he talked. But did Old Johnson? Not on your goddamned life! What does Johnson do? He says in that slow, kinda drawlin', voice of his'n, 'Gentlemen, my office is at 510 South Broad Street, in Philadelphia. If you care to discuss this matter with me, that's where I do business.' And he hung up!

"Now, does Old J. P. get mad? Does he call his damn Philadelphia lackeys and tell 'em to put Old Johnson on their black list? Does he storm and rant and rave and say, 'Listen, I'm J. P. Morgan, goddammit!'? Hell, no he don't! Him and his whole board of directors goes right out and piles into their private train and pulls up in Philadelphia and goes to Old Johnson's office, where they then proceed to do business!"

He loved that story. He was fascinated by the legendary character of Old Johnson, the man who had defied the greatest financial tycoon of his era and seen the giant come bowing to his door. Hucks used to walk past the Johnson House where the art collection used to be; during the war, the house was used for a U.S.O. Center. He walked inside several times; he could see and hear Old Johnson at his work.

"Gentlemen," he heard Old Johnson say, "the attorney for the plaintiff has made a moving summary. But he happens to have made five basic mistakes of interpretation, which I shall now proceed to enumerate . . ." Hucks could see the awe-stricken judge and the awe-stricken jurors and the awe-stricken attorney for the plaintiff stare goggle-eyed at Old Johnson as he talked. After he delivered his summary, Old

256

Johnson would pack his briefcase and walk out of the court-room. He never waited to hear the verdict; he always knew damned well what the verdict would be!

Hucks went to a junior high school in South Philadelphia. Everyday he saw the gang of boys who stood outside with their hands in their hip pockets and their hats cocked back on their heads, waiting for certain boys to come out so that they could collect their "protection money." They never bothered Hucks; they knew his brothers, and besides, they knew Hucks didn't have any money for them to collect. They waited for the boys who bought a lot of food at the lunch counter; they were the boys who had money, because the rest of the pupils usually brought a sandwich or two from home and bought only a bottle of milk or soda at the counter.

A boy named Ed was boss of the gang. Ed had gotten the idea of collecting "protection money" from a gangster movie. All of the boys acted like they were playing roles in a movie. They tried to look like Jimmy Cagney or George Raft or Paul Muni. Ed would point out the boys who had to pay the pro-tection, and a couple of his "boys" would go over and collar the guy.

"Got your protection?" the boys would ask.

Usually, the boy had it. Usually, too, he knew enough to keep the quarter he was supposed to pay them in a separate pocket. When he paid, the boys let him off, reminding him that tomorrow was another day. Sometimes, a boy would make the mistake of taking out a whole handful of change and fishing around for the quarter. That was funny; the boys would laugh, and take the whole handful of change. Some-times, some dope would say he didn't have his protection. That was funny, too. The boys would take him around the corner and give him a working over: a few punches in the

257

face and body; maybe a few kicks. If the boy didn't fall, he was reasonably well off. If he fell, shame on him! The boys would pound the heels of their shoes into his face; would kick the toes of their shoes into his groin. This was called "stomping."

Hucks didn't like the gang idea very much, and he didn't pay too much attention to the gangs until he fell for a girl in his class named Reety. She had short hair and a pug nose and nice legs. "P.L." the fellows all called her, meaning Pretty Legs. Reety was the girl friend of one of the members of a gang from the other side of Washington Avenue, but that didn't make any difference to Hucks. He liked her, and to hell with her damned other boy friend. He asked her to go out with him to movies and dances, and she said that if he was game she was too.

"You know what?" he told her once, "I'm gonna be a great lawyer one of these days, Reety."

"You square, you!" she said contemptuously, and from then on Hucks was careful not to go around telling people what he wanted to be. Only squares did that.

One night he took Reety to a dance at the Strand and everything seemed great. Ed, the leader of the gang, saw him and came over and said, "How'd you like a little guzzle?" He handed Hucks the bottle and Hucks lifted it and drank until Ed said, "Goddamn, man, I said a *little* guzzle." He handed the bottle back and Ed looked at it and shook his head. Hucks decided that Ed was an all right guy.

About twelve o'clock a bunch of boys walked in together, and Hucks could see they were members of the gang from the other side of Washington Avenue. A fight started, naturally, and Reety's boy friend saw her with Hucks. The boy friend and some of his buddies beat the hell out of Hucks.

The next day, back at the school, Ed came over to Hucks

and said, "You got the hell beat out of you by them damn Tigers. Some of the boys and me are gonna cruise into their territory tonight and stomp some of their guys. You with us?"

"Goddamn right!" Hucks said.

They rode up past Washington Avenue crowded in two big black stolen cars, like the movie mobsters used. After a while, they saw one of the Tigers. They jumped out of the car and grabbed him and beat the hell out of him and then stomped him good. They left him lying on the pavement and cruised around some more. They got quite a few of the Tigers that night.

"You ought to join the gang," Ed said to Hucks. "You're an okay guy. But you gotta have a gang to back you up against these sonofabitches around here. Else, everybody messes with you."

It seemed he had a point. Hucks said, "Okay."

"Well, you gotta be initiated. See me outside of school to-morrow."

Hucks met Ed and some of the boys outside next day. They were collecting their usual protection money. Ed threw his arm around Hucks and said, "Okay, wait a little while." Eventually, a boy wearing glasses and carrying a lot of books and eating a popsicle came out of the school building.

"See that guy?" Ed said.

"Yeah."

"Go take the popsicle away from him."

Hucks swallowed hard. Goddamn! Well, what the hell, if he didn't take it, somebody else would. You had to be rough to get along in this goddamned world.

"Hey, you!" Hucks called. The boy turned around. "C'mere," Hucks said, trying to get his voice to sound like Ed's.

The boy looked at him in fright, and then started to run. Hucks said, "Goddamnit, comere," and set out in chase of him.

259

When he caught up with the boy he grabbed his collar. "Hand over the popsicle," he commanded. The boy stared at him, terrified. "Hand it over!" The boy handed him the popsicle.

"Good work," Ed said, coming up behind him. "Sonofabitch had to run, didn't he? Bastard! Sock 'im one, Hucks."

Hucks gulped again. The kid looked so goddamn scared!

"Sock 'im, Hucks," Ed said.

Hucks hauled off and hit the guy. The boy whimpered and grabbed his face.

"Now, get the hell outa here!" Ed told the boy. The boy ran off.

Ed turned to Hucks and grinned. He put his arm around Hucks' shoulder. "Good work," he said. "You'll make out all right. Kinda hard to hit that kid like that, wasn't it? Kinda hard at first. Take a little time, though. You'll be all right."

When he was in the eleventh grade, Hucks' parents pulled him out of school and sent him to work; but he went to night school anyway, and managed to get his diploma. Right after graduation, he left home, as his older brother had done. He tried to get a scholarship to college through his ward leader, but the man laughed at him because he didn't belong to the right party. The ward leader for the other party said he'd see what he could do, but he must not have been able to see very far because he never had any success in getting the scholarship.

Hucks took himself a room in a tenement house in a different section of South Philly, and right away met a cute little bitch named Rodina Baleza. She was a pickpocket, a wild tramp, and she didn't have much sense, but she sure was a damn good listener. For a long time he hadn't said anything to anybody about what he wanted to do with his future, and so forth, but after a few bull sessions with Rodina he opened

260

up a bit and was so pleased by her response that he ended by telling her practically everything about himself.

For a while he figured he'd be decent and not try to make her, but then he said what the hell, a chick was a chick and they all had the same thing to offer. He propositioned her, and wham! she was agreeable. Just like that! He had treated her nice, and she liked the way he talked, and that was all there was to it. She didn't seem to think that there was a damn thing wrong with it. Well, what the hell! If she didn't, he sure wasn't going to try to change her mind.

"You're nice," she told him.

After a while, he figured maybe he liked her and so he said, "How about being my girl, Rodina?" She said okay, and everything was jake. They went out together and had a good time, and every so often he propositioned her again and she was willing. She didn't even need to think twice about it!

Then he was drafted. He was trained at Fort Meade, sent from there to Camp Kilmer up in New Jersey where he stewed around a while, and then was sent overseas to England where he was when the war ended. For occupation duty he was sent to Berlin, Germany, and seized the first opportunity to go to the University of Berlin to study law, under the Army's educational program.

He worked hard as hell. He sat up there in class with his eyes squinched and his brain churning, trying to catch on to everything these damned conceited teachers were talking about. The attitude of the teachers made him mad: they acted like they were superior to anybody who didn't happen to talk with a Harvard accent. Hucks wanted to tell them to go to hell, but he didn't. He stayed up late doing his homework; he practically lived in the library. He didn't fool around with the women. The boys used to ride him: "All these frauleins floating around, and you're layin' over books! Jesus, that's torture!"

261

To hell with them. He'd be making fifteen thousand a year and giving orders to phony politicians when these guys were digging ditches for a living.

The work came hard to Hucks, but what he didn't have in brilliance he made up in doggedness. He worked half the night every night, and was pretty tired during most of his classes. And some of the questions or points that were easily figured out by the smarter students slipped by him. Hucks asked some questions which the other students and the teachers thought pretty dumb. Whenever he asked a question the other guys would snigger, and the teacher would look at him with patient condescension. Then, as though talking to a kid ten years old, the teacher would give him a long and unnecessarily elucidated answer while the rest of the class kept on laughing. After a time, Hucks didn't ask any more questions.

At the end of the first report period, Hucks had failed in two subjects. He was crushed.

"You'll have to withdraw," his commander told him.

The boys in the barracks rode him to death. All that goddamned time wasted, they said. All that time spent poring over books, when he could have been out having himself a ball with the frauleins, and now he'd flunked. Hucks thought: What the hell! The riding irritated the hell out of him. Why didn't these bastards go soak their heads!

Hucks took up boxing and nearly killed the first poor guy who faced him. He was plenty tough, that was one thing! He beat every contender in the battalion, and the battalion commander called on him.

"How'd you like to represent us for the Berlin District championship?"

"I'd like it, sir," Hucks said.

The commander smiled. "Used to be a fighter myself in the old days," he said. "Army's gettin' to be a bunch of sissies now,

262

all these damn recruits comin' in. Saw you fight. Good boy. Glad to see a *man* left in the battalion."

That pleased the hell out of Hucks. The *commander!* He fought in the Berlin District matches and brought home the bacon. He was a battalion hero.

He traveled all over the American Zone of Germany boxing. Occasionally he would run across some GI students, and he'd sort of laugh to himself. "Saps," he'd mutter. There wasn't any win in school. But there damn sure was a win in boxing. He was a damned hero.

When he got out of the Army, Hucks went to New York and figured he'd get into the fight game. He fooled around a bit, got hold of a manager, and then got into a few matches. He pulled out of that racket soon enough, though, after he found out that managers and sundry parasites got most of the dough, and decided that the promoting outfits were nothing but a bunch of crooks gettin' rich off guys like him. He worked at a couple of odd jobs in New York, found he couldn't make ends meet, wasn't satisfied with the postwar country in general, and finally made his way back to Philly where he pulled into the same old tenement. He hated the goddamn place: it didn't look like he was making any progress. But what the hell! He fished around, looking for a meal ticket, and finally wound up with a job as truck driver.

"Hucks!" Rodina said excitedly when she saw him for the first time after he came back. "Say, how are you?"

"Okay, baby," he said.

"Let's see if you've changed. Hmmm. No, you look about the same."

"Only bigger," Hucks said.

She nodded. "Yes, the Army treated you right. Why did you stop writing?"

He shrugged. "That's the way it is with soldiers, you know."

She pursed her lips. Later she asked him, "How did you make out in school over there?"

"Great," he said. "Only, I'm not sure I want to be a lawyer anymore. I got good marks, and all, but I'm not sure I haven't changed my mind about being a lawyer. Might like to do something else."

"That would be a shame," she said wistfully.

"Got to get readjusted, you know," he said.

"And when will you be readjusted?"

"Hell, baby, how do I know?" He was irritated.

He thought maybe she was hurt by his tone. Well, what the hell! People ought to understand not to ask vets a lot of damn questions. Nobody felt like being shoved into anything.

"Things still the way they used to be, baby?" he asked her.

"Like what?"

"Still feel the right way about me? I'd like to see you tonight, if you do. Like you to drop into my apartment."

"Well, seems you'd ask me to go out or maybe just go for a walk or something."

"Hell, you didn't used to stand on all this formality. You wasn't always so squeamish."

"I'm not squeamish," she said. "I just think that ought not to be the first thing on your mind."

"Damn, baby, I'm a vet. We ain't used to goin' through a lot of jive first. You used to be all right. You changed?"

"No," she said. "But I think you have."

"Sure," he said. "I told you the Army changes a man."

"I don't think I like the change."

He shrugged. "Okay, baby. I ain't got time to do a lot of pleasin'. Plenty of other fish in the sea." He figured that was the attitude to adopt. Girls didn't like no weak-livered men.

"Yeah?" She looked at him a long time. "Well," she said, "I

264

guess maybe you'd just better go looking for one of those other fish, Hucks."

"Okay, baby," he said.

Goddamn chick! Getting all dignified on him! Well, she'd come off it, eventually. Chicks liked to be treated rough. They liked a fellow to be cool and act like he didn't give a damn about them. She'd come around. Before long she'd be sweet talking him to death. He could wait.

And now, in the present, he was still waiting.

2

Tonight Hucks was out on a double date arranged by one of the cute girls he had met at a store where he delivered soda. Her name was Barbara; she was fluffy-haired, a bit loud, and a lot of fun. With them were Peggy, Barbara's roommate and a student of Temple University, and her boy friend Bob, a student of the University of Pennsylvania. They sat in Hamburger Haven, just back of the Locust Theater, eating hamburgers and talking about the concert they had just left. Everybody was enthusiastic.

"Kostelanetz is great," Peggy said. She had bright eyes and looked like a college student.

"The crowd was nice," Barbara said. Barbara was pleased that she had been among a crowd of middle-class people who wore nice clothes and had nice manners. She envied Peggy a little, because Peggy was a student; but she liked Peggy very much.

"It's nice here," Peggy said. "Bob and I nearly always come here after going to a show in town. They certainly serve big hamburgers! And these onions! Did you ever see anything like them?"

"When summer comes, we can all go to the Dell," Bob said.

"They have nice open-air concerts, and afterward we can go for a walk in the park." Bob was tall and wiry; he had sharp features and intelligent eyes.

Hucks drank it all in. He felt good because he had been to a concert with two college kids. He liked this place where they were eating now: it was clean, and the people who came in wore nice clothes. He, himself, was dressed in a blue suit with a starched shirt and bright tie; he knew he looked good, as good as anybody else here. He had never been out with students before. People who came in and looked at them would think all of them were college students.

"Did you like it, Hucks?" Peggy asked.

"Me? Sure," Hucks said. One thing sort of bothered him, though; he didn't talk as nice as these college kids. He said, "It was a nice concert, except the music wasn't the kind I really like best, you know. I mean, it was nice, but I prefer the other stuff."

"Like what, Hucks?" Bob asked.

Well, now, goddamn! Hucks was a little annoyed by the question. Seemed like the guy was trying to see what he knew, or something. He said, "Well, I like that classical music better than this stuff we heard there at the concert. I mean, what we heard was nice, but I like the classical music better."

"Really?" Bob was interested. He said, "Well, you have to come over and listen to my collection sometime. I live right near the Penn campus. I've got quite a collection—operas, symphonies, chamber music. I've got a lot of Mozart; he's my favorite. Who do you like?"

"I like Mozart, too," Hucks said.

"He's the best there is," Bob said emphatically. "All other composers tire you after awhile, but not Mozart. He's always good. I have his Quintet in G, the Violin Concerto in A Major, and a whole slew of his symphonies."

266

"Gee, I didn't know you liked symphonies, Hucks," Barbara said. She looked at him with something like awe. There were evidently wide unexplored areas of her new beau about which she knew nothing.

"Sure," Hucks said. "I like all kinds of classical music, especially symphonies. Especially by Mozart. I guess I'm pretty much of an authority on Mozart."

"Yes?" Bob laughed. "Then maybe you can make me feel good about something. Some of my buddies and I argue over which of his symphonies is the best. I say the Jupiter. He says the G Minor. Some people pick the Thirty-Ninth. What do you say?"

"Hell, I like them all," Hucks said, wishing the conversation would change. "I wouldn't like to pick out any special one."

"You've heard them all?" Bob exclaimed incredulously.

"Oh, sure," Hucks said, grinning.

"Jehosephat!" Bob exclaimed. "I didn't think hardly anybody had heard *all* of them." Bob looked at Hucks with suspicion. "Say," he said, "you wouldn't be pulling my leg, would you?"

"Whadaya mean?"

"Well, I was just thinking. About hearing *all* of Mozart's symphonies. It just seemed—well, I never knew anybody who'd heard all of them, that's all."

"Well, that don't mean anything. Sure, I heard em all. Don't you believe me, or something?"

"Oh, sure, if you say so," Bob said.

Barbara looked at Hucks out of the side of her eyes and laughed. "I sorta think maybe Hucks is handing us the business," she said.

"Whadaya mean?" Hucks demanded, feeling the rising blind anger.

"You know what I mean," she said, still laughing. "I don't even think you can spell his name, Hucks."

"The hell I can't."

"Spell it then."

He burst out, "You act like I'm on trial, or something. Hell no, I won't spell it."

Peggy sat across the table, next to Bob, looking at Hucks. She said, "Well, it's not important, anyway. Let's skip it!"

"Righto," Bob said.

"What's the use a skippin' it?" Hucks asked. "Hell, don't nobody need to call me a liar. Why do I have to lie about a little thing like that? Hell, why should I try to impress you people?"

"Sure," Peggy said, watching him.

"Sure, you're giving us the business, Hucks," Barbara laughed. "Good old Hucks. I thought there was something suspicious when you started talking. Giving us the business. And us your friends, too! Mozart!"

"Kiss my ass!"

Barbara stared at him. "Well," she said, "you certainly don't have to use that kind of gutter language around decent people."

"I suppose that means I'm from the gutter!" he said. Already he felt that this fine world had exploded; the good feeling of a few minutes before was gone.

"You must be from the gutter. I thought you could at least *act* like a gentleman. If you can't, we don't have to go out together anymore."

"That suits me fine," he said, burning. "That suits me fine."

"Please, please," Peggy said. "Now, let's relax, huh? Gee! And all this started with a simple statement that we enjoyed the concert tonight. Let's forget it and stop by a nightclub or something."

268

"He makes me sick!" Barbara said sullenly. "Using language like that. Like a regular alley cat."

"Go to hell!" Hucks said. He stood up. Well, goddamn! He sure did look silly, didn't he! Goddamn! "I'm gettin' out of here," he said.

"We're all going, Hucks," Peggy said softly.

"I don't need his company," Barbara said.

"Good night!" Hucks said, and left them there.

Hucks turned onto the street. One of the kids, playing tag, ran into him, and Hucks pushed the boy. "Watch out, god-damnit!" he said. Goddamn kids! As he approached the tene-ment he heard the buzz of voices from the tearoom, and in a moment heard Mrs. Houston laugh loudly. Damn loud-mouthed woman, he thought. He went inside and walked past the tearoom, not even bothering to look inside. He happened to glance up and saw Rodina at the top of the stairs.

"Well, well, the uppity chick. How you doin' babe?"

She paused on the landing, looking at him, saying nothing. From where he stood he saw the lovely roundness of her legs, and felt a flow of syrupy heat through his lungs and stomach.

"Well, come on down, baby. Let old Hucks get a close look at you."

She did not move; she made no response whatsoever. She merely looked at him blankly, her face expressing no emotion and little consciousness of his presence. He looked at her, at her legs, at her face. Damned bitch. But a beautiful bitch. A beautiful bitch and he remembered holding her and having her, and the way they felt together, and now this other, this goddamned sissy, and the heat within him increased. For some reason he felt close to tears.

He started up the stairs. Rodina did not move. What stirred it now, this increased warmth, this great excitement, inside of him? What was it about her very bitchery, her very savagery, her very unconcern with morals or the social law, which made him weak and angry and brutal, filled with hatred and lust together?

He felt now the surge of emotion as he had never before felt it—the rising, billowing, expanding inner pressure which obstructed his breathing, quickened his heartbeat, and brought him—strangely—close to tears. He did not understand it, he did not *think* it, he merely *felt* an overwhelming desire in this instant to fall at her feet as she stood there, hold her leg to his face, kiss it, weep, and beg for her smile.

Now he had reached her; she stared at him expressionlessly, "Rodina!" he said hoarsely, brokenly, surprisingly choked with emotion. "Rodina!"

He seized her and kissed her. She struggled. As though now the spell were broken, Rodina strove to push him from her—but he held tight, impelled by the emotion he felt.

The door to Theodore's room opened. Over Hucks's shoulder she saw Theodore.

"Ted!" she called, "Ted!"

At the instant he was at her side, striking at Hucks with a lamp which had sprung miraculously into his hand. Hucks felt the crushing blow against his head and sagged, dazed, against the wall.

"Kill him, Ted!" Rodina sobbed. "Kill him, Ted! Kill him!"

The world spinning, Hucks did not know what to expect next. He did not move; he waited for the second blow.

"Kill him! Kill him!"

What struck him, dazed as he was, was the urgency and ferocity in Rodina's voice. What struck him—even now—was that he knew this was no mere figure of speech; by her tone, Hucks knew that *she wanted him dead.*

"Kill him, Ted! Ted, Ted, kill him!"

Hucks knew now that no other blows would fall. Gradually the world righted itself. He could see Theodore now, near the bannister, the lamp in his hand, looking at him. Hucks stood still, looking at him. He did not look at Rodina.

How long they stood there, Hucks looking at Theodore, Theodore looking at him, Rodina shouting, sobbing, for his life, Hucks did not know. But finally he found the will to move; finally, he pushed himself from the wall. Without a word to either of them, he walked slowly down the stairs.

CHAPTER TWENTY-THREE

RODINA LAY BETWEEN sleep and wakefulness.

Theodore would not kill for her.

He was too good (she saw him white, glowing, with wings). Juarez was wrong. She could not change; neither could Theodore change. Even if he wanted to. He was what he was. He had always been good. He could not kill for her. Therefore, he could not be what she was.

It had all been a dream that they would marry and find happiness. It was a dream, perhaps, that they had ever been happy. No, that was no dream; they had been happy at first. But they were what they were. Not for long could they be happy. He was good; she was evil. He could steal, if he had to. But he could not kill. Not even Hucks. But she could do anything. She had done everything. They could not be the same. They could not break through the wall.

Her mother had said: "You're born evil, or you're born good. Look at Judas." That was it. She had listened to Juarez, who was smart, but who did not know about being born good or being born evil. And not being able to change, no matter how hard you tried, no matter what you did. She had forgotten that. She should not have forgotten it. Her mother had told her that and she should not have forgotten anything her mother said.

He would leave her. He would see the wall, and then he would leave. Well, good. She did not care. She did not care anymore. She was tired. It was no use caring. He would leave, and it would be all right. Then maybe he would find out how to be happy. He only needed to find out that he was good, and could not love anyone who was not good. He would find out. Then he would leave. But it was all right. She did not care.

2

Dear Theodore, his wife wrote, *I'm happy that you found another job. I was fired from mine, as you know, because I was too frequently absent because of illness. I'm writing from bed: the doctor has given me strict orders not to get up, so I'll have to wait until he comes again before he can mail this for me. My biggest problem is that of nourishment: I've had absolutely no appetite lately. I've lost quite a bit of weight; you should see how thin I am . . .*

"Poor Sylvia," Theodore said. "Confined to bed."

"You should visit her," Rodina said.

"Yes," Theodore said, surprised that Rodina should suggest it.

She was a good woman, the wife, Rodina thought. She would like to meet the wife some day. Perhaps she would. Theodore would go back to her, but she, Rodina, would hold no grudge, and she'd visit them if Theodore thought it was all right. Then she'd meet the wife.

After he left she did not know what she would do. Get a job, of course. If she could. Move some place else, though; she didn't want to stay here. Move to New York maybe, or Chicago. But why think about it? She could think about that later. That was gray. She did not want to think of gray things.

Maybe she would get sick and die. Die. That would be it. Die. Then it would be all over. Soft sleep. After he was gone.

"Kill him!" Rodina had screamed. "Kill him! Kill him!" she had sobbed. And she had seemed desperately and unmistakably in earnest, Theodore thought.

Why did she hate Hucks so? Juarez had asked that question. Well, why? Theodore wondered. He was rude, uncouth, yes: but Rodina was used to men like that, she had even been his girl friend in the past. He made advances, yes: but so did many men, and Rodina was not one who would hate them for it! Why did she hate Hucks?

"Why do you hate Hucks so much?" he asked her.

She stared at him; and he noticed that her eyes filled with fear. He waited for her answer, but she merely stared at him, searching his eyes.

"He used to be your boy friend, didn't he?"

She nodded. Her lips were parted; Theodore thought that her breathing was irregular; all the time she was trying to see what was in his eyes.

"Did you love him, then?"

She looked at him blankly. She said nothing.

"Rodina."

"Yes, darling?"

"Did you love him?"

"No," she said.

He paused. Was this a cross-examination? But he was impelled onward, "Then why did you go with him?"

For a long while she said nothing. Then she said, "He was nice. He used to be nice. I wanted a boy friend; everybody had a boy friend. He was nice, and I went with him."

Yes. That was understandable; that made sense, though he was aggrieved, against his will, that she had even *liked* him at one time, kissed him no doubt, given him her body. He did not like this, but it was not the important thing: for this did not explain the hatred she now felt for him. It did not explain the look that had come over her face when first he mentioned Hucks. Why should the mere mention of his name produce *any* change in her face?

"But now you hate him."

"Yes!" she said savagely. "Now I hate him."

"Why, Rodina?"

Again the fear, the panic, the searching returned to her eyes. She seemed to be searching for his motive for these questions.

"Because he's a bully," Rodina said. "Because he's dirty and sneaky and picks on people, picks on you."

Picks on! This struck to Theodore's quick. Picks on. The neighborhood ruffian *picks on* the sweet little boy. The school nuisance *picks on* the little girl with long braids. One *picked on* people who would not fight back . . . were afraid to fight back!

"I see," Theodore said. "And that's the only reason?"

The panic filled her eyes. "What other reason could there be?" she asked, visibly terrified.

"No other reason," Theodore said. "I was just curious."

"Why were you curious?"

"Because of what happened in the hall the other day. It was obvious you hated him. You begged me to kill him."

"Oh," she said. Now she looked away. "Oh. Oh, then. I . . . was angry. He made me sick." Then she added, "I knew you wouldn't really kill him."

He was not satisfied.

Could it be, he wondered miserably, that Rodina *was* strongly attracted to Hucks? Not consciously, of course, but beneath the consciousness, against her will? For she was masochistic—everything pointed to that. And Hucks, most certainly, was a sadist. He did not want to consider the possibility, but he could not control his mind.

276

This child of twenty. He had said to her, "Rodina, let me help you." How presumptuous he had been, in his intellectual vanity, to think himself a match for the devils which had full play inside of her! Such as he could not aid her, could not know her, unless he knew her world. And this world he had never learned to know.

A man who was less than a man, and a woman who was more than a woman, he reflected wearily. There was no heart more innocent of evil, truly, than Rodina's.

Perhaps she had loved Hucks. Perhaps she still did. Perhaps his very coarseness, his very brutality, his very frustrations and hatreds, were the things which gripped her heart. Perhaps. And perhaps not (the weary hope, the tired prayer). Perhaps she loved him, Theodore. How could he know?

"Think there'll be a war?" Glenn asked, putting down the cup of tea in front of him.

"I don't know," Theodore said.

"Papers sure talk like it. Every day, the same old bull. I fought in the last one, and I sure know what it's like. This one'd be even worse. Goddamnit, the papers sure sound like one's on the stew. Every damn day."

"Yes," Theodore said. Then he said, "I hadn't thought too much about it."

"*Got* to think!" Glenn said. "That's the trouble. People won't think. *Got* to think. Can't shut yourself up in no iron castle no more, thinking you can be happy by yourself and not be bothered by what happens to other people. Not anymore. It all catches up. When the wagon comes, *everybody* goes."

"Yes," Theodore said. Professor Glenn. He smiled.

He finished the tea and sat relaxing in the tearoom. It was early evening. Upstairs, Rodina was preparing dinner. Days were longer now, and through the window of the tearoom Theodore could see the kids in patched clothing on the street.

Wonderful kids, he thought. The noise, the fights, the games, the Saturday movies. They did not know yet. They did not know. They were the ones who changed the world, and for whom the world was changed.

You old philosopher, he thought. And he felt old; old and inadequate and, perhaps, a little foolish. Forty years old.

He got up, stretched, left the money on the table, and went upstairs. The door to the room formerly occupied by Mrs. Baleza was open, and inside he saw Mrs. Davis.

"Hello," he said.

She turned to look at him. "Oh, hello, Mr. Hall. How yew been?"

"Fine," he said. "And you?"

"Oh, all right." She moved stiffly, with great effort. "M'leg's been botherin' me some. Ain't been in this room since Mrs. Baleza died. Figured Rodina wouldn't like the room rented out right away. Straightenin' up now, though. Woman wants the room."

"Can I help you?"

"No, don't figure there's nothin' much you could do, thank yew jest the same, Mr. Hall. Just a little straightenin' up. Mrs. Baleza couldn't do much messin' up, yew know. Some things in here belong to Rodina, guess yew might wanta take em to her. Dresses, sweaters, and things."

Theodore picked up the few dresses and "things." Mrs. Davis was no hypocrite, he thought, you could say that for her: she didn't even pretend she thought Rodina was going to stay in this room. That was the way it should be.

"Few things in the drawers, Mr. Hall," Mrs. Davis said. "I took most of em out, the clothes and all, but there's a few other things, pencils, lipsticks, and the like. I'll get em all out."

"Oh, don't bother," Theodore said. "I'll get them."

In the top drawer were an empty pocketbook, two lipsticks,

278

eight pencils, a compact, a pair of earrings and a string of beads. Theodore opened out his handkerchief and placed them in the center, pausing to examine the beads. He had never seen Rodina wear them. He would ask her to. He made a note of that. She would look attractive in these.

When he opened the second drawer he stopped breathing; his heart beat faster, his muscles tightened, and an alarm went off inside his head. For, in the front, beside a stack of handkerchiefs, lay two Leica cameras.

CHAPTER TWENTY-FOUR

Dear Theodore:

Remember how we used to lie in bed and listen to the plaster crumbling and falling behind the bedroom wallpaper? I can hear it now, as I write—it hasn't done that for a long time. The sound has a strange effect on me: something like hearing a half-forgotten song, made precious by a long-ago event.

I can hear many things from my bed; the doctor does not permit me to leave it. In the day time there are the automobiles, the sound of people passing by, the hucksters with their wagons, an occasional curse—the usual sounds of a South Philadelphia day. In the day, when I am not listening to the sounds, I can read or sleep, and this leaves me fresh and alert when darkness falls. Then I hear the sounds I like best of all: the distant cry of a train, the clang of a lonely street car, the murmur of a solitary automobile, the footsteps of young lovers, or, if I stay awake long enough, the clippity-clop of the milkman's horse and the rattle of his bottles.

I thought, when the doctor first confined me, that I would go mad with boredom and lonesomeness. But it hasn't been that way. I can lie here and count the flowers of the wallpaper's pattern, or the number of tick-tocks from the clock in an hour. Or I can read, or reread, the books you introduced me to. Or I can count, by their footsteps, the number of people who pass outside. Or—and here I sound too serious —I can contemplate the worth of my life thus far.

281

To say that I am never lonesome here, in this one room, in this one bed, would not be the truth. But to say that loneliness is itself unbearable—that, too, would be untrue. I have, I think, made my peace with Fate . . . however cruel I once thought Fate to be.

> With Love,
> Sylvia

He had been far away from her this last week or so, Rodina noted absently. He spoke little; he seemed always to be thinking, troubled. At times she raised her head to see him looking intently at her, a swirl of bafflement in his eyes, furrows over his brow. He moved through the days much like a man in the haze of a hangover: his eyes seemed pained by the light, his thoughts were confused and he was never in a mood for conversation.

Yes, it was beginning. Or, rather, it had no doubt begun long ago, but now it was collecting, solidifying—the realization of their identities, of what she was and what he was. She did not try to help him through those days: she wore no false smiles, nor did she try to relieve their perpetual silences by the manufacture of artificial conversation. She would let it brew. It was all right. It had to come. Now it was only a matter of time.

He went to work each morning following the half-hearted kiss during which his eyes were intent upon her own, looking, she thought, for some clue to her feelings. He wanted to know if she was hurt, she imagined. Well, she was not hurt. She was tired. It was all over. It was dragging out. She was tired of it now. She would be glad, in a way, when it was all over.

When he had gone to work she would breathe easier, though not yet freely, clean the room and then go out for a walk. It was spring now. The leaves were fresh green, and there were

282

birds and sunshine. She looked at the kids—there was a sadness because they no longer waved, no longer whistled: they were looking for the old Rodina, the Rodina of the dancing skirts. Perhaps they would not have long to wait.

Sometimes she stopped at the saloon, where the men, at least, still waved and called. It was good to be among them: men who worked and smelled of work, who were coarse and frustrated, but who liked those who respected them. She would drink with them occasionally; sometimes she would dance. They would joke among themselves, rotten joking, not minding Rodina—acting just as though she were one of them. She liked this. And when one of them, on this day or that, made a pass, she could slap his hand good-naturedly and call him a few dirty names, and they could laugh and it would be all over and there would be no hard feelings. A man might as well try. All this damn stuff about propriety, all this damn stuff about you shouldn't do this and you should do that, and ladies mustn't use that knife, was a lot of baloney, she told herself. If you were a doctor or something, and had money, maybe all you had to do with your time was to make rules like those and live by them and stick your nose up in the air, feeling better than plain people. But if you were poor, you didn't have time to be bothered by all that. You worked all day and got sweaty and came home and saw a knock-down row house and a row of kids and a wife who was sweaty from working all day, and you kissed her and ate supper and went out to the saloon to be with the boys, and if you saw a good-looking girl why not make a pass? What the hell. No harm done. Damn the rules. They had their own rules.

She felt better when her thoughts ran on like this. She had had enough of trying to change herself. Look out, Hell, here I come! That was better.

One day she strolled pretty far from home, passing a police

station, glaring at the hated cops who stood outside, passing the movie house where she had gone to see the double feature the day after meeting Theodore. She stopped and looked at the placards; she could see herself inside, see the pictures, then see herself coming out and walking on, eventually sighting the diner again. The diner. She walked in its direction. She remembered the streets, remembered the night in the soft rain, walking with her heart jumping because of the narrow escape. *Promise me you won't steal anymore.* The soft voice and the hand gripping her wrist. *Why, you're only a child!* Hearing her heart beat loudly and staring at him in hatred, not trusting him, but defiant of him, for he was an outsider. The sound of her heels as she ran off down the street.

Tapping on the window. His face: his consternation. The other days, coming down to the place he worked more or less as a lark, a joke, something different: his serious eyes and soft, patient voice: his interest in her, the talking, telling about the past and the present. That day in the hallway when he held her, after leaving her mother: *Let me help you.* And the day she came down to the tearoom, and there he was, suitcase and all. The feeling of that moment.

There was the diner: just as it had appeared to her that day after she left the double-feature. Not exactly the same: for then it had been night. It was late afternoon now. She walked into the diner. There was the waiter: Jerry his name was, wasn't it?

He looked up at her, then down, then quickly up again. He recognized her.

"Say, he*llo*," he said, "how you doin'?"

"All right." She sat down on the stool.

"Ain't you the girl came in here with Ted?"

"Yes."

"Well, Jesus Christ! Small world, ain't it."

No one else was in the diner. There was the booth. There

was the juke box. She got off the stool and walked over to the juke box. There was the record someone had played. *Laura.* She put in a nickel and pushed the button.

"That's the record Ted always liked," Jerry said.

"Yeah."

"He ain't workin' here anymore, you know. Down the street, I mean. They got a new guy, a real drip, I mean to tell you. Comes in here and talks his damn head off. Not like Ted. You seen him lately?"

"Yes."

"What's he doin' for hisself? I always wonder about him?"

"Working," Rodina said. "How about some coffee?"

"Sure. Workin', huh? Doin' what? He always had a great brain, y'know. Figured he quit that job down there and make hisself some money. We used t'talk about it all the time. I'm gonna quit m'self, one a these days. What's Ted doin' with hisself?"

"He's loading potatoes," Rodina said. "He works for a distillery."

"*Ted?* Jesus, what the hell happened? Guess things didn't turn out so hot for him, huh? He had a great brain, coulda been a crackerjack school teacher. Guess things didn't work out so well for him, huh?"

"No, they didn't work out so well."

"Damn shame. He still with his wife?"

"No. They separated."

"That right?" Jerry's eyes gleamed. "Well, whatcha know. Well, that's always the end of a man, y'know. Wife sorta pushes a man along, inspires him, y'know. Now you take me. What'd I be without my wife? I'd be a regular bum, just messin' my life away. Now I'm settled down, got some kids, buyin' furniture and stuff. Makes a difference." He looked at her. "Well, he married anybody else?"

"No."

"That right? And you see him often, huh? Well, guess maybe Ted had a lot of us fooled, eh? We thought he was just a slow, decent kinda guy, with no eyes for the ladies. Guess we sure were wrong about him, huh?"

"I guess so," Rodina said. She stood up.

"You going?" Jerry asked.

"Yes."

"Aw, stick around. I get lonesome workin' here all day. Stick around and talk. Have a coffee on me."

"No, thanks," she said.

"Aw, stick around, lady. We can talk about Ted. I wanta hear all about him. We was great buddies, y'know. I wanta hear about him."

"Some other time," Rodina said. "I have to go."

From the corner outside, she looked down the street and saw the sign: *Dranger Pharmaceutical Laboratories.* She breathed deeply and walked back toward home.

She was not surprised, when she walked into the room, to find Theodore rereading the latest letter from his wife. She said, "Hello, Ted," and began to prepare supper. She should have had it ready, she thought. She should not have stayed out so long. She could at least be dutiful.

"Are you tired, darling?" she asked him when she kissed him.

"No, I'm all right, Rodina." He looked at the letter, then at her again. He was looking for the answer to something in her eyes. "Rodina," he said softly, "I wish I knew you—really knew you."

She straightened up and did not answer. Yes, it was coming. Oh, yes. Well, it had to come. She would not make it difficult for him by trying to pardon herself. She would just let it simmer. It was all right. It had to come.

She was tired.

286

"I was reading this letter again," he said. "I think I ought to go see Sylvia."

"It would be a nice thing to do," she said.

After supper he said, "I think I'll drop over to visit Sylvia this evening. She needs company. Would you mind?"

"No, of course not," she said. So here it was.

Later he dressed. He looked very handsome, she thought, as he prepared to go. She watched him: the kind face, the fine eyes, the goodness all the way through. She felt a pull at her heart: something warm and painful was at the back of her eyes.

"I'll be back pretty late, I imagine, darling," he said. "So long." He kissed her.

"Goodbye, Ted," she said.

2

Here it was, reality at last. Rodina stood near the window, looking at the tree. She let the tears roll down her face. It could not be believed, this hot and torturous inner convulsion she felt. Yet, outwardly, she was calm. Except for the tears.

All that had gone before, all that had been dreamt, was unreal. This was the real world. Now the troubles were over, weren't they? Now she need not fear Hucks: now he could go to hell. Now she need not try to execute the design of Juarez. Her mother was dead: now she would not hear the constant indictment. She was Rodina again.

Can I still pick a pocket, she wondered idly, without either joy or sadness. Probably. She had been well trained. Only now she would know better than pick pockets in the rain. Her hands needed to be dry.

Maybe she should take a job, in the night club, say. She knew the manager, and some of the other girls who worked there. No, she did not like that idea. Things were expected of you:

five dollars per throw. No, she did not like that. Not even for Rodina; the real Rodina.

She moved to the sink to wash the evening's dishes. Theodore's plate. Afterward, she lay across the bed and looked around the room. It had been nice here. The closet door was slightly open; she saw Theodore's clothes. Ted's clothes. She closed her eyes tight and clenched her teeth.

She stood up and angrily wiped her eyes. She started to sing. She opened the door and went downstairs and sat in the tearoom.

"Hi, Glenn, old boy. How are you?" she asked him, music in her voice.

"Okay, Rodina. You seem mighty chipper today."

"Oh, I am chipper, Glenn. Very chipper. What've you got to drink?"

"You mean a shot, Rodina?"

"That's right."

"Oh, Schenley's, Old Forrester, Seagrams—"

"Got any wine?"

"Oh, sure, but I thought you wanted a *drink.*"

"Well, mix me up a glass full of half wine and half whiskey."

He whistled. "Well, pardon *me*," he said. "You must really want to go places."

"On the run," she said.

She and Theodore used to sit here so many times. There was the table where he had been sitting that day, with his suitcase. Glenn came over with her drink. She smiled and winked at him and said, "Say, Glenn, anybody ever tell you you were handsome?" She did not hear his answer. She raised the glass and drank the contents down. Almost immediately she felt a whirling in her head. I'm happy, I'm happy, she told herself. I'm happy because now it's all over, and there's no more worry, and I'm free.

288

She saw Hucks passing the tearoom. That sonofabitch Hucks. She called, "Yo, Hucks."

He paused and looked at her. He came over to the table. "What's up?"

"Nothing's up. Now, what are you doing looking at me so funny. So damned suspicious. Now, why in hell would you ever be suspicious of me? Tell me that. What're you going to do right now?"

"I dunno. I was gonna —"

"Cancel it," she said. "Grab a seat, Hucks. Join me in a couple of drinks."

"Now, look —"

"I am looking," she said. "I'm looking. I can see. Grab a seat. Keep me company."

He looked at her a moment. With some reluctance, he sat down.

"Take a drink with me," she said.

He shrugged.

When Glenn came over she ordered another of the same. Hucks looked at her. He ordered bourbon.

They touched glasses. She sipped her drink and then said, "Hucks, how are you?"

"I'm okay," he said.

"Okay? Hucks, you aren't calling me baby. How come? You always called me baby? How come you're not calling me baby now?"

"I got other babies," he said, with hostility.

"That right? You've got other babies? Well, that's okay, Hucks. If you don't want to call me baby. That's okay with me. You always were trying to be tough. That's okay." She looked at him and smiled. "Hucks, how am I in bed?"

He stared at her as though she were crazy.

"What's the matter, cat got your tongue? You're an expert,

Hucks. How am I in bed? How do I stack up beside the other babies?"

He looked at her. "You're okay," he said. He watched her closely.

"Let's go to bed, Hucks."

"What?"

"Let's go to bed. Right now. In your bed, you've got a nice soft bed, Hucks. Let's go to bed."

"You must be drunk," he said. He stared at her.

"I'm not drunk. You can see I'm not drunk. What's the matter, am I repulsive? Where's all that manhood? Here a girl offers herself to you, and you sit looking dumb. Have you re-formed?"

He looked at her, and said nothing.

"Let's go to bed," she said. "I want to go to bed with you. You don't need any wallet or anything else now. I want to go to bed with you. How about it?"

He looked at her, saying nothing. In his throat, the throbs of his heartbeat could be felt.

290

CHAPTER TWENTY-FIVE

A HUCKSTER PASSED, wheeling the big pushcart, shouting, "Any old rags! Any old rags!" Kids shouted for him to wait and rushed into their houses; this was a chance to make an easy nickel or dime. Theodore thought: One of Sylvia's "sounds" of the daytime. He walked slowly; he was in no hurry to reach Sylvia's apartment.

He thought of Rodina, the apathy with which she had greeted his decision to visit his wife. Earlier, she had objected, told him to forget about Sylvia. No more. Now she did not care. Now she seemed not to care about anything. That perpetual fog she moved in. That wall she kept between them. Such a strange girl that he loved.

The cameras. She had lied so vehemently about them. Why? Why had she wanted him to steal them, for no good purpose? Then Juarez had been right. Perhaps he was right, too, about the other things he said. How could he ever know when she spoke the truth? What could he know? He would speak or question, and she would reply with those frightened eyes wide open, and he would not know what to believe. How many times had she lied before? And why had she lied? That was the maddening question: Why?

It was apparent that she was tired of him. She made no effort to talk to him; the things they did together she did without enthusiasm. It was almost as though she were patiently enduring his presence, biding her time until he should leave.

What should he do? Leave? For her own sake he did not want to do this: for, after all, her mother had just died: she was alone, and without a job, and young. And for his own sake too; for what would he do, where would he go, what meaning would there be to life without Rodina? He could not start all over again. He could not fall in love, or even live with, anyone else. He could work, and come home and eat, and then sleep, and then go to work again. Was that life? Was it for that that man was born? How fruitless, then, was the creation.

How long ago had this begun, this disintegration? For once they had been happy: did it begin with his theft? No, there had been a subtle change even before that. The theft accentuated it, he knew. And the death of the mother—that had completed it; she had withdrawn into the shell. Was it possible that she might, eventually, emerge again? Was it possible that all this might one day be understandable and forgotten, that they would, finally, in truth, be able to find permanent happiness?

He pushed these thoughts aside. He was going to visit Sylvia now. Sylvia. He trembled; he cursed himself for being a coward. To tremble at the thought of visiting a woman, even if she was his wife.

In his mind, he saw himself standing outside of the apartment, looking up at the windows, remembering. A few neighbors passed; some recognized him and stared and whispered. For a long while he stood on the steps, staring up, filled with foreboding. Then slowly he mounted the steps, opened the door, and walked up the dimly-lighted stairs. He paused outside her door; he listened for sounds of movement within; he raised his hand to knock, hesitated, trembled, wished he had not come . . .

He saw Sylvia in bed, thin, lonely, smiling as though trying to be brave. He felt the wrench at his heart.

292

"How are you?" she asked.

"Fine, Sylvia. And you?"

"Fine."

Their conversation was awkward. On and on, the voice in monotone, the cheerfulness synthetic, the gloom penetrating. Around the room he could see things almost forgotten: the place on the bureau where his shaving kit used to lie, the drawer which had been reserved for his socks, the side of the bed where he always slept, the worn spot in the linoleum, the clean windows without the handsome curtains Sylvia had so long asked for.

And then the leaving.

He saw all this. He tried to think of something else, of something pleasant. He stopped in a flower shop, and bought a dozen roses.

"For your wife?" the salesman asked cheerfully.

"Yes," Theodore said.

The salesman beamed. "Wives appreciate a thoughtful husband."

And now, finally, here was the street, and here was the house. No neighbor stopped to stare or whisper. Was that an omen? He climbed the steps. Here was the hall, narrow and dimly-lighted. The smudged wallpaper; the squeaky stairs. And now the long hall, and there, there at that end, Sylvia's apartment, his apartment. He stopped, he trembled; his heart beat loudly. Tears welled in his eyes. He knocked.

There was no answer. He knocked again, and listened for a sound from inside. Nothing stirred. Could she be asleep? He knocked loudly, and knocked still again. No answer. He stood there dumbfounded. He tried again, and, when there was no answer, he turned slowly away from the door and walked back down the stairs.

What could it mean? Theodore wondered. Was Sylvia so soundly asleep that she had not heard him at the door? Her nerves were bad, the doctor had said. Perhaps he had given her a sedative. Or perhaps she had become worse, and been taken to the hospital.

Well, he would come back tomorrow. If she still did not answer, he would call the various hospitals to find out if she was at one of them. If this met with no success, he would try to discover what doctor had treated her, and question him. The doctor might have sent her away, to the country, for instance, where the environment was more conducive to rapid recovery. Any one of a dozen possibilities existed. He would find out tomorrow.

He was anxious but, much as he hated to admit it, relieved. He had made the trip to her house, as his conscience commanded; and yet he had been spared the torture of seeing her, talking to her, feeling renewed the acute sadness and sense of guilt. He had been spared the droning voice and sad eyes.

He felt lighter as he walked toward home. He saw the tenement, with its sagging bricks. Outside played the neighborhood children. He walked inside and passed the tearoom: there were Mrs. Houston, and Glenn, and Juarez, who waved, and others. Theodore went upstairs.

He was surprised to discover that Rodina was not in the room. Out for a walk again, he thought. He lay across the bed. In a way, he was glad Rodina was not there: he could relax. He did not feel like talking. Sylvia. In a hospital? He was so tired. This never-ending tension. I must relax, he told himself. Relax, relax, or I'll be ill myself. Try to sleep, he told himself, try to sleep. He lay still. It *was* possible to relax. He breathed deeply and slowly and felt himself sinking away from the surface world.

The door opened. Theodore saw Juarez.

"Hello," Juarez said.

"Hello, Juarez. Have you seen Rodina?"

"Yes."

"Do you know where she is now? It's about time for supper."

Juarez stared at him. Behind the watery film, his eyes were filled with bitterness. "Yes," he answered in his soft voice, made tremulous now by the intense emotion he felt. "Where she always is when you're not home. In bed. With Hucks."

The alarm clock, long-waiting for this hour, exploded in Theodore's head. He did not move. His eyes filled swiftly. So. Suddenly the bell stopped ringing and he was weary, only weary. He inhaled with a shudder.

"What are you going to do?" Juarez asked him.

"Nothing."

"She's in bed with that —"

"I know, I know." Theodore lay with his eyes closed. He felt the tremors strike here and there his body. He knew he was perspiring. All of his strength seemed gone; he lay limp. Well, there it was. There it was.

"Thank you, Juarez," he said.

Juarez looked at him a moment longer. Then he closed the door.

So there it was.

Theodore rolled over on his side, his eyes still closed. He was so tired. He should sleep. He was an old man, an old man. An old man who had fooled himself. He was tired, tired. He should sleep; God! he should sleep!

Now down his face rolled the tears. He lay motionless, on his side, letting them roll. An old, old, man. So old and weary and tired and such a fool. To have fooled himself, this way. To have criticized Sylvia. To have thought himself capable of holding the affection of a girl of twenty. Ah, the old, old fool.

And then this was over, and he lay quietly, cold. He was

295

relaxed now. He did not want to move. He kept his eyes closed. He was so tired. He felt himself slipping off the edge of consciousness. He should sleep. He was cold and relaxed. He should sleep. He was weary, oh, so weary, for he was old . . .

He sat up on the edge of the bed. In the bureau mirror, he saw his swollen eyes and tousled hair. He looked at himself, at the signs of middle age, and he laughed. It was so funny. Forty years old. In love and running off with a chippy at forty years old.

He stood up and looked out of the window. Bricks and wooden fences and this lonely backyard tree. Home.

Well, my bastard friend, what now? he thought. What now? And so Ulysses, having escaped from the Medusa, once more set sail in his attempt to reach Ithaca and the lap of his beautiful wife, Penelope!

Darkness was descending. Theodore turned from the window and went to the closet. He threw his clothes to the bed. From under the bed he lifted his suitcase, and packed his suits inside. He went to the bureau, and took out his shirts. Then he paused, smiling, seeing a shiny object. The gun.

He picked up the gun. This, he thought, would be a time for melodrama, for suicide. The naïve man betrayed. No future now. Nothing now. The gun at the temple and the blown-out brains. The end of the Drama of the Sensitive Soul. "There's a gun in the drawer. Would you use it for me?" Rodina had asked that of him.

"Ted!"

He turned, and there she stood—the wide eyes, the long black hair, the innocence, the fear. There she was. "Hello," he said.

"Ted! I didn't know you were here!"

"No," he said, "I don't imagine you did."

Her eyes fell on the suitcase. Yes, it was so. He was packing. Yes, it was so, as it had to be. Now, he would go. Now all would be gone. Now there would be no more dreams, she would be Rodina, Rodina the bitch, Rodina the pick pocket. Rodina who no longer fought herself. She felt the hysteria coming.

And then she saw the gun. Her eyes lighted fiercely and she stared at him.

"Where have you been?" he asked. "Or will you lie to me again?"

Her eyes were fixed on his. He was angry! Her heart leapt. He was angry, he was angry! Her eyes blazed into his; she leaned forward: "Downstairs, with Hucks, in bed with Hucks," she said.

His eyes fell. Her heart sank. "Downstairs in bed with Hucks," she repeated. He breathed heavily, but did not move. "Shoot! Shoot!" she cried.

He looked up at her in surprise. Shoot? He was conscious of the gun in his hand, and surprise turned to something near amusement. Shoot? The *Liebestod*?

"Coward!" she screamed, "Coward! Woman! *Shoot!*"

The word was like a blow. The amusement left his eyes. Then this had been her thought. Well, it was justified. Woman; it was justified.

In panic, she repeated, "Woman! Woman!"

But he only smiled, looked at the gun, and then tossed it to the bed.

With a cry of despair she sprang upon the gun; tears flushed from her eyes. Screaming soundlessly, she pointed the gun at him and pulled the trigger twice.

With great surprise, he felt the bullets strike into his chest. Slowly, not believing, not comprehending, he fell to the floor. Swiftly life flowed from the wounds, like water from a basin when the stopper is removed. He closed his eyes, not knowing. The last sounds he heard were a faint sobbing cry, and then the roar of another shot, seeming to come from a great distance, mingling with the clamor of a street car passing by.

3

"Names?" the detective said.

"Rodina Baleza and Theodore something-or-other," Mrs. Houston said.

"How long they been living here?"

"She's been here longer than I have, which is nine years. Guess she's been here all her life. The man's been here about seven months I guess."

"Were they married?"

Mrs. Houston laughed. "You kiddin', bub?"

Several people were in the room, including the detective and a policeman. A newspaper reporter was taking notes.

"Know anything about their backgrounds?"

"The man has a wife somewhere," Mrs. Houston said. "He writes poetry, that's all I know. The girl was a little tramp, drank, went to bed with anybody, picked pockets, stole, and so forth. Nobody was surprised when she brought him here and started sleepin' with him."

"What about parents?"

"Mother was laid up in bed nearly all the girl's life. Name was Baleza, she died not so long ago."

"Father living?"

Mrs. Houston scratched her head. "Can't say. Some say he is, some say he ain't. He was a minister, come down here to convert the sinners. Rodina's mother did some convertin' on her own. He used to come down to a bar around on Eighth Street all the time to see Mrs. Baleza—don't know why I call

298

her Mrs., 'cause they never married, way I hear it. Anyway, when he found Rodina was gonna be born, the poor guy nearly went off his hooker. Disappeared. Some say he went and committed suicide. Some say he went off as a missionary, to Africa."

"Okay," the detective said. "Guess we'll have to check on this guy's wife somehow. Got to get the last name, though."

"You can get it from Mrs. Davis. She's the landlady. She's out right now."

"Okay." He turned to the reporter. "Got everything you need?"

"Well, I've got to get the guy's name."

"Sure. Will it make a good story?"

The reporter shrugged. "These whores kill their lovers every other day, or vice versa. It all depends on how you look at it."

<h1 style="text-align:center">4</h1>

Sylvia sat before the mirror of her bureau, trying on the new hat. It was a nice hat but perhaps it wasn't quite her type. She removed the hat and fixed her hair, noting the lines in her forehead and the dark spots under her eyes. She frowned.

She thought of Theodore. Dear Theodore. What was he doing now? Kissing his beloved concubine? Or writing a letter to her, Sylvia? Or rereading, with a sad and guilty heart, her last letter to him? "I should visit her if she's sick," he would tell himself. But, of course, he would not visit her. He could not bear facing her again.

She looked at the clock. She would have to hurry. She moved quickly around the rooms: wash, dress, get out the coat, sit down again to check her lipstick and powder.

The bell rang. Howard was always on time, she thought. That could, of course, get monotonous.

She dabbed at her face with the powder puff. But there was no covering the lines, no covering the dark spots, the blemishes.

She frowned again, and felt the frustration shoot through her heart. If only she had been born beautiful, she thought longingly, as she rose to go to the door. Or rich.

5

It was the next night, when she had not seen him all day, and had gotten no answer when she knocked in the morning and when she knocked now, that Mrs. Davis used the pass key to open Juarez' door.

The room was dark. Mrs. Davis called, and got no answer, and tried the light switch, which did not work. She was conscious, first of all, of the odor of the room: dank, musty, like old unused books, with the faint clinging of stale cigarette smoke. Then gradually there came to her senses the sounds: the faint falling of rain on the window panes intermingled with the hiss of wind through the trees, green now but not yet mature in the adolescent Spring. Only after these things had come to the old, slow, wheezing woman who had cried all night because of the tragedy, did she notice, against the faint glow of the window, the dim outline of the body, brown and thin and stooped, swinging like a boxer's sandbag or a football team's dummy from the rope tied to the rickety old chandelier.